# AMPED

## MARIE LIPSCOMB

Second edition.

ISBN 978-1-957313-10-8

**Cover:** Marie Lipscomb

**Editing:** Jack Holloway

**Formatting:** Jack Harbon

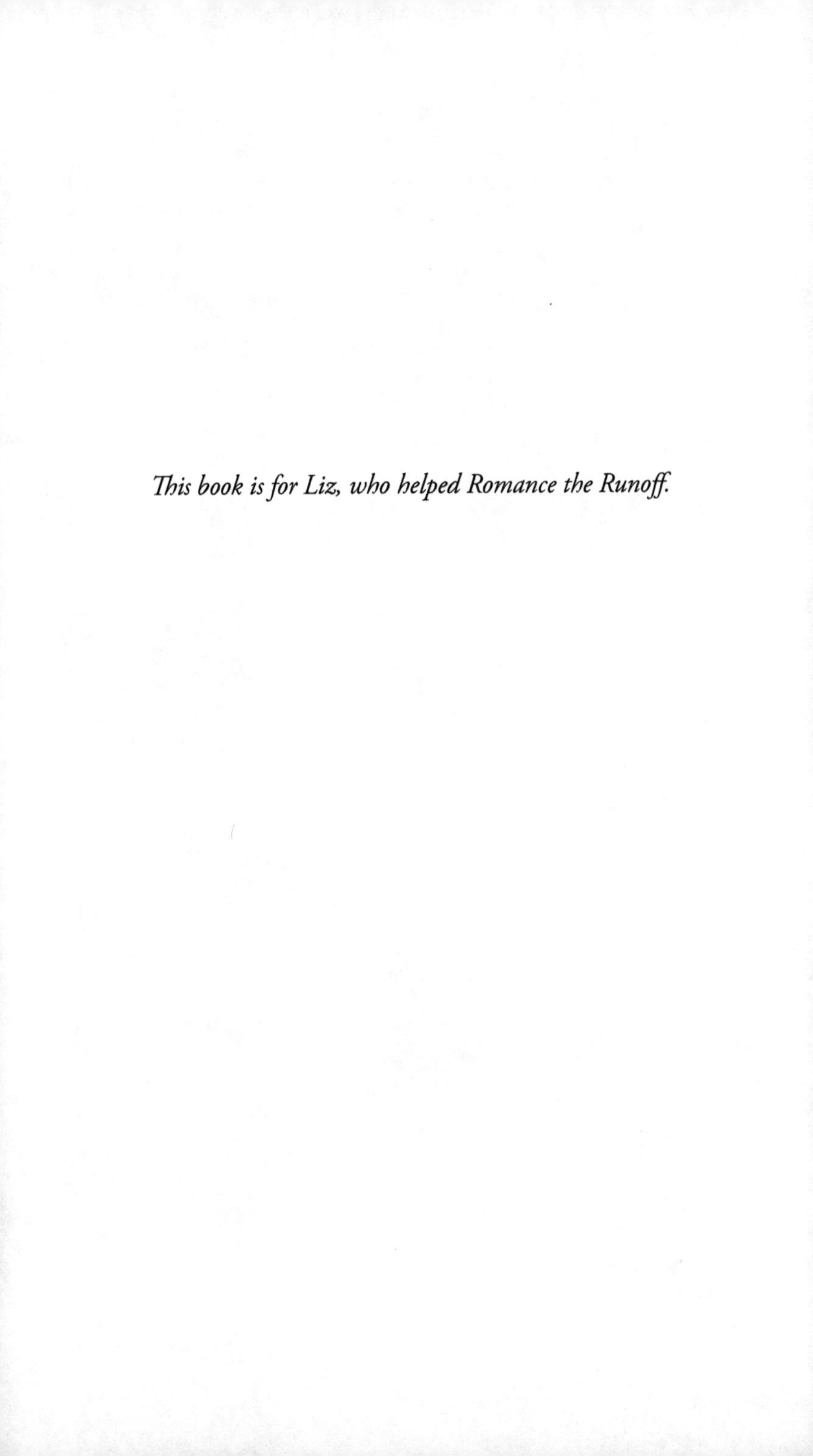

*This book is for Liz, who helped Romance the Runoff.*

# AMPED

# ONE

The soundcheck blaring from the festival's speakers hums and pulses against Liz's sternum and her heart echoes the beat. She makes her way through the backstage area, sidestepping out of the path of a bustling roadie, careful not to trip on the coils of cable around her feet. It's only the day before the festival, but already the backstage crew are grumbly and surly; completely done with the whole thing.

Especially with musicians like her getting in their way.

For four weeks Vixen's Wail have worked their asses off, preparing for the annual Halloween music festival, Ghoulfest. They're at the pinnacle of a decade-long grind to make it big, and this should be huge for them. But for Liz Larkin it doesn't really feel like the start of anything.

It feels like an ending.

How was she to know when she joined at nineteen, that the band would become her entire life? Endless cycles of practice and performance, confidence in her ability as a keyboardist, which always grows into a jarring fear that she'll never be quite good enough. Ghoulfest is the first big-ish festival the band have played and yet, everything is somehow so… samey. No matter how big the band gets, the experience is always the same, just a little more polished.

The same black loops of cable, the same flutter of pre-show nerves, the same scent of warm, sweating bodies. It might be a bigger stage, but it's just like every other show they've played.

Not to mention her appearance. Her long brown hair is always in the same flat ironed style. Black eyeliner, smokey eyes behind thick black-rimmed glasses. Black clothing which hugs her ample curves. Nothing has changed. Not externally, anyway.

"Liz? Wait up."

She stops and turns, breathing a sigh of relief as Anya, the band's guitarist, hurries toward her, darting through the backstage staff with effortless ease. Her shoulder-length auburn waves bounce as she jogs the final few steps. Anya is stunning as always, her bright blue eyes alight with excitement, the skin-tight lace of her top revealing just enough of her curvy figure that a gawking roadie trips over a box of wires. Her looks, coupled with her drive and determination to someday be recognized as one of the greatest guitarists of all time, she's a firm fan favorite of the band.

"Can you believe it?" Anya grins, breathless. "Look at us, we're backstage at a fucking festival!"

"It's amazing," Liz replies as enthusiastically as she can while hoisting her ratty backpack further up her shoulder.

"Oh, shit what's wrong?"

Okay, so maybe all the enthusiasm she can muster isn't enough. "Nothing."

"Nerves?"

That works. "Yeah, just… you know."

"Gassy?"

Liz's mouth snaps shut as she scowls, much to Anya's entertainment. She isn't the only one scowling. The backstage staff are busy, hard at work and having to walk around her and Anya as they stand there chatting. From the frustrated tuts and mutters, it's rapidly becoming apparent that they're outstaying their welcome.

"Come on, Finn said we have a trailer behind the stage somewhere," Liz mutters, turning back around to continue her journey.

"Exciting." Anya falls into step beside her. "So, what's up?"

*I'm thinking about leaving the band.* Those words press against the inside of Liz's lips, but she can't speak them, not yet, not on the biggest day of their careers so far. She's a good keyboardist, great, actually, but it was never meant to be her life. In a month she'll be thirty, a clear sign from the universe that she should find something which truly speaks to her.

Back home she has a stack of brochures for various colleges, neon pink post-it notes bookmarking the pages advertising their massage therapy classes. The brochures are all a couple of years out of date, but she's sure that for the most part all the information is still correct. It's a lot more work than she anticipated, not just learning the massage techniques, but about anatomy and first aid too. All in all, it would take hundreds of hours of training, but she could make a difference. She could help people.

"Nothing, I'm fine," she says in her usual bright tone. She glances out of the corner of her eye to see Anya raise a perfectly sculpted eyebrow at her. "I'm *fine.*"

"You're a horrible liar and you should be ashamed. It's

okay to be nervous. This is a big fucking deal. There are going to be thousands of people out there tomorrow—"

"And that's supposed to help my nerves?"

Anya shakes her head and rolls her eyes. "Well, I'm excited enough for the two of us, and hopefully it's contagious."

"Like headlice?"

The air is knocked from Liz's lungs as she slams into something. Something big and solid.

She stumbles, reaching out for the closest thing she can grab to steady herself as she battles with gravity. But it isn't enough. Her legs crumple awkwardly. Pain shoots through her ankle as it twists beneath her, but she manages to stay upright, anchoring herself on whatever it was she crashed into.

Clutching fistfuls of warm black cotton—*oh no*—she raises her eyes to look at—*please no*—the man—*nooooo*—standing in front of her. He's over a foot taller than her, husky and heavyset with big tattooed arms. His chin is covered in a bushy brown and sandy-colored beard, which almost completely hides his thick, sun-reddened neck. His eyes are pale, somewhere between blue, green and grey, like weather-worn cement. Maybe a mixture of all three. In any case, his stony eyes peer down at her, and they're definitely not happy.

That's fair. She wouldn't be either.

She lets go of his shirt, and presses her lips together. "Sorry. I didn't see you."

It's impossible that she didn't. This big, burly guy unapologetically takes up space in every direction. He's grizzled, magnetic, intimidating. And as her lips part and the world around them darkens a shade, she realizes he might just be hot.

She has always enjoyed a spot of mountain climbing.

The man doesn't speak. He just looks down at her as if she isn't worth the expended oxygen, before carrying on his path. The words "Ghoulfest" and "Staff" are printed in pumpkin orange on the back of his shirt. He's a roadie.

"Doofus," Anya chuckles.

But Liz isn't looking at Anya. She can't tear her eyes from him.

Until now, everything has seemed so samey, but whoever he is, he's definitely something new.

***

Pain in the ass performers getting in his way. Jones smooths down his shirt over his soft, round belly and continues his search for his right-hand man.

"Anyone seen Imran?" he asks as he storms his way across the stage, ignoring the persistent twinge in his lower back.

Of course, no one answers him. They're all working their butts off to get this shitshow running as smooth as possible, head-down, lips sealed. The fact that he has a carefully culti-vated reputation of being a hard-ass doesn't help. People don't tend to talk to him and that's just how he likes it.

With a low growl he turns back around, glancing at his watch. He still has an hour before he can take more painkillers but the constant throb and tightness in his thigh is getting worse. Cold, clammy sweat prickles at his back.

Distracting himself from the pain he notices she's still standing there, the woman who fell onto him. Her friend laughs as she buries her head in her hands and shakes her head. He'd be lying if he said she wasn't pretty. Full, curvy body, long brown hair, a little beauty spot above her lip. Even while this pissed off, he'd noticed.

Doesn't matter.

"Imran?" he calls, frustration growing.

"What?"

That voice is like a balm for his soul as he whirrs around to find his missing colleague. "Where've you been?"

"Trailer six. Can you believe they sent it to us without a single working lightbulb?" Imran shakes his head as his impeccably thick moustache twitches. "Unbelievable."

"It's sorted though?"

"Oh yeah. Phantasmagoria Euphoria are going to come out of that place with suntans now."

Jones blinks slowly and shakes his head. "Sorry, Phantasmagoria...?"

"Euphoria, yeah." Imran smirks and runs his hands over his floppy salt and pepper hair.

"Ridiculous." Folding his arms over his chest, Jones taps the stage floor with the toe of his boot. "So where are we up to?"

"Two more bands for soundchecks. We need to call catering and make sure they're still on for tomorrow. We have a busted speaker, three stage lights out, and I'm pretty sure Matt stole my gaffer tape."

"Business as usual then?"

"Yup."

Pulling in a long breath, Jones makes a mental checklist of everything he needs to do. For a part-time job, this gig is a bigger pain in his ass than it has any right to be. Festivals don't come along very often, but even from his limited experience, he knows this one is a cluster. As soon as he arrived at the site and saw that the artists had to walk through the same area his team were laying cables and carrying gear, he knew it was going to be a mess.

He glances toward where the woman stumbled into him. She's gone, but the sensation of her hands on him hasn't. It's been a long time since anyone touched him.

"Alright," Jones jerks his head toward Imran, rubbing the swell of his stomach as though he can erase the tingling warmth. "If you want to take a break, I've got a handle on things."

"You sure?"

Jones nods, adding a gruff "Hurry the fuck up though," in case anyone suspects he's going soft. A sharp spasm of pain shoots through his back as Imran walks away.

Gigs were easy when he started out in his teens, but lately there have been a few too many back twinges and sleepless nights caused by cramping legs. The unwelcome but niggling fear that forty is only a couple of years away presses at the back of his mind. There's only so long he can go on like this.

As familiar and comforting as this job is, he can't keep doing it forever, and the money he makes at his other part-time job at the bar isn't enough to support him. But the truth is, there's nothing else out there for a guy like him. Big, grumpy, unsociable, covered in tattoos… there isn't exactly a plethora of suited CEOs lining up to offer him cushy office jobs. It's this or broke.

So, he plows through the pain, distracts himself with work, climbing high onto the rig to fix the busted stage lights. It's cold up there, the wind whipping around him across the wide-open fields surrounding the festival site. Far below, set twenty-yards back from the stage are the trailers set aside for the bands. He doesn't allow himself time to wonder what it must be like for them; talented, pampered, living their dreams.

He closes his eyes and sucks in the cool air, gritting his teeth against the agony shooting from the base of his spine to the backs of his thighs.

"You okay, boss?" one of his team calls up to him.

The question makes him nauseous because he isn't but he'll die before he admits it.

He's the big man, the tough guy. It's taken him nearly four decades to carve out that reputation, and he isn't about to give in now. His father and older brother went to great lengths to choke the softness out of him.

"I'm fine." He grits his teeth as he climbs back down, a cold sweat settling on his brow as he commands his shaking body to keep going. There's no way he's quitting now.

By the time the final band of the night, the headliners, Vixen's Wail are called onto stage, his vision is blurred around the edges and almost doesn't see her. But when he does, his chest tightens. The woman who ran into him is part of the headlining band.

His jaw aches from clenching it so hard, his palms marked with angry purple crescents carved by his fingernails, but his heart still manages to squeeze a little as she smiles up at him.

Behind her, her bandmates smirk and nudge each other and maybe it's the pain or the fact he's twelve hours into a fifteen-hour shift, but it pisses him off. They're probably making fun of him. It happens a lot. Either people are terrified of him, want to fuck him, or they want to mock him. The first two he's more than happy to cater to, but the third he can't stand.

He quickly dismisses any hope that she might be interested in him and avoids eye contact all together. "Let us know if anything is missing. You've got nearly twice as many instruments as any other band we have playing so something's bound to go wrong."

She flashes him another dazzling smile and says, "Thank you!"

An ice chip deep in the arctic cavern of his heart begins to melt. Hers is just one of the thanks he gets from the band, but he clings to it. A tender thing he can keep to himself among all the pain and the cold, biting air.

When they head out onto stage, he allows himself to look. She's… well… gorgeous. He discovers she plays the keyboard, her fingers dancing as she makes her melodies, and he can't help but imagine what her light, skilled touch would feel like on his skin. His throat dries out as he watches her, and even though the music is blaring, pounding through the speakers, he hardly pays it any attention. His world encompasses nothing more than the sway of her hips as she plays, the way the dark-brown curtain of her hair dances along with her as her fingers spider-walk across the keys. Every breath he draws is like pulling silk over jagged rocks.

Imran's voice snaps him from his trance. "Oh fuck."

Jones blinks rapidly, honing his attention on the rest of the stage, searching for the problem. One of the band's singers runs from the stage in a fit of stage fright, and the rest of the band are beside themselves. Just what he needs. Fucking divas.

Every second they delay feels like a year as the agony in his back twists and tightens. By the time the remaining members of the band stumble through their rehearsal and head back to their trailer Jones is barely even present.

"Can you close down?" he asks Imran, clapping his hand on the man's shoulder.

"Yeah, no problem." Imran squints at him. "Are you alright? You look like shit."

He doesn't answer. He can't answer. If he admits the truth, they'll fuss over him. They'll insist on taking him to the doctor.

The pain he can handle. What he can't handle is the thought of people thinking he can't take care of himself. He limps through the darkness behind the stage, hands shaking as he pops two tablets from their foil blisters. They're a low dosage painkiller, but he so rarely takes any kind of medicine that even that feels like an admission of failure.

Swallowing them dry, he heads over to a quiet spot behind the artists' trailers. No one will bother him there and he can't spend another moment standing. As gently as he can, he drops to the ground and lies on his back, squinting at the stars peering through the clouds in the blotted ink sky and waits for relief.

# Two

Liz is the last to leave at the end of the night, and as she steps down from the trailer, she lets the door slap shut behind her. The festival site is quiet now and other than a few roadies on the stage, packing away equipment, she's alone.

Even with the drama of Étienne running off the stage and Jordan and Finn on a frantic mission to find him, she can't get excited. The music, the atmosphere, the theatrics… None of it stirs her like it used to.

She raises her face to the clear night sky and pushes out a swirling cloud of breath. The universe is speaking to her, and she can't keep ignoring it forever.

After the festival she'll tell them she's leaving. No more delays.

A wave of nausea rolls through her stomach at thought of it. She doesn't want to hurt her friends or cause them unnecessary stress, but she can't go on spending the rest of her life trudging through each day.

As she climbs down the set of three metal steps leading down from the trailer, a big, dark shape among the grass catches her eye. Right away, she knows what it is: there's a man, lying still on the ground.

She calls out, "Hello?"

Silence.

A spike of adrenaline shoots through her body as she peers through the darkness. He isn't moving.

Adrenaline turns to fear and manifests into purpose as she charges forward, letting her bag fall to the ground as she drops to her knees. With a start, she realizes she recognizes him. He's the roadie, the big guy she has been trying to steal casual glances at all evening. And he's hurt.

The thud of her heart beating against her ribs shakes the entire world around her.

"Fuck fuck fuck fuck."

She's taken a CPR course twice, practiced on the dummy and watched the videos over and over. But this is different. His life is literally in her hands.

"Okay… shit." She can hardly breathe. Taking off her glasses she tucks her hair behind her ears. "First, check the airway. Okay…"

She presses her palm against his forehead and tries to push his head back. Her heart freezes as his eyes spring open.

He bellows, *"What the fuck?"*

Sudden pain bursts across Liz's chest as his palm rams against her sternum and she's thrown backwards. The back of her head smacks against the side of the trailer. She cries out in fear as the world is flung into a maelstrom of chaos. Through the galloping beat of her pulse in her ears, and the roar of her breath as she fights to control it, swears and grunts fill the air.

"Oh shit, ah! Fuck!" He rolls onto his stomach and crawls on his hands and knees through the darkness toward her. In an instant his hands are on the back of her head, parting her hair. "Are you bleeding?"

"Get off me," she cries out, shoving against his chest. "You hit me, asshole."

"I *pushed* you. It was an accident," he kneels back, the distant stage lights gleaming in his wide, panicked eyes. "God, are you alright?"

She scowls at him, rubbing her chest with one hand while she clutches the back of her head with the other. Her hair is dry beneath her fingertips, so that's a plus. No blood.

"Do you feel dizzy?" he asks.

She shakes her head. "Just pissed off."

"I'm sorry." His big chest deflates as he pushes out a breath. "I woke up and you were…What were you doing?"

"CPR. I thought you were dead."

"What? No, I was sleeping." Any semblance of sympathy is gone from his voice. His face hardens, his mouth presses into a barely visible line, masked by the thick fuzz of his facial hair. "Why would you think I was dead out here?"

"Why would you be *sleeping* out here?"

His brow furrows as he pulls himself to his feet, grunting and grimacing, a big, grumpy bear awakened early from his hibernation. He snatches her glasses up from the ground and thrusts them out toward her. "Because I thought it was the only place where I could get a moment's peace. Obviously not."

After putting her glasses back on, Liz mirrors his scowl, using the edge of the trailer to lift herself from the ground. Apoplectic indignation boils her blood. "I was *trying* to help you."

"I didn't need your help," he snaps, storming past her

with great, lumbering steps. "Just mind your own business and leave me alone."

She lifts her fingers from the back of her head, bringing them round once more to double check for blood. Thankfully there's still nothing there. He clearly hadn't meant to hurt her, but that doesn't mean she's any less salty. Okay, most of it is embarrassment. She thought she could be a hero, but she only succeeded in waking the guy up from his nap. Whirring around to watch him, she notices he's limping. "Wait, are you hurt?"

"Leave me alone."

She presses on, jogging a little to catch up with him. He's tall and his steps, even hampered by injury, are almost twice the length of her own. "What is your problem?"

"Right now?" he grumbles. "You."

"I'm just trying to help."

He stops and turns, bearing down on her. "Listen, I don't need your help, okay? I was sleeping. I do a tiring job. I'm not just some la-dee-da fucking musician who barely has to break a sweat."

Every word he grumbles ignites a tiny fire in her blood, until her entire body is filled with a blaze. And yet, she can't ignore the way her body pulls her toward him. He smells so goddamn *manly*. Sweat and some kind of chemical-oily smell, the freshness of the earth and a vague undertone of men's bodywash. He folds his big, muscled arms over his broad chest and stares at her, as if waiting for her to speak.

She narrows her eyes. "Sorry, what?"

He sighs. "Leave. The show's over anyway. All artists should be off-site, why are you hanging around?"

Her annoyance returns tenfold. "I was leaving. I only stopped to save your life."

A muscle in his cheek leaps as he glares down at her.

"Alright, jeez. I'm going." She picks her bag up from the ground and slings it over her shoulder, muttering, "Jerk."

"I heard that."

"Good." She doesn't look back as she storms back across the stage and out of the festival site, down a short path surrounded by tall stalks of corn. The gravel crunches beneath the roadie's feet as he trails her just a couple of steps behind, shepherding her out into the parking lot.

"Why are you following me?"

"Making sure you're safe." There's no softness to his tone, but it cools off her temper just a little.

When they're out in the clear and she can see her little black car, she takes her keys out of her bag and picks up her pace. The echoing crunch of his step fades.

Almost reflexively she turns to thank him, swallowing the words at the last moment.

He stands watching her, his forearms flexing, folded over his chest as he waits under the frame of the open metal gate. To say that he looks like the type of man who wrestles grizzly bears is an understatement. He would only have to glance at a Kodiak to have it scampering off into the woods like a frightened puppy dog. And right now, all that fearsome grumpy energy is focused solely on her. "Hurry up then."

"I'm going."

He's an ass. A frustrating, temperamental ass. Yet despite knowing this, she can't seem to stop wanting to provoke him. As she slips into the driver's seat, she calls out to him. "Maybe get an early night tonight, so you don't have to sleep on the job tomorrow."

"Maybe you should fu—" His retort is cut off as she

slams her car door shut and starts the ignition, but she sure as hell sees him flip her off.

Ass.

But she can't fight back her smile. In the sanctuary of her car, she presses her teeth into the cushion of her lower lip. And though the parking lot is dark and he's some distance away, she lets her eyes wander over the big, broad shape of his torso.

There's just so much of him, as though one body couldn't contain such a surly jerk, so he had to make do with combining two together. Long legs, thick thighs, round belly, big broad chest, strong arms. The thought of being pinned beneath a titan like him makes her stomach flutter. But the thought of watching him crumble to ruins beneath her… The thought of turning all that man to Jell-o…

She pushes out a breath as her chest flutters. If this festival is to be her last Vixen's gig, she may as well go out on a bang.

In fact, she may as well go out on the biggest bang ever.

---

It's a quarter after midnight when Jones finally stumbles through his front door, worn ragged by the day. The inevitability of an even harder one tomorrow hangs like a yoke on his shoulders.

Kicking off his shoes he groans and runs his hand through his hair.

"I can't do it anymore," he whispers, releasing the admission which has played like a broken record through his mind the past two years. Ever since the pain began. "God, I can't do it."

The mirror hanging from the wall confirms his suspicions; he looks as shit as he feels. Dark circles and creases beneath his eyes, pallid complexion, and a slimy film of cold sweat shines on his brow. He's becoming his dad, through and through; a bitter, aching man who pushes away anyone before they can get too close. A bulldozer.

If he wasn't so afraid of the ghost of his father reaching out of the glass and beating him with a slipper, he'd cry.

A soft scraping sound behind him cuts off his thoughts. Roxy, his big red iguana paces her terrarium, bobbing her head. She can leave the tank at any time and wander around the house, but she likes to stay beneath the heat lamp and sleep on her hammock. The tank they had available for her at the shelter was far too small, so he agreed to take her off their hands for a couple of weeks. That was three years ago. The fervent head bobs likely mean she wants grapes. She always wants grapes.

"It's too late for treats," he mutters. He takes a step and the soft tan carpet has turned to a bed of nails.

Sucking in his breath, he presses his back teeth together, makes his way slowly to the tank and clicks off the lamp. He gives the lizard a companionable scratch at the hard arc of her jaw. "Go to sleep, Roxy. Food tomorrow."

His own belly is grumbling but he'll deal with that tomorrow too. Right now, he has more pressing concerns.

One good thing about his house—the shower is always scalding. The water pressure could wear down granite, and that's precisely what he feels like. A solid, unbending slab of a man, cold, hard and grim. As he closes his eyes and the water blasts the back of his neck, he sees the woman again, bent over him as she prepared to give him CPR. The kiss of life.

He chuckles, bitterly. It would take a lot more than a kiss to bring him back.

As he rubs a bar of soap over his soft, tattooed torso, taking care with the silver bar in his right nipple, he sighs. She might be a busy-body, but she had meant well. He shouldn't have snapped like that. Too proud to admit it was strange for him to sleep at the back of the trailers. Too strong to push her back gently. Too fucking out of it to behave like a normal human being.

The sound of her head smacking against the side of the trailer sends a wave of nausea flooding through his empty stomach. He'd panicked, shoved her back so hard his wrist ached. And then he'd thrown her off the site, and made her drive alone at night after hitting her head.

He really is an asshole.

As he lathers shampoo through his beard, he tries not to imagine her hurt, but even though the water is scalding, his blood runs cold.

# THREE

By any measure, tomorrow is a big day. Liz knows full well that she should be sleeping, but instead she sits on her bed, mind whirring. The darkened fish tank bubbles away in the corner of her room; the residence of Jim, her blue and red crowntail betta. Normally the sound of the water helps her sleep, but tonight even the usual tricks don't seem to work. She should be sleeping in preparation for the festival, but her thoughts are blistering.

A dozen brochures lay strewn across the bed. She's read them all so many times that they fall open on the pages for the massage therapy courses. She knows the entry requirements, the slight variations in their programs, the facilities at the campuses. They're almost comforting.

Almost.

Over the years she's applied to nearly all of them, starting with the one she wanted the least and working her way up, subconsciously already decided she would reject their offer of a place. Try as she might to focus on her future, she can't help but preempt her bandmates' heartache. Anya in particular would take it hard. She'd beg Liz to stay, and so, Liz rejects.

Eight years of making music, finally making enough money from it that she only has to work part-time, getting to spend every other day in rehearsals with her best friends. It's a dream for so many.

But enough hesitation. Enough putting it off for just one more week, a month, a year.

"I'm leaving the band."

The words sound so strange no matter how many times she says them, no matter what configuration they emerge in.

Because they're a lie.

No matter how many times she tells herself she's done, an excuse comes along; a wedding, a new album, a gig, a festival. She clings to excuses like a safety rope, rather than trusting her ability to swim alone.

Excuses are safe. The Vixens are safe.

She closes the brochures and lies down, watching the bubbles in the fish tank dance in the dark, and tries to think of something less disappointing.

The roadie. All that man. All that brutish strength and intimidating size. She could spend hours exploring him, finding what he likes and doesn't, letting him do the same to her. She could get to know him, coax softness from his perpetually downturned lips.

Or—and the more she thinks on it, the more she prefers the idea—she could just ask him to fuck her. Quick, brutal, a release. A goodbye.

She tries not to let herself dwell on the thought that he might just be another distraction.

The next day is Halloween, and Jones is still imagining the worst.

Despite it being way too early for the woman to arrive, Jones deliberately gives himself jobs to do on the edge of the stage, in view of the artists' entrance so he'll see her when she comes in. But tangled among his worry, some part of him— the part he thought had left him years ago—still feels a little giddy at the sensation of her hands on him. Is he really that desperate for human contact?

He kneels to tape a cable to the edge of the stage and holds his breath as pain shoots down his legs. Five hours of restless sleep didn't do anything except exacerbate it. Neither did working through the agony. He's out of ideas.

But worse than the pain is the shame. He replays the scene from last night over and over in his mind. The loud thud of the woman hitting her head haunts him. He shouldn't have hurried her out. He shouldn't have let her drive home alone.

She could have passed out half way down the highway or driven into a ditch somewhere on the backroads.

"Shit," he mutters.

"I see you're your usual cheery self today," Imran quips behind him.

The shock of Imran's voice so close makes Jones flinch, sending another spasm through his thighs. He bites down on the agony as he stands and forces himself to remain upright. "You need to start wearing a bell round your neck so I know where you are."

"But I like sneaking up on you. Especially on Halloween." Imran grins, his teeth bright beneath the grey brush of his mustache. "Anyway, I just wanted to let you know we've got about half an hour before the artists arrive and there's already a queue outside the audience entrance."

Fear sits like an iceberg in Jones's gut; cold and jagged, weighing him down. There's so much left to do. He hasn't even checked the security crew for the artists' parking lot are clear on who to allow in and who gets kicked out. "No worries."

"Anything I can do?" Imran asks.

"Uh…" Jones's heart skips as he catches sight of her.

The woman strides confidently through the backstage area dressed all in black. A long, flowing skirt swooshes against her ankles as she walks. Her shirt is cropped, showing just a couple of inches of warm, golden skin above her navel.

His mouth dries out as he tries to drag his gaze away from the sway of her full, curvaceous hips. She's a pain in his ass, he reminds himself, always under his feet or refusing to mind her own business. At least she's alive.

She turns her head to glance at him as she strolls past, her big, dark eyes framed by thick cat's-eye glasses, giving her that sultry librarian look. And there's something in her expression. It's in the way her perfect lips curve, the way her dark eyebrows crinkle, and her chin tips out toward him. Amusement? Maybe a little teasing? Confidence.

It's a look which says she knows he'd tear down the stage splinter by splinter, just for the privilege of being her throne.

*Woof. Down boy.*

The combination of relief, and the simple fact that she's downright gorgeous is a powerful one. If he didn't know any better, he'd think the look she gave him was an invitation to follow her.

He dismisses the fantasy as quickly as it enters his mind and focuses on hard facts. Jones may have a reputation as an asshole, but deep, deep, *deep* down he knows he's capable of being a somewhat decent man. Okay, maybe not with humans, but even with his meagre social skills, he knows he should apologize again while things are a little calmer.

"You want me to brief security for you?" Imran presses him.

"Uh, no. I'll do that." Jones clears his dry throat. "I'd rather do the important stuff myself so I know it's done right. Can you finish up here while I head out back?"

"Sure thing." Imran grins. "I'll do what I can to save your old bones."

"Fuck off," Jones growls as he makes his way across the stage. But even he has to silently admit that standing is far easier on him right now.

He switches his focus to what he'll say when he approaches her:

*Hello there, just wanted to apologize for being such an ass...*
*Hi, sorry about your head.*
*So, you're alive! That's good.*
*Shit.*

By the time he reaches Vixen's Wail's trailer, he has to dry his palms on the sides of his shirt. He shouldn't be this nervous. Maybe because apologizing admits fault, which requires more vulnerability than he's comfortable with permitting himself.

Or maybe because historically, admitting he did something wrong resulted in him getting his ass whooped.

The creaking of the trailer door chases away those unwelcome thoughts.

"Is there a reason you're lurking out here?" the woman asks, eyes narrowing with understandable suspicion as she stares down at him from the top of the stairs. "Or am I interrupting your naptime again?"

Jones's forces a long breath as his jaw tightens. Even three steps up she's barely above him, and yet her attitude she may as well be ten feet tall. "No, actually. I came to speak to you."

It takes every measly crumb of his decency not to stare at the strip of bare skin above the waistband of her skirt. But in the back of his mind images play of him dropping to his knees to kiss her there, inching her top a little higher, pulling her skirt a little lower… An unwelcome twitch strums inside his boxers.

"What did I do now?" She folds her arms over her chest, pushing her breasts together.

"Nothing. Shit, can you get off my case for one—" He exhales slowly and tries to calm himself. "I came to apologize."

Her eyes widen. "Oh, okay. This should be good." White teeth flash against the berry-pink cushion of her lower lip, pressing against the tender flesh and making his cock ache. "Come in. It's cold out here."

He does as he's told, but deep down he knows this isn't a good idea. Yet every cell in his big, brutal body drives him up those steps. He no longer cares about the pain or that he hasn't briefed security, or even that he desperately needs this job. Jones is no longer in command.

The artists' trailers are all identical inside and he knows them well, but as he stoops beneath the threshold, somehow everything is different. The air is thick and hard to breathe, scented with a soft, pleasant sweetness he can't quite place.

Jones dips his head a little so his beard brushes his collar and hides the heat crawling up his throat. "You're here early."

She smiles. "Yeah."

"Do you always arrive early, before a gig?"

"No. Just today."

The woman crosses to the other side of the trailer and sits on the couch, which is fixed in an L-shape to two adjacent walls. She leans on one hip and lifts her legs so she's reclining on the couch. Some part of him—the site manager part—balks at the sight of her feet on the upholstery, but since he's here to broker peace he lets it slide.

"Okay," she grins, opening her arms wide to rest them on the back of the couch. "Let's hear it."

He shifts his weight between his feet, unused to feeling this small. "I'm sorry."

"And?"

He raises an eyebrow. "You're enjoying this."

"I like watching men beg."

He's not completely clueless. She's flirting with him, and he's more than happy to oblige her. It's been a while since anyone has. He swallows hard and tries to keep his voice level, despite the pulse of his jittering heart. "Fine. I'm here to apologize for pushing you so hard last night. I woke up, panicked, and reacted badly, but I didn't mean to hurt you. And I'm sorry I sent you out driving by yourself when you could've had a concussion. That was shitty of me."

It could be a trick of the light, but he could swear her expression softens a little. Her appearance slips from ridicule to genuine surprise, and back again before he has time to fully convince himself of it.

"I was worried about you last night," he adds. "I couldn't stop thinking about y—about what could have happened to you."

There it is again, that devastating shift. Except this time, it sticks a while longer. Her eyebrows tilt a little. "You thought about me?"

He doesn't answer.

She lowers her eyes. "What if I told you that I thought about you last night too?"

How is it possible for a granite heart to soar? It's a momentary lightness, a giddy swell in his chest which almost pushes his lips into a smile. "Well, I suppose that depends on what kind of thoughts you were having."

It could mean anything. She could mean that she thought about putting in a complaint to his bosses, or hell, even the police. But he doesn't think so.

"I had a lot of thoughts." Swinging her legs down from the couch, she stands. "But mainly I thought about doing this."

His body braces with the expectation of her pressing herself against him, but she simply walks past him, taking all the air from the room with her. She leans over a countertop and peers through the white horizontal blinds covering the trailer's window. They're pulled down but they aren't closed. She arches her back a little, sticking out her ass as she raises onto her tiptoes.

He takes a step toward her, as if pulled by an invisible rope.

"I was thinking about how we could make it up to each other, for last night," she says, eyes darting back and forth, searching the area outside the trailer.

Another step.

He could be fired for this. He's expected to maintain a level of professionalism with the artists, and right now he's so far below that level he feels the flames of Hell flickering against the soles of his feet.

Jones can lug heavy speakers across the stage, hoist lights up onto their rigging, and has wrestled with big, tough metalheads all his life, but he's not strong enough to tear his eyes from the smooth curve of her round ass as she bends over the counter. Between the hem of her skirt and her cropped top, her back is warm and tanned. His fingers flex with the need to touch her. "Oh, you were?"

"Would you like me to tell you?"

"Never much been one for words. Why don't you show me?" He takes another step, leaving just a couple of feet between them. He's close enough he can smell her skin, the soft scent of her conditioner.

She glances over her shoulder and fixes him in a dark-eyed stare. "Come closer."

Heat pours over his body, like molten metal coating every inch of him as she lifts her skirt. She isn't wearing anything underneath and he's never hated his back pain as much as he does right now.

Two years ago, he would have fucked her until she couldn't stand. He would've taken his time with her, licked her, fucked her. He would have had her coming so hard her fingers would still be trembling when she tried to play her keyboard tonight on stage.

Nothing good can come of this.

*Leave,* he tells himself. *Go to the staff restrooms and jerk off while thinking of her. Nothing more. I can't do this. I can't. I can't take another step toward her.*

But he does.

# FOUR

L iz's breath stalls as his rough hands caress the curve of her ass. She isn't even sure of who she is anymore.

Liz Larkin is never this brazen.

Liz Larkin doesn't throw herself at gigantic asshole roadies without even knowing their name.

But perhaps that's been the problem all along. Liz Larkin has never truly lived the way she wants to. She has done what was expected of her and not a thing more.

Electricity tingles along her spine as she bows her back to his touch. She expected his hands would be callused, toughened by hard work, molded by brutality. She didn't know they could feel this good; rough, warm and oh-so strong.

"Look at you," he whispers, his voice edged and rough like chips of flint. "So beautiful. So goddamned sexy."

The rush of breath from his big, broad chest prompts her to release her own. "We need to hurry."

He tuts dismissively, skating his rough palms up the backs of her thighs. "I'm not about that. I want to take my time with you. I want to savor you."

A shudder of pleasure rolls through her body as he uses his thumbs to part the lips of her pussy. But once the shock subsides it isn't enough. She tries to back onto him, tries to angle her hips so his fingers brush against her clit, but he gives her nothing. She presses her teeth together, biting down the frustration and need tangling in the pit of her stomach. "My band could be here any minute. Just fuck me."

"I'm not going to fuck you," he growls.

Rejection stings, but she isn't about to let him know that. "Then don't waste my time."

As she pushes up from the counter and attempts to stand upright, the roadie's hand presses against the small of her back, urging her down. Firm, but not forceful.

Liz glances over her shoulder at him, her heart racing and stomach fluttering. She gulps down a hard-fought breath as the room dims and shimmers around them.

His pupils are ink-black and blown out, his mouth pressed into a thin line. His big chest rises and staggers back down. "You stay right there. I'm not done with you."

She nods and has to bite her lip to stop herself from moaning. This shouldn't feel so good. She wanted to watch him crumble, but she's the one falling apart.

The roadie keeps one hand on her back as he slides his fingers of the other hand between her folds. A low growl escapes him as she gasps.

"You feel so fucking good," he says. "So hot and wet. I want to watch you come."

"Yes. God, yes."

His fingers stop just shy of her clit. "Tell me you want it."

"I want it," she snarls through her teeth, pushing back against him.

"See, you got me in here expecting me to beg you. But

the tables have turned somewhat, haven't they?"

A low groan escapes her as he removes his hand from her altogether "Bastard."

His low chuckle stokes the fire in her belly. "This is just a game, okay? You're mine until I make you come, but if you tell me to stop I will, without hesitation. Understand?"

"Yes."

Big, black boots step between her feet, gently kicking her ankles apart so she's spread open for him.

"Hurry."

"Now, now. You're being a brat," he tells her. His hand glides up her back, following the path of her spine as her skin tingles beneath his touch. "Unless you want this to stop, I don't want to hear another word out of you other than you gasping my name. It's Jones. That's all I want you to say. Jones. You hear?"

She nods, biting into her lip. "Yes, Jones."

"Good girl."

He slides two fingers either side of her clit sending a shiver of pleasure through her body. Just the sensation of someone else's hands on her is enough to make her knees quake. "Oh God."

"Oh God who?"

This asshole. She'll kill him. "Jones."

"Not so hard, is it?"

He keeps teasing her, his firm, callused fingers stroking the area around her clit, but never touching it directly. His hand completely covers her pussy, warm and heavy and rough. Her pleasure builds quickly, hastened by the taboo of what they're doing, and he seems to know it. He keeps her teetering on the edge of an orgasm, tethered to him. Her pussy muscles clench, desperate for release.

He draws out every sensation, savoring her squirms, her whimpers.

Her stomach drops as something catches her eye out the window, a flash of long blue hair blowing in the wind as two figures walk down from the stage, heading toward the trailers. It's the band's cellist, Jordan, and beside her is their new singer, Étienne.

Liz and Jones are seconds away from getting caught.

"Faster," she gasps. "They're coming."

He doesn't scold her for breaking his rules. Instead, he brings his fingers together, letting them slide over her swollen clit.

"Oh fuck," she gasps, her knuckles white as she grips the edges of the counter. "Jones."

She cries out as she comes, pressing her ass against the round, warm curve of his belly as he keeps strumming her clit, coaxing out every last second of pleasure.

"Good," he whispers, smoothing his hand over the base of her spine.

Trembling, Liz stands upright, letting her skirt fall back down to her ankles as she scrapes her hair over her shoulder. "Thank you."

"I'll hold them off," Jones mutters. His cheeks are rosy and pink above the coarse hair of his beard. "I'm sorry."

And with that, he leaves, boots stomping across the floor. The door smacks against its frame, plunging the trailer into silence. He didn't even ask her name.

Each breath is a battle as she watches him out the window. He blocks Jordan and Étienne's path to the trailer, giving Liz a few precious moments to regain her composure. Shit. As if she could ever feel the same way again.

She doesn't even know if she won the game she set out to

play. Does what happened between them even count as seduction?

As the roadie storms away her heart presses against her ribs, urging her after him. Somewhere in his hurried departure there was an apology, wasn't there? She has no clue what he was apologizing for.

She achieved what she set out to do, a fitting send-off after almost a decade with the band. Time to regroup, refocus.

The trailer door creaks open, snapping her from her thoughts. She forces a smile and greets her bandmates. "Happy Halloween!"

<hr>

He's worked backstage at gigs and festivals for almost twenty years, but this is the first time since his rookie season that Jones has stood shaking in the shadows as the bands play.

What was he thinking?

Every second that passes could be his last on the job, and then what? He still has his shifts at the bar, but it isn't enough. Too intimidating for a comfortable job, too broken for a physical one. On Mondays he volunteers at the local animal shelter, which he loves with his whole damn heart, but it's not like he can do a job like that and get paid.

He rubs his face with his hands. "Fuck."

He needs to apologize again. He needs to go back there and try to get a minute alone with her and grovel his ass off. Apologize for hurting her last night, apologize for his inappropriate behavior since pretty much the moment he met her. Even then, he wouldn't be surprised if he was fired. She has every right to demand his head on a platter.

"You look rough," Imran yells over the bone-jarring racket coming from the stage. He keeps his thumb over the button of his walkie-talkie, never once taking his eyes from the performers onstage.

The smoke machine by Jones's feet spews out another wave of dense fog. Phantasmagoria Euphoria are about six hours into their first song—or so it feels. Not that he's complaining. There's only one more band left for the evening, and it's the last band on earth he wants to see.

"I always look rough," Jones replies, wincing as just the effort of speaking sends a spasm of pain down his left ass cheek.

"Okay, now I know something's wrong. You haven't told anyone to fuck off in the past three hours."

"Fuck off." The words barely roll out of him. His pulse flutters at the very back of his throat, making his breath shake. He may as well just quit now, confess to Imran and take back at least some control.

"Half-hearted, unconvincing… a little superficial. I give it a two out of ten."

"No," Jones snaps, clenching his back teeth. "Really. Fuck off."

"Alright, that's a ten. What's wrong?"

His stomach churns as his blood runs cold, like a goddamn shaved ice machine. "I think I fucked up."

"Shit…" Imran sighs before giving the signal for one of his team to switch out the guitarists' instruments. "Did you forget to brief security? I had a feeling you would."

"No, I… wait." The chill spreads, freezing his lungs solid. "Ah, crap."

"You might still have time." Imran claps his hand on Jones's shoulder and pushes him gently in the direction of the entrance. "Just pray no rabid fans are out there stalking yet."

He's a dead man.

As Jones hurries away from the stage his heart is pounding. He would have hoped that security would know not to let anyone in without checking their passes and making sure their names were on the list. The company they hired is supposed to be shit-hot, the best of the best... but then again, so is he.

Ignoring the pain, he lumbers down the steps on the side of the stage, his breath blowing hard as he hurries. If he's quick about it he might not have to see her right now, he can figure out what he's going to say.

"Jones!" Imran's voice calls behind him as he reaches the base of the stairs. "Before you do that give Vixen's Wail their five-minute call. They actually only have four and a half minutes."

"Can't you do that?"

Imran points at the walkie talkie in his hand before speaking into it "Okay, send the coffin through the trapdoor. Phantasmagoria Euphoria are on their last song."

Shit.

He runs back up the stairs and through the chaos backstage, baring his teeth as spikes of pain shoot through him. He needs to be fast, draw as little attention to himself as possible. He lumbers across the lot and raps his knuckles on Vixen's Wail's trailer door without even climbing the steps. "Five minutes. This is your five-minute call."

Right, done. He turns and bolts, unable to face her again, and heads out to the security tent by the artists' entrance.

Damage control. That's all he can do now.

# FIVE

Liz silently thanks Jordan and Étienne for distracting the rest of the band. They're so busy getting cozy with each other that no one seems to notice the shift in her. If they do, they're too caught up in the drama to say anything. Their big bearded drummer, Finn, is excitedly reading comments from their fans on all their social media sites, but the buzz in the trailer still isn't enough to rouse her.

The only time she has felt anything lately was during those few, frantic minutes with Jones, but she can't pin down exactly what those feelings were. Lust, certainly. Curiosity, indignancy, elation? Excitement.

That was it. For the first time in a long time, she was excited.

*"Five minutes! This is your five-minute call."*

She nearly jumps out of her skin at the sound of his voice on the other side of the door. Thankfully, the call has the same effect on the rest of the band.

Regroup, refocus. He didn't even want her name. She got what she wanted.

She stands and rotates her shoulders. The others are on edge, running through their warm-ups and getting themselves psyched for the biggest performance of their careers. The creak and slap of the trailer door makes her jump again, but it's only Jordan heading outside.

What would Liz even do if the roadie walked in here? She couldn't look at him, but it would be equally as unbearable to look at anything else. He's impossible, a magnet charged both ways, simultaneously drawing and repelling her.

"Hey," Anya says as she approaches, a magenta pink guitar pick clenched between her teeth as she tousles her auburn waves with her fingertips. "Nervous? It's going to be okay."

Liz shrugs a shoulder and continues smudging her eyeliner with the tip of an applicator. Is she that transparent? "I'm good."

Anya removes the pick from her teeth and shakes out her arms. "Alright, but if you need to talk…"

"I know. Thanks." The band are always there for each other, always stressing the importance of talking things through rather than letting resentment simmer.

An ache in the pit of her stomach gives her pause. She loves them. She truly does. And she *could* tell them about her decision to leave the band right now. Whether she *should* is another question entirely.

The thought occurs to her that maybe she's robbing the others of the chance to know this is her last gig. Perhaps it would be better to tell them now, give them time to adjust, and a chance to mark the occasion.

But they're excited. So, so excited just to be there, playing music together with their friends and no matter how much the secret burns in her chest, she can't bear to pass along that pain. Not yet.

Just a little longer.

"Alright, gather round," Finn calls, lifting his arms and stretching so he drums his fingertips across the ceiling. "Where's Jordo?"

"She went out," Liz says, folding her arms over her chest as she leans against the countertop where she and Jones… well, *the* countertop.

Finn makes a little sound of disappointment at the back of his throat and scrunches his nose. "Well, Étienne listen closely and tell her what I say, okay? You can be my secretary."

"You got it," the new singer says, shoving his fingers into the pockets of his painted-on jeans.

"It's been…" Finn raises his eyes. "God, it's been almost a decade since we were teenagers playing out of my grandma's garage."

Oh jeez.

A twinge of nostalgia tightens Liz's chest. Back then Anya wasn't even part of the band. They had a different guitarist—Danny, a total jerk who turned out to be even worse than her rock-bottom opinion of him. He and Jordan dated for a few months, but their breakup left the band in tatters. At least the cellist has Étienne now. He seems nice. Cute too.

The total opposite of the man whose touch Liz still feels, rough and savage between her thighs.

Finn continues, "We honestly sucked back then, but even on that first day I knew we were something special. And now, all these years later, here we are, headlining Ghoulfest. I can't even tell you how proud and honored I am to play alongside you, or… I guess behind you." He chuckles. What a dork.

"No matter what happens on that stage tonight, we're Vixens. Now and always. And… Aw, shit, I love you."

Liz swallows the lump in her throat. She was definitely right not to announce she was leaving today, not while Finn is so set on giving her a major case of the feels.

"Fuck it," Finn says pulling Étienne into his arms. "I'm nervous, I need a hug."

The band shuffle together, tangling their arms until they're one enormous multi-limbed entity. Liz is crushed between their lead vocalist, Mia, and Étienne's creaking leather jacket.

"Alright," Liz groans as the air is squashed from her lungs. "Let's go."

"Let's fucking rock this," Finn bellows from the center of the huddle.

After a barrage of similarly effusive platitudes from the rest of the band, Liz turns, desperate to keep her eyes from the countertop where she can still see herself, bent over.

*"Last call. Vixen's Wail to the stage."*

Jones's voice sends the memory of his touch jolting through her body. She's thankful for her thick stage makeup which hides the heat creeping across her cheeks. It's show-time, just an hour or so to go and they'll be out of there, far, *far* away where she never has to see him again.

Even if she wanted to.

Which she absolutely does not.

As she and the band make their way out of the trailer and step into the electric night air, Liz's heart stops. She suspects the rest of them feel theirs freeze too, though not wholly for the same reason.

Standing not ten feet from the trailer, facing off against each other, is Jordan and their former guitarist, Danny.

"Shit." The word bursts from Liz, dragging all the air in her lungs along with it. Did she somehow think that dickhead into existence by thinking about him for five goddamn seconds?

And what's worse, Jones is standing a little way back, his arms folded over his big chest as he watches the scene with a scowl. He stands slightly askew, leaning a little to the right as though he can't put his weight down fully on his left side.

Liz barely even registers the commotion with Danny as Finn and Étienne rush over to help Jordan. They can handle themselves, but she can't tear her eyes from Jones.

He's an enigma. Rude and surly one moment, kind and caring the next. Even when she was pinned down by him, dominated by him, he made it abundantly clear she was still in control.

*Unless you want this to stop, I don't want to hear another word out of you other than you gasping my name.*

Her stomach drops as his stoney eyes slide over to her. There's something in those eyes, the way his lids hang as heavy as the corners of his mouth. There's something wrong.

It's the same look as the patients in the videos and career guides for the massage therapy courses have in their eyes. It's the look she sees in the mirror when she contemplates giving up her dreams and staying in the band so she doesn't have to tell them she's leaving. It's the expression she imagines the Vixens will wear when she finally plucks up the courage to tell them.

Pain. He's hurting.

And yet, his gaze remains fixed on her. His chest rises sharply, as though preparing to speak. It's as if there is no festival or conflict going on around them. It's just them, alone again but neither of them willing to break the silence. In place of words, she offers him a smile.

Sudden movement breaks the spell. Jordan's fist darts out, connecting with Danny's jaw and sending him staggering back. Jones is on the jerk in an instant, pinning his arms behind his back and marching him back toward the stage.

It's far hotter than it has any right to be, Jones's tattooed bicep flexing, his deep voice growling threats as Danny whines and protests.

She barely even notices the roar of the crowd beyond the stage as they wait for Vixen's Wail to perform.

T he security personnel do their best to avoid eye contact as Jones and the trespasser approach the gate. He isn't going to yell at them for letting the man past—after all, he isn't completely blameless himself—but what's important is that they *believe* he'll tear into them.

Having a reputation as a bastard without actually being a bastard is an artform, and Jones is the goddamn master.

The pain shooting down his back, ass, and thighs makes him sweat, forces him to bare his teeth. Whatever. It only adds to the effect. Tonight, he'll be restless, and not just because he can't stop thinking about the woman, or worrying about what he's done.

"She hit me," the man hisses, trying to twist his arms from Jones's grip.

"I saw."

"Well, are you going to throw her out too?"

"No."

The man sneers as they reach the gate and march past the

guards standing there, engrossed in whatever they have written on their lists or the contents of their coffee cups, or counting chips of fucking gravel on the parking lot floor.

"You know," the guy says. "This is probably the high point of your entire life. Sad, isn't it?"

This is a tactic Jones hasn't heard before. He lets the guy go, but remains in the gateway, blocking his path, arms folded and stance wide. "Is it?"

"Yeah. Here you are—what, fifty? Fifty-five?"

"Thirty-eight." He doesn't even know why he answers, but he does.

The man bursts out laughing. "Holy shit, dude. You're not even forty and you're crumbling. Just a sad, pathetic, ugly bastard whose whole job is to do whatever those people…" He points over Jones's shoulder. "What the beautiful people, the people with the talent, tell you to do."

The slew of insults hardly dents Jones's self-esteem. It's nothing he hasn't said to the mirror every day for the last two years.

"Hm." Jones grunts and tilts his chin toward the parking lot. "See you later then."

"That's it?" The guy's face cracks with a broad, shit-eating grin.

Jones considers. It doesn't *have* to be it. The desire to pluck every single straggly hair from this asshole's little black goatee is a persistent one, and the longer he spends out here, the less time he has to spend trying not to stare at the keyboardist.

But that would leave Imran and the rest of his team short.

Jones sighs. "That's it. Go."

The asshole cackles, shaking his head. "Loser."

He reaches out a long, slender arm and pushes firmly against Jones's shoulder, proving the point that there's nothing Jones will do to stop him.

As Jones's body sways from the gentle impact, a red-hot poker rams through the base of his spine and down, all the way down to the back of his thigh. It turns his jaw to steel, his skin to scalding vapor. Every light on the stage must have blown out all at once, because the world is plunged into darkness as his stomach lurches and acid splashes the back of his throat.

Pain. Pain like he's never felt before.

A voice in the darkness speaks to him—probably the asshole—but the words are meaningless.

Back when he got his tattoos, he breathed through it, distracted himself by staring at the little drawings on the walls, and reading the names of the inks lined up on the counter; raven black, blood red, mystic blue, starlight white, snot green…

He tries it now. A deep breath in, a broken one out, polluting the air just by pulling it into him.

People gather around him, security guards, and other roadies. The word 'ambulance' echoes through his mind, spoken by a faceless bystander.

"Fuck off," he groans and barges through them, as flaming arrows pelt his lower back.

Jones can admit many things about himself. He'll admit he's a waste, a disappointment, a downright awful, ugly son-of-a-bastard.

But he'll never admit he's hurting. Not to anyone.

# Six

"Holy shit!" Finn laughs for about the fiftieth time since they left the stage. His hair is soaked through with sweat and his cheeks are shiny and pink. "Ho-*lee* shit."

Liz smiles as she pulls on her hoodie and draws a deep breath. All things considered it was a great gig. The perfect ending.

The rest of the band have already left, hurrying home to their loved ones to tell them all about their magical, dramatic night. From the way Finn throws his unzipped backpack over his shoulder and steps on the backs of his shoes, he's just as keen to get home.

Liz takes her time. She doubts her betta fish waited up to ask about her day.

She scrubs the thick makeup off her face and moisturizes, feeling a hundred times more refreshed. It's getting pretty late, but she's not tired. Right now, she feels like she could run a marathon. She feels free.

"Do you want me to walk you to the parking lot?" Finn

asks, holding his phone in his hand. The screen flashes with a picture of his wife and the words *incoming call.*

"I'm good." Liz shrugs. "There are still plenty of staff around."

"Alright, see you at the meeting next weekend." He swipes his thumb across the screen and puts the phone to his ear. His face lights up as he heads to the door. "Hi beautiful! Yes, it was awesome. Holy shit! I'm on my way home right now…"

The trailer door slaps shut, leaving Liz alone in the silence.

"I'm quitting the band," she says beneath her breath.

When she phrases it like that it sounds like giving up an addiction, a habit which has consumed her life for years.

Slinging her bag over her shoulder, she casts one last look around the trailer to make sure they haven't left anything behind. Considering there are eight Vixens now, they try to keep things tidy whenever they play venues like this.

It's like leaving a hotel room after a vacation. A decade-long vacation.

She steps out of the door and into the cold, crackling night. Backstage staff are still milling around, striking the stage and setting up for the second day of the festival.

But something draws her eye from them. A figure she half hoped she would never see again.

Jones.

He stands alone, eyes screwed shut, hands braced against a massive black amplifier. His heavy breaths and grunts break through the air.

"Are you alright?" Liz asks.

His eyes open and a sharp inhale raises his chest. He puts his boot on the lever of a battered red hand-truck lift and carefully tilts the amp toward him, staggering beneath the weight. "I'm fine. It's just busted."

He doesn't look fine. Despite the lift bearing most of the weight of the equipment, he staggers and limps beneath the load. A glossy film of sweat shines on his skin.

Liz presses her lips together as her brows furrow, but she can't just stand by and watch him struggle. "Do you need any help?"

"No."

He's lying, but there's little she can do. Her breath burns in her chest as she walks toward the entrance, and the slow crackle of the hand truck's wheels on the gravel stays steady ahead of her.

"Thank you," she calls out to the security personnel on the gate. "Have a good night."

They bid her goodnight, their tones bright and cheerful, but as Jones comments that he'll be back in just a few minutes, something shifts.

"Just lock him out," one of the staff mutters, much to the amusement of the others.

"Yeah, change the locks too."

"Asshole."

Liz casts a scowl over her shoulder.

The furrows in Jones's brow are etched even deeper as he battles with the heavy load of amps, fighting with the dolly to get them across the lot. He makes his way slowly toward a big silver truck. When he reaches it, he pulls down the back and stands for a moment, leaning his weight on the vehicle as his eyes glaze over.

Liz pauses. "Are you sure you don't need any help?"

"Certain." He doesn't even look at her. He just stares at the amp, as though he can will it onto the truck bed telekinetically. A muscle flexes above the brush of his beard as he clenches his jaw.

Letting her bag fall to the floor, Liz walks over to the side of the amp. "Well, tough shit. I'm helping anyway."

Jones releases a heavy sigh but finally concedes. He gives a little grunt as he pushes his weight up off the truck. "It's heavy."

"I'm strong."

"Alright. Lift with your legs."

"I know."

"I can't afford to be sued."

"I wouldn't." Liz frowns as he lowers himself to a half-squat beside her. His features tighten, eyes crinkling and his complexion reddening as he grips the handle on the amp. "You okay?"

Jones sighs. "Stop asking."

Being so close to him again makes her stomach tighten. Just a couple of hours ago she was at his mercy, bent over, exposed, loving every moment of it. Her cheeks redden.

"Alright, on three," Jones grumbles. "One, two, three..."

Liz hoists the amp, groaning as her arms strain to lift the heavy weight. The first couple of inches are relatively easy, but suddenly the weight is more than doubled. A sharp cry pierces the air, and her heart plummets as the expensive-looking equipment crashes to the floor.

"Fuck!" Jones snarls, pressing his palms to the gravel as the tendons in his neck bulge and strain. He gives a strained, agonized cry. It's like a scene from every werewolf movie she has ever seen. She half expects him to grow fur and claws.

Liz's heart races, her aching fingers curling as she fights back the urge to reach out to him. "What is it? What's wrong?"

"Nothing."

"It's clearly not nothing. You're hurt."

"No. No." He keeps his head down, refusing to look at her. Every syllable is forced out between bared teeth. "Just go."

"I'm not leaving you here like this." She pulls out her phone with shaking hands, fully aware that this was exactly how every monster movie damsel ended up getting mauled. "I'm calling an ambulance."

"Don't." His protest bursts from him like the crack of a whip, giving her pause. He sighs and closes his eyes. "Please, don't."

"Jones…" she says his name softly, reaching out to cup her hand over his big, round shoulder. He radiates heat through the black cotton of his shirt. Fortunately, it feels like there's just skin and hard muscle beneath the cotton… no fur. "You are hurt. I think you need to see a doctor."

He breathes slowly through his nose. "I can handle it. It's bad enough I had to ask to leave work early. I… don't…"

"Jones…"

He raises his eyes to meet hers and the pain in them twists her heart.

"Tell me what hurts."

He grunts in frustration as his lips press together into a thin line. "My back."

Liz's muscles relax just a fraction at his reply. It isn't much, but it's an answer; a fragile beam of light shining through his otherwise impenetrable defenses. But she could have guessed it was his back just from his limp, his crooked stance, his goddamn irritability.

"Is it always this bad?"

He gives a barely perceptible shake of his head. "This is worse."

Veins throb in his neck and forehead, as though the act of answering is just as painful for him as the physical agony. The tips of his fingers are bone white as he presses his palms against the earth.

Hurried footsteps behind Liz draw her attention. A tall, slim man with warm brown skin and a thick grey moustache, jogs toward them. She vaguely recognizes him as another one of the roadies.

"Jonesey?" the man calls out, concern apparent by his empathetic tone. "You alright?"

"Oh, for fuck's sake, tell him I'm fine," Jones seethes beneath his breath.

"Who is he?" Liz whispers.

"Imran." He frowns, swallowing hard. "He works with me."

There's little time to process what's happening as Liz stands and smiles at the approaching man. Jones is opening up to her, barely beginning to trust her. She has to do whatever she can to keep that door open.

"He's fine," she says brightly as Imran approaches. "He just needs a minute."

The man narrows his eyes in suspicion. "You sure?"

"Yeah," Jones grunts from the floor. "Just thought I heard a clunk coming from underneath the truck."

"Ah, right." Imran's moustache twitches as he folds his arms over his chest. He smiles at Liz. "Well, I can't help you with that, I'm afraid. No good with clunks."

Liz chuckles. The guy seems perfectly amiable, and she has no idea why Jones wouldn't want him to know. Still, if she's to maintain the hard-won shred of trust, she needs to respect his wishes.

Jones grunts as he pantomimes looking at the chassis of the vehicle. "Imran, while you're here, make yourself useful and give her a hand with the amp."

"Grumpy bastard, isn't he?" Imran grins at Liz.

"He sure is."

"Imagine working with him."

"You deserve a medal. And a raise."

Jones grumbles something inaudible from the ground as Liz and Imran squat to lift the amp. It doesn't take long for them to hoist it onto the truck bed and secure it with pillows and straps. When they're done, they pull over the bed's cover and lock it with a snap.

"Alright," Imran sighs, wiping his palms on his thighs. He turns to Jones and raises an eyebrow. "You found your clunk yet?"

"Not yet."

"Well, good luck with that. I'll see you tomorrow, yeah?"

"Yeah," Jones says. "See you."

Liz smiles politely as the men say their goodnights and Imran leaves. The night air grows thick and heavy as Jones relaxes his shoulders and ends his charade with the truck.

"Is it no better?" Liz asks, crouching back down beside him.

Jones shakes his head sullenly.

"Okay. Here's what I want to do." She reaches out to him once more, but this time she lets her hand trail across his shoulder blade, keeping her touch light and soothing. "I want to take you to urgent care and have them check you over."

"No, I—"

"Please?" More gentle, soothing circles.

He looks into her eyes and with every thundering heartbeat which lunges against her ribs, the muscles in his shoulders relax.

"What will they do to me?" he asks.

Liz frowns. "I'm not sure. But you can't keep on like this, not if it's getting worse." Her heart drops as he lowers his head. She can't just leave him like this. Even if he gets up now and can walk away, the next time he feels this kind of pain he might be alone. "If we go, I promise I'll stay with you the entire time."

His shoulders hunch as he pulls in a slow breath. "I don't want them to keep me there overnight."

"They won't. I promise. It's just urgent care. We can just go, see what they say, get a prescription and leave. And then you can decide what you want to do. But at least you might know what's causing it."

He bows his head again and rocks his weight back onto his knees. An agonized groan bursts from his lips as he lifts his hands from the ground. His wide palms are dented, pockmarked by the gravel.

Liz's hand slips from his shoulder and drifts in mid-air. He's hurt, grumpy, downright petulant and yet, she can't help craving the warmth of his skin beneath her touch. As soon as it's gone, she misses it.

"Who are you?" He asks.

"Oh." She can't help but chuckle after all they've been through, he still doesn't know her name. "Liz."

"Okay, Liz." He mutters her name like a curse as he uses the corner of his truck to lift himself, clinging to the edge of the bed to keep himself upright. "I'll go."

"Thank you."

"But if they try to keep me overnight, I'm not staying."

Relieved, Liz stands. "Your shoelaces are untied," she says. "Be careful."

"I don't tie them," he hisses through gritted teeth. "Can't—uh, shit."

She steps close to him, pressing her hip to his thigh to offer him support. He feels so sturdy and warm against her, and as he leans his weight onto her a little, she can't help but notice the hard strength in his tattooed arms, the round, softness of his stomach as she reaches around to help him into the passenger side door.

"I can drive," he grumps even as he climbs into the seat.

"I know," Liz replies, handing him the seatbelt so he can buckle himself in. "But I want you to take it easy for a minute."

In truth, she's afraid. She's afraid his back will spasm again and he'll lose control of the vehicle. But she can't tell him that. She barely knows him, but she already knows he's proud to a fault, unwilling to accept help, eager to prove he can do things by himself.

It does occur to her that she's vulnerable here too, but if he had wanted to hurt her, he has already had ample opportunity. Back in the trailer he was respectful, insistent on her boundaries. He didn't just ask her consent, he relished it.

As his hardened gaze turns to her, her stomach tightens. For the first time since her ill-fated attempt to perform CPR on him, they're at eye-level, their faces only inches apart.

He's nothing like any of the men she has ever been with before. On a scale of Étienne to Finn, her previous partners have leaned closer to the prettier end. But Jones makes even big, burly drummer, Finn seems soft and delicate by comparison. Jones is a gruffly handsome, sentient refrigerator with a tumbleweed balanced on top of it.

He's all scowls and surliness, tattoos inked across muscled biceps and sinewed forearms, grubby black shirt stretched across his soft round stomach. Liz's heart thrums as she helps him buckle in, and when his stony eyes fix her in a scowl her throat dries out.

"Your car will get stuck here when they lock the gates," he tells her.

"I'll get it in the morning."

But until then she's riding with him, wherever that road takes her.

The hospital is lit up like a beacon as they approach. The sight of it is enough to make Jones queasy. Every cell in his body urges him to run. As they wait at a stop light, his fingers twitch with the urge to grip the door handle and get the fuck out of there.

How many nights has he woken up sweating, with visions of those stark white corridors haunting him? He can still see it. Whenever anyone asked why he looked so goddamn awful the next day, he would never tell them about the nightmares.

His father taught him not to discuss his dreams.

*"No one cares, Ted. Just be quiet and eat your breakfast."*

*"… but I was high in the clouds, dad. They were pink and purple—"*

*"Eat. Your. Damned. Breakfast. Ted. Before I feed it to the whelps. Goddamn, I should feed you to their mama."*

No matter how his dad yelled, Jones knew the mama dog

would never hurt him. She was a sweet girl with doleful eyes who let him hide with her and the pups when his dad was rampaging.

But still, he learned silence quickly.

When he did speak it was about what was real; a lost pup in a litter, a guy coming to buy two dogs for his hunting team. The Joneses didn't discuss dreams or hopes or anything gentle like love.

So, he never told anyone about his dreams. Not even the ones which terrified him. Not even long after his father was gone.

"At the risk of sounding like a broken record, are you okay?" Liz smiles at him from the driver's seat and his heart lurches.

When did they pull up?

They're in the parking lot, a way back from the other cars where she has been able to find two empty spots next to each other. Easier for her to maneuver the ungainly truck, and probably—if she needs to—the ungainly man inside the truck. He silently prays she won't have to help him.

"Uh…" He clears his throat, and sets his expression back to his usual heavy-browed scowl. "Yeah."

"Is the pain any better when you're sitting?"

Honestly, no. He wants to crawl out of his own body, to scream, to do anything, *anything* to stop this goddamn pain. Two years. Two fucking years of crawling across the carpet, of passing out from exhaustion rather than falling softly to sleep, of the world spinning around him whenever he bends to lift something.

But he hasn't set a toe in a hospital—or an urgent care, or whatever she wants to call it— for a long damn time. Not since twenty-one years ago.

The sight of his father being wheeled away on the squealing bed haunts him. Jones just stood there; torn between the relief that his dad was gone… but terrified by the fact that his dad was *gone*. Theodore Jones Senior, the strongest man he knew.

So strong even when Jones was fully grown and taller than him by a head, he still felt insignificant beside him. He could never push him back, never stop that juggernaut from coming for him.

People went into hospital and didn't come back. Even the strongest, the meanest, the one he thought would never die.

Hell, he half expects the doctor to just to walk him round back with a shotgun over their arm. Put him out of his misery.

Prickling heat swells beneath the surface of his skin as his chest grows tight. "I'm fine."

She raises her eyebrow skeptically, as if she's already cracked the code. "Do you want me to come inside with you?"

"Yes." He balls his fists so she won't notice his fingers are trembling. Every muscle in his body is taut, tense, on the verge of snapping. "Please."

"Okay." She smiles and just for a moment his heart lifts and a fraction of the pain is forgotten. "Whatever you need."

As she gets out of the truck and closes her door, he breathes for what feels like the first time all day. He steps out after her, walking slowly across the parking lot on splintered-glass feet.

"I hate hospitals," he mutters, more to himself than her, but she raises her face to him and gives him another reassuring smile. If she carries on like that he won't have to walk. He'll just float beside her.

"Well, this isn't really a hospital. This is in-and-out. I don't think they even have overnight beds."

He doesn't really need Liz to support him as he walks, but she does it anyway, letting him lean his bulky body against her. She's warm and soft, the scent of her hair conditioner comforts him even as it makes his heart beat harder. Her arm snakes around his lower back, exactly where the pain radiates from, but if he told her she'd take her hand away and he doesn't want that. Her touch gives him something to focus on, something soft and comforting in his hard, barbed world.

The hospital doors slide open, a hungry mouth beckoning its meal, but she forges on ahead, gently guiding him inside. It smells just like he remembered, a chemical sting right at the back of his nose. Cold, clinical, filled with hard metal slabs to die on.

A lady at the reception desk peers at them both over her spectacles, her lips pursed as if to say *what are you two doing up so late?* Her perfectly set short bobbed hair sits like a silver helm on her head.

"Hi," Liz smiles as she leans against the desk. "He's having back pain."

The receptionist's eyes slide to Jones. "Insurance."

He hands over the card in his wallet which he has never used before, covering his name with his thumb.

Nobody calls him by that name. Nobody gets to. The sound of his first name makes his stomach churn.

The woman behind the desk doesn't even blink as she sets a clipboard with a handful of documents fastened to it on top of the desk and slaps a white ballpoint pen on top. "Okay, Mister Jones. Fill these in."

"Okay."

He takes the clipboard and limps over to a gunmetal-grey chair in the corner of the room. Even without sitting he can tell the rough fibers of the blue seat cushion will poke through his thick khaki pants and scratch his thighs. Besides, it's more comfortable to stand. Liz sits opposite him, so far down there's no way she can see what he's writing, but he still leaves the section marked *'first name(s)'* blank.

The rest of the form is fairly simple but as he works through it, he can't shake the feeling he's being watched. "What?"

Liz shifts a little in her seat. "Do you need help with any of it?"

"I can handle it."

It comes out gruffer than he means, but then again, so does everything. Her nimble fingers curl around the thick, bunched material on the sleeve of her hoodie as she lets her gaze trail around the room, her deep-brown eyes settling on the various posters and health warnings on the walls. She presses her toes onto the speckled-white tiled floor, bouncing her leg as she waits.

He can't stop watching it; the motion of her body. It takes him a good minute to realize he has finished the form as he stands there, lips parted, eyes transfixed on her, on the way her thigh moves. She's intoxicating.

But what would she want with a man like him? Sure, in the trailer she had invited him to touch her, back before she knew about his pain, his weakness. Back before she had seen him shattered and whimpering on the ground.

Liz is a goddamn rock star, beautiful, talented. She could have anyone she wants. He knows he's the bottom of the barrel, a release, a challenge, single-use only.

Jones doesn't need her anyway. He doesn't need anyone.

He snaps himself out of it and heads over to hand in his clipboard. The receptionist barely looks at it before she hands it back.

"You missed the first line."

Jones swallows hard and turns back to Liz. She's still transfixed by the posters on the wall, her arms folded over her chest, that leg still bouncing.

He turns back to the sheet and uncaps the pen, scrawling his name as quickly as he can.

*Theodore Jr.*

# Seven

Liz presses her back to the wall and tries to keep her attention on anything other than the giant, grunting man on the black-padded bed. Jones lies on his back, knees bent as he stares at the ceiling. Under the doctor's guidance he pulls in a deep breath before raising his left leg as high as he can, gripping the edge of the pad and baring his teeth.

"Sciatica," the doctor announces as Jones groans and lowers his leg. "Your sciatic nerve is pinched, probably by a herniated spinal disk. It's fairly common and usually treatable at home."

Liz's heart settles as the doctor walks away from the table, pulling blue latex gloves from her hands.

"What do I do?" Jones growls. "How do I make it stop?"

Liz taps her thumbnail against her teeth as she wrestles with her conscience. It's wrong to let her eyes wander over his body as he's lying there hurt, but no matter how many times she tells herself to stop, she just can't find the will to do so. His big broad chest inflates and deflates slowly and the urge to climb on top of him is overwhelming. To feel all that man between her thighs, ride him until she makes him feel just as good as he made her feel, back in the trailer.

*How was that only today?*

"Alternate hot and cold compresses," the doctor says, scribbling notes on another clipboard. "I'll give you a print out of some stretches you can try, gentle exercises. And I'll write you a script for some painkillers and muscle relaxants."

"Thank you," Liz says as she tears her eyes from Jones. She silently prays that the unforgiving fluorescent lights don't show that she's blushing.

"And try to limit strenuous activity," the doctor concludes, like a spoilsport. "What do you do for a living?"

"I'm a roadie," Jones groans, raising an arm to press his palm against his forehead. "And a barman."

The doctor nods slowly and sympathetically. "I would strongly suggest you take a break from any kind of heavy lifting, twisting, bending, that kind of thing. Take it easy but keep up the gentle movements and stretches. If the pain hasn't subsided in two weeks, book an appointment with your orthopedic, okay? Your prescription will be at the front desk in a few minutes."

"Okay. Thank you," Jones's voice is little more than a whisper as the doctor heads out of the room and the loud, hollow tap of her shoes fades down the hallway. When he and Liz are alone again, he grumbles, "I don't have an orthopedic."

Silence descends like a thick blanket, smothering Liz as she waits, backed up in the corner of the room. The clock on the wall reads 11:02 but that can't be right. It must be four hours behind at least.

Her eyes are raw, her skin cold and tingling. She's fizzing from the outside in. The thunderous sound of the festival's amps and the roar of the crowd still rattles in her chest. The pressure of Jones's fingers between her thighs still teases her. There's no way it's only 11:02.

She pulls out her phone to check the time and finds the clock is actually three minutes fast.

Jones sighs loudly from the table, still staring at the ceiling. He runs his callused hands over the thighs of his khaki cargo pants. "What do I do?"

Liz's heart squeezes as he rolls his head across the pillow to face her. "Well, first we go and pick up your script."

"No, I mean about work. I can't afford to take time off—"

"I know," she says gently, taking a step toward him. "I know. It's a lot to take in. Which is why we're just going to take it one step at a time."

He sighs again and turns his head to face the wall. Liz almost sighs with him but she gets the feeling that showing her frustration will only cause him to clam up further. He's scared, she can tell. Scared about what this means for his job, his livelihood. And no doubt tired of the pain.

"Step one, we get your script. Easy as that."

"Oh, right." He gives a bitter chuckle and winces, sucking in a breath. "And then?"

"Then we find an open pharmacy and get your meds."

"Liz." His big chest swells as he tightens his grip on the edge of the bed. When he speaks, he spits the words through his gritted teeth. "I'm tired of hurting."

"I know." She takes a cautious step toward him. He reminds her of a great wounded beast, roaring and snarling because he has a thorn stuck deep in his paw. "The medicine should help, and then we'll get you home and—"

"You don't have to come with me." He screws his eyes

shut as he groans and pulls himself up into a sitting position. "I'll just drop you off at your place and head home by myself."

A queasy sense of unease rolls through Liz as she puts her hands securely in her pockets. "Do you live with anyone?"

"No."

The answer worries her, but confusingly, gives her a strange and vague sense of relief. "I don't know if it's a good idea for you to be alone. Especially while driving."

"I'm always alone," he grumbles as he stands briefly, before lowering himself back down to the bed with a shaking breath. He scowls as he notices the concern etched across Liz's face. "My feet are asleep. I'll be fine."

"Yeah, so you keep telling me."

"Well, if you'd listen then I wouldn't keep having to."

"Because I know you're not fine."

"I don't need you." Gritting his teeth, Jones lifts himself from the bed, his face twisting into a mask of agony. "I don't need help."

She lunges forward as his knees buckle, offering her arms for support. Having him press down on her shoulders, bearing the weight of him, is like trying to stop a landslide, but somehow, between them they manage to keep him upright.

"Fuck," Jones whispers, defeated. His brow grows heavier as he stares down at his feet.

"Come on," Liz says gently as she wraps an arm around the base of his back, and lets him rest his arm across her shoulders. "Let's go and get the script."

"Alright," he says, resigned to his fate.

"You don't have to do this," Jones mutters from the passenger seat as they pull up outside his house. It's a single-family home, almost identical to the ones either side of it, except his is stripped bare of any kind of decoration or color. White vinyl sidings, white window frames. Empty white flower pots line the uneven path to the white front door. It's as if all the color has been leeched from it.

"I know," she tells him. "You keep saying."

She lets her eyes fall to the paper bag in his lap. The folded-down opening to the bag is screwed up tight, wrung and ripped by his big hands. He hasn't opened it yet though. If she were the one in pain, she would have swallowed the painkillers dry in the car, but he seems almost nervous to even look at them. A printout, given to him by the lady at the urgent care's front desk, sits on the dashboard, unread.

"Are you sure you're comfortable with me being here?" she asks.

A small, bitter breath of laughter shakes his chest. "Do I have a choice?"

"Yes. Of course you do. If you want me to leave, I'll call a lift and get picked up right away." She turns in the seat to face him. "Back in the trailer you respected my boundaries. This is no different. If you want me to go, I'll go."

It might be the dim light cast from his porch light, or maybe a trick of her weary, stinging eyes, but she could swear he turns a shade darker. "No, it's fine. You can stay the night."

"I'll sleep on the couch, or on the floor or wherever. I just don't think you should be alone when you're hurting this bad."

He nods slowly. "You probably shouldn't sleep on the

couch though. Roxy sleeps there sometimes. You don't want to wake up to her crawling all over you."

"Is Roxy your dog?"

"Yeah. Sort of."

Liz's heart lifts a little. Maybe there is a little softness to that flinty edge of his. "I don't want to be pushy."

"You *are* pushy. But maybe I need a little pushing."

"Just a little?"

"Shut up and get out of the truck."

Liz has to bite down on her lip to stop herself from laughing as she opens the door and climbs out. She hitches her bag onto her shoulder, nestles the truck keys in her hoodie pocket, and peers up at the three bright stars shining down on them. As always for the time of year, the frogs and crickets are silent, and the cool night air makes it far easier to sleep than in summer.

Her adrenaline from the show—and the pre-show in the trailer with him— still crackles in her veins, but its effect is waning. She'll be asleep soon.

In a virtual stranger's house.

She should be far more nervous about that. But perhaps this is who Liz Larkin really is. Besides, they've been through so much together already. Not exactly strangers.

*"Ah fuck."*

At the sound of Jones's struggle, she heads around to the other side of the truck. He climbs out slowly, placing his huge brown boots tentatively on the asphalt. The moment he sees her his face hardens again.

"I'm f—"

"Fine," she finishes. "I know."

"Good." He slams the door shut and holds out his hand toward her.

On instinct, Liz reaches out and takes it, her heart stuttering at the sensation of his big, rough palms. He has the type of hands that could tear dictionaries in half, or turn a person to a quivering wreck with just the lightest touch—

"Keys," he grunts.

Liz frowns. And then her giddy heart drops. He wasn't offering her his hand to hold at all.

*Oh no.*

The heat on her cheeks could melt tungsten as she darts back her hand and reaches into her pocket. "I'm so sorry."

"I need to unlock the front door."

"Yeah. God, I'm…" She hands over the keys and pushes an errant strand of brown hair from her forehead. "Shit. Sorry. It's been a long day."

Perhaps it's another trick of the light, but for a moment, one *fraction* of a moment, she could swear he almost smiled.

---

Jones has had plenty of people—men and women—in his home over the years, but never one who had to basically carry him over the threshold.

They step inside and close the door, cocooned in the warm, well-maintained space. The walls are white, the carpet a sort of pale tan. It's bright and inviting, but Jones is all too aware of the ghosts who haunt the corners of his childhood home— like the presence which sits like a watchman on guard in the dented La-Z-Boy recliner. Memories rattle their chains at him as he lumbers into the room, leaning his weight on her small frame. If his dad really was there, he'd be ridiculed.

"Holy shit," Liz exclaims as her eyes roam the living

room and settle on Roxy's terrarium.

It's so late that the big red iguana isn't even head bobbing for grapes. She's asleep, slumped over her favorite log, her scaly face a picture of reptilian serenity.

Not many, but a few of his partners have been either grossed out or terrified of Roxy. Jones's lungs ache as he waits on Liz to gauge her response. Not that it matters, he tells himself. Not that Liz is even his partner.

Maybe if she's scared, she'll leave. Leave him alone.

Which is what he wants.

He thinks.

"Is *that* Roxy?" Liz says at last, her fingers curling to a fist. She presses her knuckle to her teeth as a broad smile lifts her cheeks.

"Yeah," Jones grumbles, pain almost crushing the fluttering feeling in his chest as he kicks off his boots by the door. "That's her."

"What is she, like four… five feet long?"

"Five and a bit. Eighteen pounds." He runs his index finger firmly beneath the rim of his lower lip. "She's big for a girl, abandoned at the shelter where I—" Why is he telling her this? Why does it matter to him that she knows? "She was at the shelter."

Liz shakes her head slowly, her eyes transfixed on the lizard. "I don't understand how anyone could abandon her."

"Things happen, things people can't control." He shrugs, the pain subsiding a little. "It could have been that someone bought her when she was small and didn't want her anymore once she grew. Or you know… maybe they lost their job or their house, or her owner passed away or got sick. She was healthy and well taken care of when she was dropped off. I try not to judge."

Liz makes a small hum of contemplation in her throat, her dark eyes still fixed on the terrarium. Slowly a corner of her mouth turns upward. "She looks happy."

"She is. Warm, comfortable, and spoiled fucking rotten. She eats far better than I do." He smiles a little, but forces it down before she has a chance to turn and see it.

What is he doing?

His guard is slipping and he can't allow that to happen. It's as if he can see his father out of the corner of his eye, sitting in the recliner and shaking his head as he taps the ash from his cigarette into his fifth empty bottle of the evening. Jones's stomach clenches, preparing to run, hide, shut out the world.

Liz chuckles quietly. "Oh, wow. Food. I haven't eaten since breakfast. I forgot all about it."

Heat flares along Jones's spine, but it isn't the sciatica. It's an urge. An urge to make her comfortable, to protect her, provide. "Are you hungry?"

"Not really. More burned out than anything."

He nods, faintly disappointed. "Well, I suppose we'd better figure out sleeping arrangements."

She turns to face him, tearing her eyes from the sleeping iguana, and his chest buffets. He'd forgotten just how pretty she is, or rather, he hadn't let himself remember. In the warm glow of the heat lamp, her brown eyes are a myriad of shades; whisky and tobacco, deep, rich earth and tiger's eye gemstones, framed by the dark rim of her glasses.

The little beauty spot above her lip tightens a knot in his belly. He wants her, wants to cup her face in his big, clumsy paws and touch his thumb to her beauty spot.

"Well, it's a small house," she says. "Let me guess, only one bedroom?"

"Two, actually."

Though there's only one he would ever be willing to sleep in, and it's the smallest one. His back tightens, and with that tension comes the spasms. Fingers hot and sweaty around the top of the paper bag, he grimaces and steps across the living room to switch off Roxy's light.

"Oh, okay, cool," Liz says lightly. "Well, I guess I'll take the spare."

"No." He lumbers back toward her and through the door into the kitchen. "It's not—we can't use it."

The master bedroom is piled high with his dad's stuff; mountains of tools, paperwork, clothes and bad memories.

Jones could move them. He knows he should. But that would mean touching them. God only knows what ghosts he'd awaken if he kicked up the dust in that room.

"I don't mind sharing," she says.

Jones reaches into a cabinet and takes out a glass, pouring water from the faucet to wash away the acid in his throat. He sets the bag and the printout on the countertop and turns away from them.

Liz's eyes follow his every movement.

"You want water?" he asks.

"Uh. Yeah."

He tilts his head toward the cupboard. "Fill your boots."

"But my feet will get wet," she deadpans.

Fuck. He lifts the glass to his lips to hide the smile so desperate to emerge. He's supposed to be annoyed that she's here. He's supposed to be pushing her away and insisting he's fine on his own.

But he can't.

"Are you sure this is okay?" she says as she stands on her

tiptoes to reach the top shelf of the cupboard where he keeps the taller glasses. "Me being here?"

He takes a sip, and averts his eyes to avoid the elongating curves of her body as she reaches. Instead, he finds himself side-eying the bag on the counter. His heart thrums as he considers the implications of taking the medicine. Strong painkillers. An admission of defeat. Muscle relaxants which will strip away his control.

He has half a mind to flush them down the drain but she'd probably stop him. Hell, she'd probably drive him right back to the hospital, have him explain to the doctor what he's done and then take him to the pharmacy to pick up more. Shove the pills down his throat and clamp his jaw shut until he swallowed.

"I think it's weird," he mutters.

Blunt but honest. It's weird having her in his home. It's weird that there's no expectation of sex, despite his incessant urge, and it's doubly weird that they already crossed that boundary. If he concentrates, he can still vividly recall the way her pussy felt beneath his fingers, the way she shuddered and tensed as she came. He can still feel the fluttering weightlessness in his chest. There isn't a single fucking thing about this which doesn't feel weird.

"Are you going to take your meds?"

"Don't you ever stop prying?"

She frowns and fills her glass from the faucet. "I want you to feel better."

"Why?"

"Because." She raises the glass to her lips and drinks as he waits for an explanation.

The pulse of her throat as she takes gulp after gulp is as hypnotic to him as the sight of her bent over the counter. If she were any other woman he'd invited into his home, he would be kissing her there, feeling the softness and warmth of her skin beneath his lips. If she were anyone else, they'd probably just fuck it out of their systems, here in the kitchen, before he called her a cab home. But no one else has seen him this vulnerable, and for all their passion in the trailer, they never kissed.

Perhaps she doesn't want to kiss him. He certainly wouldn't want to. And yet she's here, in his home, drinking his water, trying to jimmy his life open like a busted lockbox. There has to be some ulterior motive.

He gets tired of waiting for the explanation as she gulps. "Because what?"

She holds up a finger as she swallows the last mouthful. When she's done, she gasps, sets her empty glass in the sink, and scowls up at him. "Why do I need a reason? I just want you to be okay."

"Bullshit."

Frustration swells in his chest as he glares down at her. People don't just care. Not about him. His back throbs as he steps away from the counter, putting a few paces between him and the paper bag which at this point may as well contain a tangle of angry pit vipers. His breaths are shallow and sharp.

"Jones," she says softly. "You should take them."

She's trying to calm him, but his name on her lips does the complete opposite. Memories of the trailer collide with a fresh wave of agony. His left thigh bone is a rod of burning hot iron, and the pinch at the base of his spine is enough pain to make the world spin. "I can't."

He flinches at the memory of his father's voice in the back of his mind, yelling *"Can't or won't, Ted?"*

She takes a step toward him. "They'll help you."

"I don't need help." The air burns as he gulps it down. "Just go. Just—"

"I'm not leaving you alone tonight." Her words are punctuated by the soft thud of her bag falling to the kitchen tiles. "Come here."

He freezes at the sensation of her hand sliding around the back of his shoulders, and before he has time to realize what is happening, her body is pressed to his, her arms around his neck, her palm stroking a smooth circle around his shoulder blade.

"Hey," she says gently. "It's okay. You don't have to do anything you don't want to."

His body revolts, tensing with the need to get her off him. Jones doesn't do this.

Jones doesn't hug.

He doesn't need them.

Doesn't deserve them.

And yet, he's helpless as he bows his head to press his face to the warm, soft cradle between her neck and shoulder. The scent of her, the gentle perfume of her conditioner; sweet vanilla, honey, and almonds. For the first time in a long time, he can breathe.

He doesn't put his hands on her. If he did that, he would die of old age with them still resting on her. Nothing but her word would convince him to let go of her. He doesn't deserve that luxury. But he lets himself be held, and he breathes, and moment by moment, the hard, jagged edges of flint begin to erode.

"I'm fine," he mutters.

Just for that moment, there might be an atom of truth to it.

# EIGHT

He's a mystery.

Jones is so big and sturdy he looks as though he could stand up to a hurricane, and pull a mountain apart with his bare hands. Yet his hands tremble as he throws the pills to the back of his throat.

He glugs down a full glass of water to chase them, and then stands, staring out of the window into the empty blackness beyond.

"You okay now?" Liz asks as she wraps her arms around herself. Exhaustion is catching up to her, and when her energy is this low, she gets shivery.

He doesn't answer. By now he's probably tired of her asking. She can hear herself being annoying.

She watches him a moment longer, realizing it isn't the darkness he's looking at, but at the man staring back at him in the reflective surface of the glass; tired, stooped as he braces a palm on the edge of the counter, the dark circles beneath his eyes telling her everything his lips refuse to. Tired, hurting, grumpy Jones.

"We should sleep," she says.

He nods in agreement and sets his glass in the sink beside hers. "Yeah."

He leads the way through the house, down a short hallway to three doors. "Bathroom," he says, barely raising his hand to point to the leftmost door. "Off limits," he says to the one in the center. "Mine," to the one on the right.

"Got it."

He flips on the light in his bedroom and steps aside to let her in. The scent of him is concentrated in there, a masculine spiciness; leather, black pepper, and woodsmoke. It ties her stomach in knots. On one side of the room is a small, dark fireplace, surrounded by a protective tarnished brass grate. There's a chest of drawers, and a slatted, white closet door.

His bed is huge, taking up almost half the room, made up with cozy grey comforter and so many crisp white pillows.

Nothing has ever looked so welcoming.

"I'll take the floor," she says, doing a decent job of masking her disappointment.

"No way." He stands in the doorway, his broad frame filling the space. Her stomach double-knots.

She should be too worn out to be horny, and yet, the strain of his forearms as he braces himself in the doorframe turns her throat to sand. The way his shirt clings to the round curve of his belly, stokes an ache between her thighs, a desperate desire to explore him. To touch him. If he wasn't hurting, she'd jump into his arms, wrap her thighs around him, and have him carry her to the bed.

"You take the bed. I'll take the floor," he says.

"But you're hurt."

"It's easier for me to get comfortable down there."

"Are you sure?"

He doesn't answer.

"Okay." She nods, swallowing hard.

It could be a combination of exhaustion and the medication, but his eyelids are hanging low and heavy. He gestures lazily toward a smooth oak chest of drawers. "There are shirts and pajamas you can wear in the second drawer if you want to get changed. I don't have a toothbrush for you…"

"It's fine." She pats the bag slung over her shoulder. "I have one."

"Okay. I'm going to take a shower. I won't be long. You can get changed."

Her eyes trail after him as he turns and heads back out into the hallway. A second later the bathroom light clicks and the low whir of the extractor fan rumbles deep in the bones of the house. She stands alone in his room. Unsupervised.

Not that there's much to pry into. The only things on top of his drawers are a digital alarm clock, and a small blue bowl, half-filled with loose change. There are no ornaments, no photos, no clutter. If she'd had a million years, she never would have guessed Jones's home was minimalist and neat, unlike hers. If he stepped into her room, he'd know almost everything she loved.

Sliding open the second drawer, she's faced with a patchwork of uniformly folded t-shirts and plaid pajama bottoms. She picks out a pale blue shirt and the stretchiest pair of bottoms she can find. Jones is a big guy, but his hips and thighs aren't quite as full and thick as hers. She tosses them onto the foot of the bed as she pulls off her top.

The constant whoosh and occasional heavy splashes of water tells her he's in the shower. She changes quickly but doesn't bother to close the door. The thrill of standing naked from the waist up, exposed in his bedroom, pebbles her skin, tightening her nipples. He's naked too, not ten feet away from her, water sliding over his body, caressing every curve, trickling down each burly inch.

Everything in the room smells like him; the air, the soft cotton of the shirt in her hands, the bed sheets. It's intoxicating. Perhaps it was all part of his plan back in the trailer, to give her just a taste of him, enough to get her hooked, but not enough to satiate. She sighs as she pulls on the shirt and the soft Jones-scented fabric settles against her skin.

She wriggles her skirt down past her hips. In all the excitement she had completely forgotten she went commando, and she's wet. The warm slickness of her pussy spreads as her thighs glide together. A needy ache spreads through her as she lets her hands trail through her dark patch of damp curls, to her swollen clit. It would take so little to get her off. She could be done before he even gets out of the shower. And maybe then she'll stop wanting him, at least for a while. If nothing else it'll help her sleep.

She climbs into his bed, sinking into the softness of his mattress as she begins to stroke herself. It's wrong. But God, that only turns her on more. Closing her eyes, she can see him, his face between her thighs, licking her, savoring every inch of her.

*I don't want to hear another word out of you other than you gasping my name.*

"Jones."

*Good girl.*

A shaky breath escapes her as she circles her clit with her fingertips, imagining his tongue. Her thighs tremble beneath the comforter as she chases her orgasm, clenching her pelvic muscles, curling her toes.

"Oh," she gasps. "Fuck, Jones."

"Oh, shit."

Liz's eyes open wide at the sound of his voice, and the world falls out from underneath her. Jones stands in the doorway, completely naked but for a tiny grey hand-towel wrapped precariously just beneath his stomach. The makeshift garment is fastened only at the very top corners, flaring open wide at his hip to reveal the entirety of his thick, muscled thigh.

"Sorry," he mutters, avoiding her eyes. He takes his hand and rubs his forehead. "I think the medicine is… it's doing something. I think maybe I'm dreaming. I forgot you were here."

Liz is frozen, her eyes wide, her hand still resting on her pussy beneath the bedsheets. Does he know what she was doing? She doesn't dare move. "You're not dreaming."

He squints. "Oh. Shit."

Her eyes trail over his body, his broad shoulders, the full curves of his chest and the pinkish-brown peaks of his nipples. One of them is pierced, the shining-silver bar gleaming among the downy dark-blonde fuzz covering his chest and stomach. His belly is round and soft, and his hips are wide and curvy. The heroic hand-towel is fighting a losing battle to contain him. His skin is flushed pink and gleaming, scrubbed clean, steam coiling from his shoulders. Droplets of water drip from his beard and run over his chest and stomach in rivers.

He's still the drier of the two of them.

"I forgot to take a big towel," he mutters as if he can read her mind. "And pajamas. God. I feel drunk."

Her heart is racing. "It's probably the muscle relaxer."

"Yeah."

It's hard to tell whether the pink on his cheeks is from

the hot water or whether he's blushing. Liz certainly is. One of his big hands clutches the towel at his hip, the other rubs his forehead as he stares at the corner of the room. "I'm just going to grab some clothes."

"Sure."

He edges his way around the bed to the chest of drawers, his eyes focused on the carpet, as if looking at her will turn him to stone. Slowly, Liz's hand recoils, and she places it on the mattress beside her. Guilt churns her stomach, as well as the unease of not knowing. There's every chance he couldn't tell what she was doing beneath the comforter, and that his embarrassment comes purely from his own state of undress.

"Is the pain any better?" she says, hoping he can't hear the tremble in her voice.

"A little. I think it's helpin—shit." He gasps as he fumbles with a folded shirt and the towel falls open, just enough for Liz to catch a glimpse of his round, pale ass cheek. "Fuck."

As much sympathy as she has for him, she still has to press her lips together and try not to laugh as he struggles to cover himself, but both their efforts are a lost cause. The towel drops away completely, landing silently on the floor.

His back is to her, but she can clearly tell his hands are cupping his cock. His ass and the backs of his thighs are covered in the same blond fluff as his torso

"I'm so sorry," he mutters.

"It's okay." She bites her lip. Her pulse is beating so hard she can feel it fluttering in her throat.

Jones's ass is spectacular, a veritable dump truck, the eighth natural wonder.

Jones and the Giant Peach.

She bites down harder to save herself from laughing.

"You've seen my butt. I'd say this levels out the playing field a little."

His shoulders slouch as he lowers his head. "I guess so. Shit. I'll be back in a minute."

Liz clamps her palm over her mouth as Jones begins to sidestep back around the bed, facing away from her the entire time.

The bathroom door clicks shut, and she dives out from under the covers, pulling on the blue and white plaid pajamas she had left at the foot of the bed.

---

Jones's mind is fuzzy. He stands in the bathroom holding his pajamas, staring at them as though they contain the secrets to the universe. Gasping in the thick and warm air is like trying to breathe in feathers.

Even without the pills, none of it makes sense. Yesterday she was just some performer at the festival who caught his eye. He thought he'd never see her again. Today she's in his bed, making herself at home, wearing his pajamas, and—he thinks, though he can't let himself fully believe it—touching herself.

Despite the fact he just showered, he bends over the sink and turns on the faucet, splashing cold water over his face. He's weightless, off balance, blindsided. If he wasn't so damned terrified, he'd be giddy.

Dressing is somehow harder and easier. For the most part his pain is deadened, but it takes longer than normal to fully understand the intricacies of his pajama bottoms, flipping them this way and that, turning them inside out twice before realizing it doesn't matter. At least she can't see him stumbling around on the tiled floor.

When he's dressed, he gives himself one last glower in the mirror, heads back into the bedroom and does his best to act normal. Liz sits on the edge of his bed, folding the tiny grey towel he'd used to cover himself.

"Are you absolutely certain you don't want the bed?" she asks.

"I'm sure."

"Well, if you change your mind during the night, tell me. I don't mind switching."

"Thanks. But I won't." He takes a couple of comforters from his closet, unfurling one on the floor. While he prepares his sleeping space, she heads to the bathroom. For a moment it feels as though they're real, together, that this is just their lives.

This situation could not get any weirder. He's simultaneously growing comfortable around her and in a constant state of unease. With anyone else he wouldn't give a rat's ass if they saw his body. He'd have walked out of the bathroom naked, hard, and ready to fuck.

But not her, no matter how badly he wants to, though he doesn't understand why. She's stunning, sweet, and there in his bedroom, but as much as his body craves her, there's something else telling him to hold back.

*Because I'd disappoint her.*

He takes a couple of pillows from the bed, positioning one for his head and the other for his hips. With a groan he lies on his side, wedging the pillow between his knees to ease the tension.

Okay, if he's honest with himself, he wedges the pillow a little higher than usual, letting it rest against his tight, heavy balls and his semi-hard cock. It serves the same purpose. A release of tension. An outlet for his ache. If he tilts his hips just a little it sends a bolt of pleasure through him.

"You okay?" she says as she steps back into the room.

His pajamas are quite possibly the least sexy pajamas in the world, but on her they're somehow hardwired straight to his cock. She picked out the stretchy ones, which hug her curves faithfully, showing off the thickness of her hips and thighs. She isn't wearing a bra, and her breasts jiggle as she walks, her nipples pressing against the pale fabric.

He bears down harder on the pillow.

"I'm fine," he says, his voice a little deeper and huskier than before. "Just go to sleep and stop worrying about me."

"Alright." She shuts the door and flips off the light switch, plunging the room, and his heart into darkness.

"No!" His breath catches in his throat as he stares into the black, and immediately his mind starts to race. Faces staring back at him, things slithering across the carpet toward him. Cold seeps into his lungs.

Only a moment passes between Liz switching off the light and her flipping it back on, but to Jones it's a lifetime.

She stares at him, eyes wide. "What's wrong?"

He's pathetic. He knows it. Six foot four, easily over three hundred pounds, almost forty years old and still afraid of the dark. He swallows hard and tries to steady his breath. "I can't sleep in the dark."

"Oh, no problem," she says. And nothing more.

She doesn't mock him. She doesn't question him. And as the bed springs squeak and the mattress judders, he finds himself relaxing.

Jones breathes deeply. "Thank you."

"It's okay," she says. He can't see her, but she sounds like she's smiling. "Honestly, I prefer sleeping in the light when I'm in a new place. Sometimes I wake up confused and I panic."

He knows she can't see him, so he lets himself smile. Whatever those pills were, they seem to be working. He feels mushy, warm, and oh-so heavy.

"Jones?"

"Hm?"

"Thank you for letting me help you."

*Don't get used to it*, he thinks. But he doesn't say it out loud. He isn't talking to her.

# NINE

The clock on top of the drawers reads 10:25am when Liz opens her eyes again. Dazzling brightness assaults her eyes, both from the glaring overhead light, and the rays of golden sunshine streaming through the cream-colored curtains.

A soft snore from the floor brings everything flooding back.

Liz rubs her eyes and tries to make sense of it all. She seduced a roadie, got finger-banged, played Ghoulfest, took the roadie to urgent care, came to his house, met his lizard, masturbated in his bed, got caught, fell asleep. All in all, not a bad Friday night.

She yawns and rubs her stomach. It's been over twenty-four hours since she last ate anything, and right now she could chew her own arm off.

Rolling over to the edge of the bed, she peers down at the sleeping man. He's on his side, curled up a little, his features softened by sleep. It's the first time she has ever seen him not scowling. His brow is smoothed, his lips relaxed, a picture of gentle serenity. But she knows first-hand how startled he can be when he first wakes up.

"Jones?"

He doesn't move.

Taking the pillow from the bed, she uses it as a probe, letting one corner graze across his bicep. "It's morning."

He growls softly and twists his head to bury his face in the pillow, swatting at her with his hand. "No."

"It is," she says quietly, reaching down with her hand to gently jostle his shoulder.

"Stop it," he mutters, without even opening his eyes.

She presses her lips together and tries again. "I'm hungry."

"Eat then."

Exasperated, she raises her eyebrows and sighs. "Fine."

Let sleeping bears lie. She throws off the comforter and climbs out of bed, her toes curling in protest as she steps onto the chilly floor. It's carpeted, but the cold still seeps in. Poor Jones. But he seems comfortable enough, and if not for his thorniness, he'd almost look sweet.

Her phone battery is dead, the screen black and lifeless. She puts it on charge, takes her glasses from the top of the drawers and makes her way across the room. As soon as Liz opens the bedroom door, she hears a distant skittering noise, and a second later the enormous lizard is stomping down the hallway.

"Oh, hey Roxy," Liz whispers.

The iguana bobs her head up and down in response.

"You're probably hungry too, huh?"

More head bobs. Liz glances at the bedroom door and contemplates attempting to wake Jones again. She can't be sure, but she gets the distinct feeling that depriving him of sleep will result in even more grumpiness.

Instead, she reaches down to stroke the top of the iguana's head. "Let's just see what we can rustle up together, shall we?"

She half expects Roxy to follow her to the kitchen, but the lizard just stares at the bedroom door, probably confused as to why a different primate than the one who normally feeds her has emerged this morning. It gives Liz time to find her way around the kitchen, exploring the various cupboards and drawers. Everything is stacked neatly, matching dark blue plates and bowls, uniform rows of cans in the pantry. There are clear plastic tubs with their contents labeled; pasta, flour, rice, cereal. Everything in its place.

She's starving, and cereal isn't going to cut it, so instead she opens the refrigerator and takes out an egg box. Soft, grainy lizard's skin brushes against her leg as Roxy scrabbles against the salad drawer with her front claws, almost halfway into the refrigerator before Liz has a chance to stop her.

"Hey! Hey, no," she tries to block the lizard's path with her legs, wedging herself into the fridge. "This isn't a place for lizards."

Undeterred, Roxy continues her desperate bid, her sharp claws raking across Liz's calf. Jones's pajamas bear the brunt of most of the attack, but the scratches sting all the same. Fingers gripping the fridge door, Liz sucks in a breath and bites down on the pain.

"Roxy… Jeez. What is it? Is your food in here?" Liz huffs. She doesn't really know what iguanas are supposed to eat, and without her phone she can't look it up. Fortunately, Jones is the label king, and she spies a Tupperware box on the bottom shelf, helpfully marked "Roxy food".

"Oh, hey, look," Liz says enthusiastically as she snatches it up. The lizard stops her assault almost immediately at the sight of the container. "Okay, okay. You get breakfast first, I get it."

Her ankle throbs as she heads into the living room with the iguana trotting dutifully beside her. She pulls off the lid and peers at the vibrant salad inside; green alfalfa and what could possibly be chopped up collard greens, yellow mango, white slices of peeled apple, long yellow strands of spaghetti squash. Red and orange nasturtium flowers garnish the top.

"Wow, you're a gourmet. He wasn't kidding about you eating well," she says as she tips the salad into a large food bowl in the terrarium.

The iguana climbs up and begins to enthusiastically munch her breakfast as Liz finds the switch for her heat lamp and turns it on. She smiles as she watches Roxy. Outwardly, Jones is so gruff and hard-edged, but she's beginning to see the cracks in his armor, the soft parts he's trying to keep hidden. Though why he seems so intent on coming across as an asshole is beyond her.

How can the rude, abrasive man who never smiles be the same man who meticulously prepares salads and flowers for his adopted lizard?

"What in the hell is going on out here?" Jones grumbles from the doorway.

Liz doesn't have time to turn around before he speaks again.

"Shit, stay there."

"What?" She freezes as though she just stepped into a minefield and the slightest moment could be the end of her. Breath burning in her chest, she turns her head to the location of his voice.

But he isn't in the doorway anymore. A cupboard door slams in the kitchen, sending a fresh wave of concern through her body. The fear that she gave Roxy the wrong thing entirely, that some poisonous concoction was stored in the Tupperware, coils every muscle in her body.

"What did I do?"

Jones returns a moment later, groaning as he drops to his knees behind her. "Just stay still."

"Did I hurt Roxy?"

"What? No."

The frantic beat of her heart is echoed in the throbbing pulse at the back of her calf. She realizes with a start that he's gently rolling up her pajama leg.

He hisses as he pulls in a breath. "You're hurt."

"I'm fine." As soon as the words leave her mouth, she snaps her lips shut.

"You're bleeding on my carpet."

"Oh." She almost loses her balance as Jones cups a hand around her shin.

"Bend your leg back if you can."

She can, but she has to hop around awkwardly to retain her balance. As she struggles, Jones lowers her foot, until her toes rest on his thigh.

"What happened?" he mutters as he rummages through a turquoise plastic first aid kit on the floor.

"I just opened the fridge and she wanted in. I guess I got in her way."

"Hm." He grunts as he tears open a packet on an alcohol wipe. "This might sting."

"It's—Ah!" Stars burst in the blackness behind her eyelids as burning agony flares across her leg. Her mouth opens in a silent scream until the burning subsides. "Okay. It's okay. Fuck."

"Told you."

She glances over her shoulder and her breath catches in her throat. He's kneeling right behind her, his face mere inches from the curve of her ass, her foot resting on his thick, muscled thigh. It should feel weird to be this close to him, and yet, he touches her with such gentle familiarity it sets her at ease. And he's careful; so gentle with her she could happily let him take care of her all day.

"I'm going to have to do it again," he says. "I'm sorry."

"That's okay."

The second time she's prepared. She presses her lips together and screws her eyes shut, breathing through the sharp, burning pain. But beyond the sting there's comfort; the tender warmth of his hand holding her shin, the gentle sensation of his thumb drawing circles on the side of her calf.

She focuses on that, and it makes her breathless.

"Good," he tells her, and her skin crackles at the sound of his voice.

"How bad is it?"

"Six big scratches and a couple of grazes. None of them look deep."

She forces out a breath. "I think your dog is rabid."

It could be a trick of her ears, but she swears he gives a monosyllabic chuckle. "I'll have a word with her."

Was that… *a joke?* She didn't know he could even do that.

She adjusts her balance, placing her hand on his shoulder as he begins to wrap a bandage around her leg. "Thank you."

"Don't mention it. I heard you crashing around out here and thought you were wrecking the place."

"Most of the noise was Roxy."

"That sounds about right." He ties off the bandage and gives her shin a gentle squeeze. "Done."

She closes her eyes and tries to steady her breath. His hands are so warm, so big and coarse, and yet so gentle. She sets her foot on the ground and turns to face him.

If she wasn't blushing before, she certainly is now. He gazes up at her from his knees, his hair a little ruffled on one side where he lay on his pillow, his eyes at the level of her stomach. A tingling sensation spirals through her abdomen. "Good morning."

"Morning," he replies, his voice quiet and hoarse.

For one moment, she almost reaches out, cups his face in her hands and kisses him. Just a moment. The flutter in her stomach spreads, filling every part of her with need. Instead, she takes a step back and turns her head to the terrarium where the iguana is making fast work of her meal. "Thanks for patching me up. I'm just glad I didn't hurt her."

He groans as he stands and makes his way back to the kitchen. "We'll call it even," he says. "Grab some breakfast and I'll take you to go and pick up your car. I'm sure you're keen to get home."

The flutters dissipate.

---

Jones may be bigger than Liz, but he sure as hell doesn't make half the noise she does. He winces at the clattering dishes, the scrape of wooden cutlery on his nonstick pan before she drums it three times on the edge, the incessant humming while she cooks. She somehow manages to crack eggs louder than anyone he has ever known.

And yet, every time he glances at the time and realizes they don't have much longer before he has to leave, his stomach sinks a little lower.

She doesn't take her eyes off her cooking as she speaks. "How's your back this morning?"

"A little better."

She smiles. "Good. Remember to try to do the stretches on the information pack the doctor gave you. And alternate hot and cold compresses."

"Yeah."

"Thank you," she says with a smile. She tilts the skillet toward him so he can see the scrambled monstrosity she's cooking up. "Omelet?"

If he's honest, any other time he'd eat it just to see her smile, but he isn't feeling charitable this morning. The pain might be dulled by the medicine, but his sense of failure hasn't.

"Just coffee."

"It says not to take your medicine on an empty stomach," she says, patting the leaflet they neglected to read last night. "We probably shouldn't risk that again."

"My stomach won't be empty. It'll have coffee in it."

She huffs a little, but returns her attention to the skillet. "Have you told your work you aren't coming in today?"

He spoons instant coffee into his mug and stirs in a dash of creamer. Her eyes burn against him, but he can avoid them all day if he has to.

"Jones…"

"Eat your omelet."

"You need to rest."

"I need to work."

She sighs heavily and scrapes the heap of egg onto her

plate as he pours boiling water into his cup. Ridiculous. They've known each other less than two days and they already bicker like an old married couple.

"How's your leg?" he asks, trying to sound unbothered.

"It hurts a little, but I'm okay."

"Hm." He takes a miniscule sip of scalding coffee, hiding his concern that she's hurt, and guilt that he still feels the firm, smooth texture of her skin on his fingertips. Her warmth, her scent, just the comfort of being near her. None of it was his to take. He flexes his fingers to be rid of it, but to his dismay, finds the sensation of her has seeped into his bones. Shoving his hand in his pocket, he tries to forget. "So, what are your plans for today? You're not playing a Ghoulfest, so…?"

"Oh." Her eyes widen. "What day is it?"

"Saturday."

"Shoot." She leans back against the counter. "We were supposed to have a band meeting this morning."

Another sip. Guilt sinks deeper, settling like a lead weight in his gut. If she hadn't stayed to take care of him, if he hadn't been such an inconvenience, if he'd only stayed strong for a couple more minutes she would have been on her way after the festival. She wouldn't have missed it. "I'm sorry."

She shrugs. "It's fine."

But there's something in the way her gaze loses focus as she stares at the edge of the opposite counter. Something she can't say aloud. He knows better than anyone that if something is "fine" it definitely isn't.

"Come on," he says, setting his almost full mug on the counter. "I'll get you to your car. I'm going to be late."

She shovels the last bit of her breakfast into her mouth

and battles to swallow. "Shit, okay. Give me five minutes to get dressed."

His fingers flex again, but this time with the urge to reach out to her as she passes, to wrap his hand around her arm and pull her up against him. But he resists. He watches her as she limps quickly to the bedroom, her bandaged leg making her gait a little stiffer than normal.

What an asshole he is.

But at least this way she'll be out of his life. He can go back to getting through each day, without having to worry what she thinks of him.

He sighs as he takes two pain pills from their bottle, picks up his mug again and throws them to the back of his throat as he sips the cheap, bitter coffee. It's for the best.

***

"Your car survived the night," he says as he pulls up beside it, filling the silence in his truck. Raindrops speckle the windshield and large pools of grey water sit on the uneven gravel lot. Great. It's going to be a muddy second night at the festival.

"That makes three of us." Slowly her fingers curl into a loose fist. "Tell Roxy, no hard feelings, okay? It was nice to meet her."

He nods once.

There's a lot Jones wants to say, but nothing he'll even admit to himself. Still, it presses at the back of his throat, a petulant, persistent need to speak, to ask, to *beg* if she asked it of him.

*Can I see you again?*
*How can you bear to be around me?*

*Will you stay a little longer?*

A force at his back pleads with him to inch toward her, to pull her to him, kiss the lips he can't stop imagining the softness of. He barely knows her, but he misses her even before she's gone.

"Well…" She breathes heavily, breaking his trance. "Thanks."

He should be the one thanking her. She left her life behind to take part in his, just for a little while. Just for one night, where he didn't feel quite so alone. But as the passenger door slams shut, he knows his time is up.

He waits until she has left, until he can no longer see her little black car driving away and she's completely unreachable before he gets out and begins his march across the cold, soggy parking lot. The sky is heavy and grey above him as he checks in with security and makes sure they're set on who gets backstage and who doesn't.

"You alright?" Imran asks, tucking a pencil behind his ear as he crosses the stage. "Did you find your clunk?"

"What? Oh, yeah," Jones says. "Everything's fine." but in truth, something inside him feels very, very broken. Business as usual, really.

# TEN

Anya's voice is an octave higher than usual, piercing through the phone's speaker. "Where the fuck have you been? We've been so worried."

Liz grimaces and holds the phone away from her ear as she sits on her bed. Jim the betta fish swims around flaring out his gills at her in contempt. She probably deserves it. "I was at a friend's house overnight. My phone died."

"I was just about ready to kill Finn for leaving you alone last night. Jesus. I've been scouring the local news looking for reports of your murder."

So dramatic. "I'm sorry."

Anya sighs on the other end of the phone. "I'll send out a group text and let them know you're safe. You missed the meeting."

"Oh, right, yeah." Not that it matters. She won't be in the band much longer. "Anything interesting?"

"Just welcoming Étienne officially, talking about what that means for the band, how royalties will be divided going forward. Pretty important legal stuff, honestly."

"Ah."

"Are you okay?"

"Yeah, just—" A sharp gasp on the other end of the phone cuts Liz off.

"When you say you spent the night with a friend, do you mean a friend or…?"

"A friend," she says as plainly as she can. "Just a friend."

"What's his name?"

Liz narrows her eyes and leans back on the pillows. "Nice try."

"Please."

The secret of Jones sits like a weight on her chest. Speaking about him out loud might help unload some of the burden. Because honestly, could she even consider him a friend? A five-minute-stand? Yes. A pain in her ass? Most definitely. Can she still feel the tingling echo of his touch on her, still feel that delicious, agonizing heat between her thighs? Yes.

Yes, she fucking can.

"I'll see you at rehearsal on Monday."

"Ugh," Anya sighs. "Fine. Coffee after?"

"Sure. See you then." And with that, Liz ends the call.

She sighs and lies back on her bed, swiping through a hundred different notifications. Promotional emails, matches on dating sites she no longer gives a shit about, messages from their forum. No matter how many apps she opens and closes, how many asinine posts she scrolls through, she can only think of one thing: that big grumpy roadie with his perfect round ass and sparkly nipple.

Grumpy, abrasive, irresistible Jones.

It'll be late before he gets home and sees the note she left in his room. She knows very little about him, but she knows for certain that his bullheadedness won't allow him to admit to his job that he's hurting. He'll charge through the whole shift until he collapses again, and this time she won't be there to help him.

She lets her phone fall onto her chest.

It was such a corny note. So uninspired. Just 'call me' and her number. She'd ignore it too.

Still, she picks up her phone, scowling at the empty screen. And that's how she spends the day. One moment her mind is made up, she doesn't care if he calls or not, doesn't care if she never sees him again. The next she's unable to keep from checking.

Something has to change.

Jones was exciting, but that's over now. Time to move on; from him, from the Vixens, from everything. After she's showered and all traces of him are scrubbed from the surface of her skin, she pulls out her laptop from beside her bed and opens one of her bookmarked pages. She's wrapped in a towel, water droplets still dotting the tops of her arms when the page loads.

*Monroe Massage Therapy Training.*

The college is four hundred miles away, two states over. It would be a clean break, plunging her into the unknown, alone and free to shape her life into whatever fits her best. Her application has been filled out for months, saved in her drafts. All she would have to do is hit send.

So, she holds her breath, and clicks.

Her hands tremble above the keyboard. The world fades to black for a second as the realization hits her.

<<*Thank you for your application. We will be in contact to arrange the next steps within 3-5*

*business days.*>>

It's done.

After years of holding back and constant excuses, Liz Larkin has applied for college. And not just any college; Monroe, the last one on her list, four-hundred miles away. The school is less than a mile from the ocean and offers everything she's ever wanted. She put it last because she wants it most.

It's simultaneously a huge mistake and a massive leap forward. The hope she'll get accepted is distorted by that overly cautious voice in the back of her mind which tells her she'll be relieved when the rejection inevitably comes.

The cheerful chirrup of her cell phone breaks her reverie.

It's past midnight; the Jonesing hour. The scratches on her calf sting and she almost knocks the catalogs from her mattress as she dives to retrieve the message.

It reads simply:

*What?*

That's it. If she didn't read it in his familiar gruff, curt tone she'd be insulted. But it's him, unmistakably. And it makes her smile. She bites her lip as she types her reply: *I said call me. This isn't a call*

He replies right away:

*I don't call.*

*Of course you don't.* She chews her lips as she types back. *How do you feel?*

...

Three dots bounce over and over, telling her that he's typing, their rhythm is equal parts maddening and hypnotic. And then they disappear.

No matter how long she stares at the screen, or how many times she puts her phone face-down and picks it back up again, they don't come back.

"What am I doing?" she sighs, as she runs her hands over her head, her still damp hair leaving moisture on her fingertips. Nothing good can come of this.

Jones never smiles. He never laughs.

And in any case, she's going to college.

Hopefully.

He shouldn't be half as curious about him as she is, but…

"Fuck," she sighs, switching off her phone and tossing it onto the teal cushion of the wicker chair at her dressing table for good measure. Out of reach but not out of mind.

There's every chance she'll be four hundred miles from him in a few months, surrounded by new people, forced to make new friends. Far, far away, where hopefully the devastating impact of a heavyset man with a nice beard and a ridiculous ass can't reach.

She closes her eyes, and makes a mental note to search for backup colleges on the opposite side of the country. Just in case.

---

Jones groans as he sits back against the trailer's bench and lifts his throbbing feet from the floor. The hiss and pop of a bottle cap being removed is just about the most beautiful thing he has ever heard. It's the disgustingly early hours of Monday morning and Ghoulfest is finally over.

"Here's to the end of a shitshow of epic proportions," Imran toasts as he slides a beer across the table.

Jones barely has energy left to raise the bottle. They've definitely had worse years, where absolutely everything has gone wrong; most notably the pyrotechnic disaster eight years ago, of which they do not speak. But those were still physically easier. Since Liz left on Saturday morning, he has taken his meds every day, though after stripping the stage the past two nights, they barely even take the edge off.

Still, he made it mostly intact, even if she did walk away with a tiny chip of his heart.

With a groan he sits forward and clinks his bottle against Imran's before taking a sip. "I don't know how much longer I can keep doing this." As soon as he speaks, he regrets it, a moment of weakness, of vulnerability.

"Alright," Imran says with a grunt as he sits opposite, leaning his elbows on the black fold-down table between them. "I've worked with you for how long?"

"On and off, eight years," Jones shrugs.

"Right, and in that time, I've known you like to give off this impression that you're an untouchable, grumpy bastard, but this is the first time I've seen you actually really miserable. What's going on?"

Jones scowls. "Give off the impression?"

"We all know it's bullshit," Imran chuckles before taking a swig. "You turned your life upside down to look after a lizard nobody wanted, you volunteer with puppies on your day off, and cover for everyone's asses when we fuck up. Your soft side is pretty well fucking hidden, granted, but everyone knows it's there. You ain't fooling anyone."

Clamping his jaw shut, Jones glances out of the window into the darkness. Though he tries to focus beyond it, his own reflection stares back at him, tired, broken, and just as Imran said, miserable.

He can't tell him about the pain, because honestly, he knows the answer and he knows full-well he can't afford to take time off work. But that's only half of it. The sciatica is sharp, vicious agony, but there's also a constant low-level ache in his chest. One she left there.

Jones pushes out a heavy breath. "You're married, right?"

"Happily. Fourteen years next June." Imran's eyes widen. "Fuuuuuck."

Something between a longing sigh and a disdainful growl rolls through Jones's chest. "How did you know? Like, in the beginning how did you know you would work together?"

"Well, I wasn't sure in the beginning, or rather *she* wasn't sure. To be honest I think I annoyed the ever-living shit out of her."

"Understandable."

Imran's moustache twitches as his lips curve beneath. "But I knew I loved her pretty quickly. And one day, I just knew I wanted to spend the rest of my life with her, and by some miracle, she felt the same way about me." He sits forward, his deep brown eyes fixed on Jones's. "Jonesey? Are you asking someone to marry you?"

Panic darts through his chest. "No. God no."

"Oh my God, it's that woman you were with the other night? Wasn't she a performer? Vixen's Wail, right?"

"Stop it," Jones shakes his head, feigning disgust. "I've met her twice in my life. Well, three times if you count her walking into me."

"But you like her?"

"I didn't say that."

"But you're not denying it." Imran laughs and claps his

hands once. "That's it isn't it? You like her and you're not sure what to do with all these normal human feelings, because you've lived your entire life in grumpy old bear mode."

Jones drains his beer bottle and makes to stand. "Fuck this, I'm calling a cab."

"The fuck you are," Imran grins, pulling the top off another bottle and sliding it across the table.

Jones has no chance but to catch it before it slides off the ledge. Cold condensation presses against his palm, as tempting a siren song as any after the night he's had. He sits back down and huffs.

"Okay," Imran says, trying unsuccessfully to shake his grin. "So, you like her?"

Jones doesn't blink as he stares dead ahead, peeling the label from the bottle.

Imran dips his chin, his eyes burning into Jones's. "I'm taking that as a yes. Have you two…?" He raises his eyebrows suggestively.

"No…" It's only half a lie. "Her name is Liz. She spent the night at my place on Friday night, and before you get excited, she slept in my bed and I slept on the floor."

Imran's nose crinkles as he chuckles. "Do you have Liz's phone number?"

"Yes."

The man's smile widens. "Alright, here's what you say to her, and listen very closely because it's complicated and you want to get it right." He leans in a little closer. "You make sure you stay up on your hind legs, and say, in your nicest, most human voice, *Hi Liz, how are you?* And then, maybe she'll answer, and then—"

"Yeah, I get it," Jones sighs. "I know. I could just talk to her but…" he shakes his head and fights back the urge to look at the broken man in the window. "She's kind. Really, really kind and she barely knows me but… she cares. She likes Roxy, and… I think I maybe want to let her into my life a little."

Imran grins. "I knew you were a softie."

"If you tell anyone…"

"Yeah, yeah unspeakable evil, pain and suffering, hellfire and brimstone. I know."

Jones glowers but carries on. "I don't want to mess her around. I don't want to have a one-night stand with her and then blow her off."

"So don't?"

"It's not that simple."

"Isn't it?"

"No." Jones takes a swig. "Fuck, Immy, who would want me? Who would want to wake up every morning beside a man like me?"

He despises himself harder for a moment, despises the concern which etches across Imran's features, despises the beer for settling so quickly in his empty stomach and letting his thoughts flow so freely. And most of all he hates that it seems to be a crack in a great concrete dam he can only cement over for so long. It can't hold forever, so he lets a little out, just enough to release the pressure. "I feel like I'm this big dark cloud. I hang above everyone bringing cold and grim misery."

"Jonesey… that isn't—"

"I know what I am. I've slept with people. A few people who like storms. They want to dance in the rain, flirt with the danger of being struck by lightning, but no one wants rain all the time. No one wants to spend their life with this," he gestures to himself.

"Look, I know you've had it rough with your mom and dad and—"

Those words chill his blood. He plugs the hole in the dam and lets the flood subside. Far behind the barrier, buried deep in the sediment are the bones of his father, and the dark unexplored waters his mother inhabits. She had known Jones for all of thirteen days before she left him and his dad in search of a life she could bear.

She wanted the sun back.

"Let's just talk about something else." Jones sighs.

Imran frowns on the opposite side of the table. "Buddy, I think I've seen the worst of you…"

He hasn't. Not by a long way. Yes, Imran has seen him stressed and overworked, exhausted, grumpy, even downright furious. But never once has Jones allowed him to see the worst; his pain, his fear, his aching-to-the-bones loneliness. No one, neither Imran or any of the people he has known for years has ever been permitted to see his weakness.

No one except Liz. A near stranger. One he can't stop thinking about.

Imran sighs before reaching into his pocket and pulling out a black leather trifold wallet. He pulls out a cream-colored business card with dogeared corners. "I know what you're going to say. You're going to say you don't need it and you'd rather be seen dead than see a therapist, but…" he slides the card along the table.

Jones can only stare as he reads the card; *Doctor Kim Shepherd. Cognitive Behavioral Therapy.*

"You're serious?"

"I've been seeing her for two years now and it helps just to talk to someone and put things in perspective."

"I don't need—"

"Put it in your wallet."

"I don't have it on me," he lies.

Imran sets his bottle down and narrows his eyes. "Alright, but just… consider it. Okay? I've known you a long time, and yeah, there are definitely dark clouds and more than a few rumblings of thunder, but I think there's far more light to you than you can see, Jones. And I bet you anything she can see it too."

Jones taps his finger on the card. "Yeah, but she's paid to say she sees it."

"I'm not talking about her."

---

The sky is milky violet when the men finally emerge from the trailer, stiff-legged and fuzzy-headed. Jones places the heels of his hands above his ass and stretches his back a little, wincing as the pain lances through him.

The carcass of the festival stage stands sentinel in the morning mist, a behemoth picked clean, but not before taking so much from him.

"Hey," Imran says, his voice a little too loud as he stumbles down the trailer steps. "You forgot this."

Jones turns, feigning surprise as the man holds out the business card. "Oh. My mistake."

But it wasn't. Not at all. Still, it's late and he isn't in the mood to argue. He slips the card into his pocket.

Later, when he's alone at home he sticks the card to his fridge with a magnet, beside a note he has tormented himself with all weekend. Liz's phone number. Just one more thing he desperately needs but can't allow himself to have.

Perhaps it's the beer, or the late hour, but he's almost

tempted to cave. Almost, until he glances at himself in the window's reflection and remembers who he is; Theodore Jones Junior, unworthy of both.

Glancing at the clock on the wall, he grimaces. In less than six hours he'll be expected at the animal shelter and he knows already he'll be in pain. A sleepless night to finish off what a hard weekend of work started. He pours himself a glass of water and sighs, taking his pills out of their orange bottles on his counter. They sit in the palm of his hand; one round white painkiller, one pink oblong muscle relaxer, so small and yet, so monumental. He swallows them back, gulping the water and tries to block out his father's voice chastising him in the back of his mind. Liz would be proud of him. He tries instead to focus on that.

# ELEVEN

It's a chilly post-rehearsal Monday afternoon when Liz and Anya pull up in a parking spot outside Maclean's Café.

"Something's wrong," Anya says as she unbuckles her seatbelt and climbs out of the driver's seat of her car.

"I'm fine." As soon as the words leave Liz's mouth, she snaps her lips shut and climbs out of the passenger side. Thoughts of Jones she's working so hard to shut out, bellow for attention. He hasn't called or even texted since Saturday night. Which is a good thing… maybe. At least it removes one complication, however small. Monroe is considering her application and she doesn't need to be distracted by him.

No, the biggest complication is standing right in front of her, her very dearest friend. But today is the day. Today she'll tell Anya her plans and prepare to bid her whole life goodbye.

The guitarist sighs and pulls open the café door, enveloping them in the rich, comforting scent of freshly ground coffee and freshly baked pastries. They step inside and find a table close to the window.

"Don't bullshit me," Anya says, shrugging off her crimson wool coat to reveal a faux-distressed Vixen's Wail tee beneath. The slogan "Anya Supremacy Society" is written in vivid hot pink across her chest, each of the first letters towering over the others.

For the first time in days, Jordan finds herself laughing. "Are you for real?"

The guitarist shrugs. "A fan sent it to me."

"The acronym…"

"Yeah," Anya casts her a look of incredulity. "That's why I wear it."

"You need to rethink everything about that slogan."

A waiter steps up to their table, glancing between the pair of them. He's a young guy, slender and clean-shaven with dark blonde hair and eyes far wearier than any kid his age should have. "What can I get you?"

"A large mocha for me," Anya says.

"And just a water," Liz adds. "Please."

"No problem," the waiter mutters as he jots down their order in a pad. As he turns, he glances back at Anya. "Nice shirt."

"See?" Anya beams, turning back to Liz.

She can just about manage a half smile as she sets her phone on the table top. "I stand corrected. It's a great shirt, obviously as it appeals to you and precisely one teenager."

Anya narrows her eyes. "Okay, there's definitely something wrong with you. Any other day you'd love my ass shirt."

The instinct to deny it springs to Liz's tongue, blocked only by her tight-lipped smile. She nudges the corner of her phone, rotating it a couple of degrees, so the sun's reflection doesn't shine quite so brightly on the screen. Easier to see notifications that way.

*I've applied for college. I want to leave the band. I'm leaving you.*

The words ring clear in her mind, but so does the image of Anya's disappointment. The look of betrayal on her face.

"Who is he? What's his name?" Anya asks, a wry smile pulling at her crimson lips.

Today is not the day, Liz decides. But she can't leave her with nothing. Anya has known her for over a decade, and she knows something is up.

"Jones." His name leaves her like a long-awaited exhale, a release, the perfect distraction from the uncomfortable truth. Even his name feels good on her lips.

The guitarist's smile spreads as she leans forward. "That's it. Just Jones?"

"Just Jones," Liz nods, heat rising on her cheeks.

"Mysterious."

"Yeah." She can't help but smile. "You've seen him actually—"

"It's the Ghoulfest roadie, isn't it? I knew it." Anya gasps. "Fuck yes, Nic owes me a dollar."

"You placed a bet on me?"

"Well, we kind of all knew it. It was pretty hard to miss." Liz frowns. "We?"

"The Vixens. All of us. Thank you…" Anya grins as she accepts her coffee from the waiter. "You were clearly smitten. I mean, come on Liz, we're your best friends."

The words are a knife to the heart. Liz thanks the waiter as he sets an expensive-looking glass bottle of water on the table in front of her, with the cap already twisted off. Fuck, should have specified tap. There isn't even a brand name on the bottle so it must be expensive.

"So…" Anya presses. "What happened?"

Liz glances at her phone. Nothing. "He got hurt at the festival so I took him to the hospital and then drove him home."

"Is he okay?"

"Yeah… well… maybe? But I stayed the night at his place and—"

"Holy shit!" Anya hisses, loud enough to catch the attention of the elderly couple sitting in the corner of the café. Undeterred by their obvious disapproval, Anya continues. "And then what?"

"Nothing," Liz shakes her head. "I slept in his bed and he slept on the floor."

"Aw, shit. But that's good. That means he respects boundaries. You like him though?"

"I do…" The hesitancy in Liz's voice gives them both pause. "He's good looking, and he tries really hard to seem intimidating but I think deep down he's really kind and gentle."

"Hold on," Anya waves her hand in the air as though swiping away the last few words. "Is this one of those he-treats-you-like-shit-but-you-think-you-can-change-him situations?"

Liz picks up the cap from her bottle and rolls it absentmindedly between her thumb and forefinger. "No. He was a little grumbly when he was hurt, but other than that he was kind of sweet, in a just-awoke-from-hibernation kind of way. I think he has a past and issues he hasn't worked through yet. I know I can't fix them for him."

"As long as you're sure."

Liz sighs. "Well, it doesn't really matter anyway. I left him my number and asked him to call, and other than a couple of texts asking why I left my number I haven't heard from him."

"Ah," Anya wrinkles her nose as she sips her coffee. "Well, that does suck."

"It does," Liz sighs, drinking her fancy water straight from the bottle. She glances out of the window, her eyes focusing on the sway of the bare tree branches outside. "Anya, he had the most beautiful butt."

Anya perks up. "You saw his butt?"

"I can see it even now, whenever I close my eyes."

The guitarist snorts a laugh, nudging Liz's ankle with her foot. "I knew you were holding out on me. Just promise me you won't do something ridiculous like quit the band and run away with him."

Liz chuckles, hiding the panic bubbling in her chest. "God, no, never."

"Good," Anya smiles. "I don't know what I'd do without you. And if he never calls you, he's missing out." The guitarist sets her coffee mug down, oblivious to the riot of terror and guilt coursing through Liz's chest. She grimaces and stares into the cup. "I think this is a cappuccino. I swear I ordered mocha."

"You did."

"Huh." She shrugs on her coat and flicks her auburn hair over the collar. "Well, if it's okay with you, I have an errand to run. Wanna come with?"

Liz chuckles as she screws the cap on her water bottle. They came in the same car so it's not like she has much choice. "Where are we going?"

The guitarist leaves ten bucks on the tabletop and waves to the waiter. "Animal shelter."

"Wait…" Liz follows at her heels. "Why?"

The two women walk out of the café and back onto the street where Anya's car is parked close by.

"Because I have a bunch of blankets and towels which I don't need anymore, and the shelter uses them for the animals." Anya flashes a smile and adds before she ducks into the car. "And I'm—no, I *might* be thinking about getting a cat."

Liz climbs back into the passenger seat holding the water bottle between her knees as she fastens her seatbelt. "A cat?"

"Yeah," Anya chuckles. Her eyes drop to Liz's lap briefly as they pull out of the parking spot. "Wait… you stole the bottle?"

Cold fear hits like a tidal wave. "I thought you paid."

"I did. For my coffee." Anya cackles suddenly. "That's what they serve the tap water in."

Liz's eyes widen. "I thought it was bottled water."

"Are you for real? It doesn't even have a label."

"I thought it was some fancy kind of… Fuck. Anya, you let me drink right from it."

"I thought you were being like a cool rock star or something."

"Shit," Liz hisses, fighting back a laugh of her own. "Okay, so add that Maclean's café to the list of places we can never go to again."

"Um, excuse me, I paid for my coffee. Don't drag me down with you, criminal."

"You're my getaway driver," Liz laughs. "You're just as guilty as I am."

Her phone vibrates in her lap, and a small white envelope

symbol appears on the screen. Liz's heart leaps. She presses the symbol as her breath burns in her chest.

>> *From: Monroe Massage Therapy Training*

>> *Subject: Your application.*

A wave of nausea presses against Liz's throat as she prepares to scroll down, as she freezes, as she glances out the corner of her eye at the woman in the driver's seat.

Not today.

She hits the trash can icon in the top right of the screen. And then she breathes.

"You okay?" Anya asks, turning her head toward Liz but never taking her eyes from the road.

"Yeah," Liz smiles, hiding the tremble in her voice. "Never better."

Anya tsks and shakes her head, but the corners of her mouth are dimpled as she fights back a laugh. "My best friend, nothing but a common thief."

The words hurt more than they should, beating against Liz like heavy summer wind just before a storm. Anya *is* her best friend, and the rest of the Vixens are as good as family. She glances out of the window and watches their familiar world blur by. The same streets, the same sights. The mountains she could trace the peaks of in her sleep which stand sentinel on the horizon. It fills her simultaneously with dread that the day will never come, and comfort that perhaps it doesn't need to. Life isn't quite what she wants it to be, but it's still good.

Her heart is just about settled as they reach the animal shelter and pull up in front of the little hut with a sign above the door reading 'shelter office'.

They've made an attempt to make it look cheerful. Children's drawings of the animals are displayed inside an A-frame poster standing out front, and though it's early November, multicolored twinkling fairy lights decorate the office's roof and window. But even with the car doors closed, the persistent, desperate barks can be heard, muffled but no less heartbreaking.

"I don't know if I should go in," Liz mutters. "I'll only want to adopt everything."

"Oh, please." Anya twists around in her seat, her green eyes wide and pitiful. "If you don't, I *will* adopt everything. I need you to rein me in. I'm only allowed to get one cat."

A deep sigh fogs Liz's window. "Alright, but if I cry you have to buy me ice cream."

"Thank you," Anya beams. "But promise not to steal anything else while we're in here, okay. It's a charity."

"You're such a jerk," Liz scowls playfully as she opens the door and climbs out of the car, setting the contraband water bottle in the cup holder between their seats.

She helps Anya carry the bundles of old towels and an array of blankets out of the trunk of her car, before delivering them to the lady behind the desk in the office.

"Thank you so much," the woman beams. She's perhaps in her fifties, with silver strands in her espresso brown hair, and dark, kind eyes. "These come in handy, especially with the colder months coming up."

"Don't mention it," Anya smiles. "And if possible, can we take a look at the cats you have for adoption?"

Liz hangs back, scanning the information posters on the walls; pleas to spay or neuter your pets, enlarged images of various horrific bugs and parasites, advertisements for fun runs and bake sales to help raise money for the shelter. Her eyes pass over them all, and drift across to the window at the back of the office, looking out on the rows of kennels and cages.

It's dreary and depressing, an endless landscape of grey metal and concrete. Occasionally a black nose or a white paw pokes out from between the bars. But in the center of it all, there is a man. His broad back is to her, as he bends a little at the waist, lavishing attention on something she can only assume is a dog. The word "volunteer" is printed on the back of his dark green shirt in blocky white letters.

He squats and she can see the animal fully; an enormous Pitbull, all muscle and sleek sandy brown fur. Its ears have been cut into sharp points and its tail cropped to little more than a nub. Pale scars streak across the dog's back and sides, but it bounces on its paws as it slobbers all over the volunteer, causing the man's shoulders to shake with laughter.

Liz can't help but smile. Despite the evidence of cruelty and misery all around her, there's good in the world. There are good people who spread joy, who give up their time to help and plant kindness. And as the man brushes off the seat of his pants and clumsily stands, Liz's heart damn near leaps out of her chest.

Jones.

His name remains on her lips, silent and impossible.

The Jones she met was a hard man, never smiled or laughed, but this man radiates joy and endearing softness. He ruffles the top of the Pitbull's head with his big, strong hand and gently takes the leash from between its jaws.

He has to be an identical twin or something, she reasons, an identical twin who also doesn't tie his bootlaces and wears the same oil-stained khaki cargo pants as Jones.

"Hey, Liz," Anya says as the woman behind the desk jingles a large bunch of keys. "You coming?"

"Yeah." She bites down a smile and rakes her hand across her hair as butterflies flutter through her stomach.

"Oh," the woman from behind the desk chuckles as she glances out of the window. "Looks like the boys are out there playing rough. Don't worry, they're both completely harmless."

Liz's eyes remain fixed on Jones as he pats his chest, encouraging the dog to stand on its hind legs and place its paws on his stomach. The affection in his smile as he gazes down at it and gently strokes the dog's mangled ears makes Liz's heart kick against her ribs.

Unsmiling, grumpy Jones was handsome, mysterious, an enigma, but this… the man smiling out there is beautiful outside and in.

<hr>

Mondays are always Jones's favorite days.

As Teddy walks to heel like a National Dog Show champ, Jones can't help but smile; something he does often at the shelter. Because for every gut-wrenching, soul-crushing sadness, there's a dog like Teddy.

Ordinarily the big, boisterous dog would have almost brought him to his knees and left him broken. Not today. Today he's more himself than he has been in a long time, a near-stranger in his own body. In the movies he watched as a kid, time travelers would return home exhausted, only to find their world had altered. The grass would be blue, cars replaced by spaceships, pterosaurs gliding through the clouds.

Jones's world altered too; the edges not quite so hard and unforgiving.

The soft crunch of gravel and the sound of voices pull him back into check. He stands straight. "Sit," he says firmly, gesturing to the ground with an open palm. If Teddy is to be adopted and find the home he deserves, he needs to be on his best behavior.

The dog's butt hits the concrete with enthusiastic force, the nub of his tail wagging as he licks his chops. He knows all too well what Jones has in his pocket.

"Good boy," Jones smiles, handing him half a chicken training treat. "Stay. You can have the rest in a minute."

The visitors draw closer, but he pays them little notice. Jones keeps his attention on Teddy, the end of his leash looped tight around his hand. The last thing he needs is for the big doofus to jump up and slobber all over them. He'll never find a forever home that way.

"Stay," he reminds the dog.

Teddy cocks his head to the side, his body trembling a little with the overwhelming instinct to play and bounce. But he seems to be keeping himself in check. For now.

"This is one of our volunteers," Dana from the office announces cheerily as the visitors draw closer. "And the handsome young man beside him is Teddy, one of our long-term residents."

Jones raises his head to nod a greeting, but his heart empties.

It can't be, and yet it is.

How is it possible for Liz to look even more beautiful each time he sees her? Her long, dark brown hair is swept up into a ponytail, her thick-rimmed glasses speckled with tiny drops of rain. He knows he made a point not to mention he volunteers at the shelter so she hasn't come to speak with him. Just a coincidence then. Just one more instance of her appearing right in front of him when he least expects it.

And she's smiling. She's smiling at him.

"Hi," she says, barely louder than a whisper, her dark eyes fixed on his.

The redhead beside her makes a little audible gasp and Jones's ears burn as warmth floods his cheeks. He sort of remembers her from Ghoulfest but she clearly knows about him. Liz has obviously told her, but he has no idea if that's good or bad. There are so many questions he wants to ask; how has she been, why is she there, is her heartbeat skipping the same way his is? The cold, wet press of Teddy's nose on the palm of his hand snaps him out of his thoughts.

Dana chuckles. "How long has Teddy been with us now?"

"Fourteen months," Jones says grimly, tearing his eyes from Liz.

He can't keep them away from her for more than a few seconds.

"Why so long?" Liz asks.

Jones sighs. "Well, he had a rough start. Really rough, actually. He was in bad shape when he came here." Gently, he runs his hand over the dog's scarred side. "He wouldn't let anyone touch him, didn't trust humans."

"He trusts you," she says.

"Yeah," Jones smiles before catching himself. He clears his throat. "But we're struggling to find him a home. He has the disadvantage of being big and scary-looking, older and kind of ugly. I guess we had a lot to bond over."

His attempt at self-deprecating humor only deepens the crease between Liz's eyebrows. Shit.

"And you share the same name," Dana reminds him, as if he isn't painfully aware.

His heart drops a little lower as Liz's eyes narrow, and he braces himself for mockery. Looking the way he does with a name like Theodore is only a small part of the reason he never goes by his forename, but it's the one people latch onto. The other part he keeps hidden.

"I don't think he's ugly at all," Liz says. "I think he's very handsome."

She raises her eyes from the dog and holds Jones's gaze, sending the butterflies in his stomach soaring. The corners of her lips arc into a fleeting, knowing smile, telling him she doesn't just mean the dog. Even his battered self-esteem can't convince him otherwise.

Dana jangles her keys against her palm. "If you'd like to know more about our dogs, I'm sure Jones would be more than happy to show you around while I take Anya to see the cats."

Liz and the redhead exchange a glance which stretches to infinity as Jones waits. A knot at the base of his belly tightens, and his throat turns dry. Either she refuses and walks away from him, or she accepts and they're left alone. Both options terrify him.

"I'd love to," Liz says. "If that's okay?"

Jones simply nods. With his throat deadlocked and his heartbeat drowning out the rest of the world he can't do much more.

As Dana and the redhead walk away, the cold air thickens, until it's barely even breathable anymore. Jones stares at the ground by her feet, the world around them blurring as heat crawls up his neck.

Liz clears her throat. "Can I pet him? Will he let me?"

"You can try," Jones says, his voice rough in his parched throat. "Don't approach him though, let him come to you."

"Okay, she nods.

This is easy, he tries to convince himself. He talks to visitors all day. He can think of her as just that. Just one more visitor.

That she seems to wield the one and only battering ram which can burst through doors he's kept locked for decades is momentarily forgotten. "You can stand or crouch, but don't lean over him."

Another nod. She lowers herself down to a crouch, her weight balanced on her toes, and holds out her hand. Jones's heart jolts as Ted stands and hurries toward her, the remnants of his tail wiggling with enough force to shake his whole back end. He trusts the dog not to snap, his body language is calm and happy, and he trusts Liz not to frighten him, yet Jones's pulse races. His muscles tighten, ready to stand between them should he have to.

He cares. He cares about them both. Deeply. The revelation makes his heart empty, because he shouldn't. One day Teddy will find a new home and he won't need Jones anymore. And Liz... he doesn't deserve her. The fact she's here means nothing.

The cacophony of doubt dissipates as Liz's hand coasts gently down Teddy's chin and throat, and down to rub his chest. She's gentle, respecting the animal's space, showing him that she isn't a threat. The Pitbull flops to the ground and rolls onto his back, legs sticking up in the air like a giant dead bug.

Jones chuckles as Liz smiles up at him and it takes longer than it should to remember to fix his face. But once Teddy's back leg starts kicking and Liz starts to laugh, Jones finds that this smile is far harder to remove.

A small, barely perceptible twinge of pain streaks through Jones's back and thigh as he crouches opposite Liz and joins her in scratching the ecstatic pitbull's belly. "He likes you," Jones smiles, meeting her gaze.

The air crackles between them, and then as her fingers glance over his, lightning strikes, shooting through his veins. His breath catches in his throat as she smiles and places her hand over the top of his.

"I like him too."

Can she hear the tremble in his breath? Can she feel his racing pulse through her fingertips? If she does, she doesn't say. He's spent his entire life trying to make himself as cold and hard as possible, yet with barely any effort at all she melts him every time he sees her. And they keep stumbling into one another. Perhaps that means something.

"I'm glad I got to see you again." He has to drag every word from his narrowed throat to his clumsy tongue. "I'm sorry I didn't call. I didn't know what to say."

She nods slowly. "I wouldn't have known either." A corner of her mouth lifts and curves into a half-smile as Teddy wriggles beneath their hands, desperate for more attention. Her hand slips from his as she scratches beneath Teddy's chin. "You look good."

"Me or the dog?"

She laughs, a lovely sound which only makes him smile harder. "You. Although Teddy is very handsome too."

"I feel good."

"Is the medicine helping?"

He nods.

"Good."

*Can I see you again?*

The words dance in his chest, following the rhythm of his frantic heart but doubt hits like a tidal wave. She had his number too, yet she didn't call. And he can't blame her. He can't stand to be around himself either.

The soft crunch of footsteps stills his heart as Dana and the redhead appear from between the rows of cages.

Liz stands and turns to face them. "Everything okay?"

"I'm mad at you," the redhead grumbles as she approaches. "You weren't there to rein me in."

Liz cringes. "What's the damage?"

"Three cats."

"Anya!"

Jones stands as Teddy rolls onto his belly but keeps low, watching their conversation and cocking his head to the side.

Dana chuckles. "We just have a little paperwork to go through, and then I'll bring the carriers around."

Liz laughs and shakes her head. "You are unbelievable."

"I have literally no self-control," Anya cringes.

Jones steps back, and Teddy follows him dutifully, though his attention remains on the women. Maybe he's projecting, but he can almost see the pain in the pitbull's eyes as he watches Liz, knowing there's someone just in reach who he longs so desperately for. Riding high on hopes he can scarcely believe himself.

"What about Teddy?" Dana asks Liz. "Do you think you could take him?"

Liz glances over her shoulder towards them. Jones's heart is a concrete slab, still and heavy in his chest. He silently begs with her, pleads for her to see the good in him, give him the chance to prove he's worthy of her time and her love.

She presses her soft lips together. "I'm sorry, I can't."

At once he's certain she's talking about both him and the dog. He can see it in her eyes, the way she can't even look back at the pair of them as she heads back to the office.

Jones isn't good enough for her. He knew it even before now. It was a fool's hope to think otherwise.

"Come on, Teddy," he says, picking up the leash. "Let's take a walk."

# Twelve

Liz curls her fingers against her palm, trying to savor the memory of the warmth and weight of Jones's hand as she follows Anya back toward the office. Her heart races, every breath unsteady and uncertain, as words she longs to say block her throat.

If not now, then maybe never.

"Hey, give me a minute," she calls to the two women ahead of her.

Anya's eyebrows raise. "You okay?"

"Yeah," Liz nods as she begins to turn. "Yeah. I'll be back in a minute."

She jogs back to the spot where she saw him last, searching down the mono-toned rows of kennels and pens. Dogs bark, some of them jumping up to greet her as she passes by, but Jones is nowhere to be found.

Doubt nags at her, tells her she doesn't even know why she's looking for him or what she'll say when she finds him. But another far more persistent voice tells her she can't just walk away from him, not when the universe has brought them together once more.

"Jones?" she yells as she rounds a corner, freezing as the enormous Pitbull skitters back away from her, yelping as though she just kicked him.

"Hey, hey!" Jones cries out, stepping between the two of them.

Liz takes a step back, her heart hammering against her ribs and her pulse pounding in her ears. "I'm sorry."

"You just spooked him," Jones grumbles as he crouches down beside the dog and pets his chest. "You shouldn't be so loud around them."

"I'm sorry."

His eyebrows stitch together as he raises his eyes to meet hers. "What's wrong?"

Shame burns on her cheeks as she breathes hard and fast. "I… I don't know."

Jones stands, concern etching deep across his brow. "Liz? What is it?"

"Do you feel like perhaps the universe is telling us something?" She waits for him to respond, but he simply stands and watches her. "Maybe I'm wrong, but Jones, I feel *something* when I'm with you, and I don't know what it is, but I… What if we tested it? What if we … I don't know."

He makes a monosyllabic grunt deep in his chest, but doesn't say anything more.

Liz's hope plummets. She already made one questionable decision when she deleted the email from Monroe. Chasing down a man who doesn't seem to be remotely interested in her is the second, but she can still walk away with most of her pride. She shakes her head and turns back to walk to the office. "I shouldn't have come back, I'm sorry. Let's just forget—"

Her words are cut off by the warmth and strength of his hand around her wrist, the giddy sensation of being spun, and then the shock of his lips. His lips on hers, heat and softness, the world dropping from beneath her feet and everything, *everything* falling into place exactly where it should.

It seems to surprise him as much as her. His grip on her wrist loosens, falling to his side, but she catches his hand and laces their fingers together. Then something inside him breaks free.

He kisses her like the world will end if he stops. The fingers of his free hand tangle in her hair, while her hand rests on his chest as his pulse leaps beneath her touch. In answer Liz's heart pounds against her ribs, calling out to his, beckoning him closer, deeper, hoping against hope it never ends.

He releases her hand, and his strong, tattooed arm drops to wrap around her waist, pulling her against his body, the heat and strength of him pressed against hers, heart to heart, soul to soul.

The hand in her hair drops to cup her cheek, and he breaks away to whisper "I'm sorry," against her lips.

"Why?" She's drunk on him, eyes half-lidded, lips throbbing with the aftershocks of his destructive kisses. Her glasses fog, but as the world becomes clearer and she can see him fully, her heart lunges as though now it knows what it's like to be close to him, it can't live any other way.

"I should have asked."

She raises onto her tiptoes, seeking his lips again. "My answer would have been the same."

This time he's gentle, as though she'll be crushed if he

kisses her with that same desperate ferocity. So she presses forward, fusing her body to his, balancing on the tips of her toes so he doesn't have to bend down so far.

Dogs bark around them, and the cool fall air tangles their breaths in clouds, but against him she's warm. She's burning.

The cold, slimy press of Teddy's nose against her elbow pulls them back to earth. Jones laughs quietly as he pats the dog's head. His cheeks are flushed pink, his eyes usually such cool stony grey are dark and hazy.

"I want to see you again," she says.

He pulls in a breath which doesn't reach further than his throat before he exhales. His eyebrows stitch together again. "Are you sure?"

How can a man so big and burly seem so close to shattering? How is this the same man who bent her over the trailer's counter and claimed her as his with such confidence? Jones is an enigma, one she's finding more and more she longs to solve. "Super sure. If you are."

He can't look at her as he says, "I don't know that I'm good enough for you."

"Why don't you let me decide that?" She raises up onto her tiptoes and kisses him gently on the corner of his mouth as his lips curve beneath hers. She's an addict. Now that she has seen his smile she craves more. "You really do have the most handsome smile."

He glances away, dipping his chin. "You'll make me blush."

"Good."

A quiet chuckle jolts his chest. "Liz… I…" He turns his attention back to the Pitbull sitting by his feet and waiting patiently. Slowly, he strokes the dog between the ears. There's still hesitancy in his voice. "I work most evenings."

Ah. Liz forces a smile. "It's okay if you don't want—"

"I do. I really do." He raises his eyes to the clouds, unable for a moment to even look at her. There's something deeper than rejection. Something more than just not wanting to go. He's afraid, she realizes, holding himself back, denying what he so clearly wants.

"Okay," Liz says gently. "How about I swing by your place one morning this week and we get breakfast?"

Finally, his eyes return to hers. "Yeah. Yeah, I'd like that."

She tightens her grip around the lifeline as he clings to it. "Cool. Which day works?"

"Wednesday?" The word leaves his lips, barely louder than a graveled whisper. "Is that too soon?"

Any doubt she had about his enthusiasm disappears. Liz smiles. Jones isn't playing it cool, and honestly, she doesn't want to anyway. If she's staying, she's taking every damn thing this town has to offer. "That sounds perfect. Wednesday at ten? It'll give you a chance to sleep in if you're tired after work."

"Make it nine," he counters, the color returning to his cheeks.

Liz raises onto her tiptoes to brush her lips to his once more, just a fleeting kiss, but it sends sparks to the pit of her stomach anyway. "See you then."

The ache for him begins almost as soon as she walks away. A force deep inside her chest begs her to turn back. One more kiss. One more smile. But she doesn't. She makes her way back to the office, avoiding Anya's sidelong glances and wry, knowing grin.

That evening Jones tries in vain to fill his lungs as he paces behind the bar. He's four hours into a six-hour shift and dangerously close to wearing a canyon into the floor. "What the fuck am I supposed to do?"

Imran perches on a barstool, his elbows braced on the wooden bartop. "I don't know. Anyway, about that drink?"

"What do I even talk about?" Jones asks for at least the third time. "I can't let her know who I really am."

Imran's brow creases. "What are you talking about?"

"She thinks I'm…" Jones waves his hands in mid-air as though he can conjure the image of the man she believes him to be.

"A puppeteer?" Imran sits taller, his eyes wide and alert with purpose. "Wait, no… a wizard?"

"No, shut up."

"To be fair, you'd probably be a better wizard than you are a bartender. You've got the beard for it at least."

Jones's scowl breaks as he glances down at the pristine ten-dollar bill pinched between Imran's fingers. How long has he left him hanging while he's been pacing? "Oh. What do you want?"

"Beer," Imran sighs. "Actually, better make it two."

It takes all of twenty seconds for Jones to retrieve the bottles from the fridge and set them on the bar top. Fortunately, Calico Jack's is dead on Monday nights. Jones doesn't have to be good at the job. He just has to be there.

Still, the owners insist on him wearing the full get-up. An eyepatch over one eye, a flouncy shirt which shows off a deep-plunging V of hairy chest, and tattered, cropped pants which flap against the backs of his calves. He even has a fake green macaw strapped to his shoulder. He cringes at the thought of Liz walking in and seeing him here. She's already found two of his three workplaces and the last thing he needs is for her to see him looking like this.

"I should cancel," he mutters. "I'll let her down gently, tell her I had other plans and forgot them."

Imran sets his bottle down. "… I thought you liked her?"

"I do." Jones's heart lurches at the thought of her, the way her glasses fogged as she kissed him, the way her soft, full lips pulled at his with so much urgency. Something twitches low in his belly. "I really like her, but the fact still remains that she's not going to want me when she gets to know me better."

"Are you afraid of her finding out what a grumpy bastard you are?"

"No, she already knows that." Jones pulls up a stool behind the bar and perches on the edge, wincing slightly. The pain meds are beginning to wear off and as blissful as relief has been, the knowledge that the pain is only hidden, rather than cured, is just as agonizing. He manages a long breath. "I told you the other night, I'm not good enough for her. I know I'm not." He shakes his head. "I've never even been on a date."

"Oh… well they're nothing to be afraid of. Best not to overthink it. You just go and hang out and ask her questions about herself and talk about yourself."

"No, you don't understand. Immy, I've never said yes to a date before."

"Why?"

"Because…" He raises his eyes to the ceiling, to the cracking red paint and the gently flickering faux-candelabra hanging above him. "No one has ever made me think that maybe I could be worth spending the time with."

When he lowers his eyes, Imran's thick eyebrows are stitched together with incredulity. "Did you call that therapist?"

"No."

"I really think you should."

He's thought about it, weighed up the pros and the cons, yet the card remained untouched on his refrigerator door. "I don't know… it's not really *me*. I'm just better off alone." Jones inwardly winces as his father's voice emerges from his lips.

On Tuesday morning he's pacing again, only this time he's in his own kitchen, hands shaking as he holds the business card in one and his cell phone in the other. He punched in the number ten minutes ago, but his thumb still hovers above the call button.

"Ridiculous," he whispers. "I don't need therapy. I just need to come to terms with the fact that I'm not worthy of her. Let her go."

A noise from the living room stills his heart. He freezes, fully expecting his father to appear in the doorway demanding to know why Jones is being so loud, why he's wasting his time on women when he could be out earning a living, getting his hands dirty like a real man. Instinctively, he tucks the business card behind his back.

Roxy swaggers into the kitchen, a yellow nasturtium flower petal stuck to the side of her lips. Ever the graceful eater.

Jones releases a sigh and shoves the thoughts of his father to the back of his mind. He resumes his pacing, stepping over Roxy as she makes her way to the corridor to sleep in a sun spot.

His dad is gone, for better or for worse. He has been gone for more than two decades. Jones is free to work on becoming the man he wants to be. Whoever that is.

# THIRTEEN

"We kicked so much ass at Ghoulfest," Finn grins, sitting in the center of the couch as the rest of the band settle in Anya's living room. "And it's opened up a lot of opportunities for us as a band."

Mia nods slowly beside the drummer. "We can't do them all, so we need to consider our options carefully. If we can't all agree then we'll go with the majority's decision."

Liz's attention wanes almost immediately as Finn pulls out a notebook and launches into a long list of events they've been invited to, highlighting their conflicting dates and travel plans. Whether they play another festival three states over, or a dive bar downtown, or apply to play at esteemed reviewer Armand Corvo's annual industry party in the new year, it's all the same to her.

Since the band found out about Anya's adopted cats it was unanimously agreed that their Tuesday night meeting would be held in her tiny living room and Liz can tell hers isn't the only mind that's wandering.

Anya lies on her stomach in the middle of the floor while

two ginger kittens run riot around her, batting her hair and attacking her feet whenever she puts her toes down. Tamika the bassist sits in an armchair over by the cluttered bookshelves, her eyes scanning the titles and lingering on the knickknacks. Étienne is cross-legged on the floor beside Nic, the pair of them fussing over a beautifully demonic-looking, one-eyed, black tomcat. Jordan the cellist sits opposite, her eyes fixed on Étienne the whole time, a subtle smile curving her lips.

Having a couple in the band again is… weird. Jord and Eti keep things *mostly* professional—when they're not making out on stage that is—but the constant eye-fucking is hard to miss. Liz lets her gaze lose its focus, and immediately her thoughts go to Jones.

The chemistry between them, and the excitement is like nothing she has felt for a long time and she'd be lying if she said she wasn't counting down the hours—fourteen and a quarter—till she gets to see him again. Perhaps the attraction is purely sexual, because God knows he rocked her world that day in the trailer, but she's certain there's something more.

She doesn't know much about him but his grumpy façade is already cracking. It helps that he's kind to animals too. When Roxy scratched up her leg, he took care of her with just as much tenderness. The gentle, soothing caress of his hand on her calf occupies her mind just as the memory of his hand bringing her to orgasm while he pinned her to the countertop.

"Liz?" Anya says sharply.

Snapping herself out of her thoughts of him, Liz becomes acutely aware of the rest of the band staring at her expectantly. Heat flushes her cheeks as she tries to swallow and moisten her bone-dry throat. "Hm?"

"How does that sound?" Finn asks. "You in?"

"Yeah. I'm in."

No doubt he hears the hesitancy in her voice because the corners of his eyes crease as he smiles and shakes his head. "Alright. Well, that's that part of the meeting over with. Now I guess we need to decide on a setlist for Armand."

Étienne stretches his back, twisting to the side as he grunts, "I vote for a symphonic metal cover of *Total Eclipse of the Heart.*"

"God no—" Mia snaps her lips shut and stares off into space. Her eyes raise as she imagines the song. "Actually…"

Étienne sits back and flashes a proud smirk toward Jordan.

As the band's conversation turns back to business, Liz's mind returns to Jones.

---

It's around midnight when she texts him from her bedroom; a short message reading simply *I'm looking forward to seeing you.* She sets her phone face down on the bed and tries to focus on literally anything else. Her phone's chime is like a penny hitting the bottom of a wishing well.

*Me too.*

And then another:

*I can't sleep.*

Her temples burn as she reads the message again and again. He can't sleep. He's telling her he can't sleep. He's awake. He will be for some time. Is it an invitation? A simple statement? She shouldn't reply. She absolutely should not reply. She thinks it even as her thumbs dart across the keypad: *Do you want to move our date forward?*

Her heart races as she sets the phone down on the bed and drags in a breath. She closes her eyes and tries to will some sense into her head. What she wants and what she should do are two totally different things. Opposing forces, pulling her apart.

She needs to put on pajamas and get into bed. She needs to try to recover her deleted emails and prepare to tell the Vixens she's quitting the band. She needs to focus on a billion different things which aren't Jones.

But she *wants* to get dressed, go out to her car, drive to his place and do everything she has imagined since the moment she collided with him. She wants a release for the nervous energy coursing around her body. She wants him.

Closing her eyes, she squeezes the power button on her phone for a moment. Not long enough to switch it off, but almost long enough to convince herself of her good intentions. The message tone chimes.

*11281 Fairview Road.*

"Fuck." She can barely breathe as she stands and unwraps her damp towel. She can't do this. It doesn't feel like the start of something casual. Already she's in too deep with him, and God help her, she's *feeling things.*

She shouldn't do it, but she is.

Rummaging through her drawers she finds her seldom-used nice matching black lace underwear set and a half-full box of condoms. The bedroom pulses around her as she gets dressed and quickly blow-dries her hair.

"Sorry Jim," she whispers to the fish as she throws her toothbrush and a pair of clean underwear in her overnight bag. "I'll be back in the morning."

---

Jones's knee judders as he sits on the couch, waiting, panicking, regretting. It's been half an hour since he texted her his address, a clear invitation, and she still hasn't replied.

He shouldn't have done it anyway.

It was a moment of weakness, a moment where he let his libido take charge and abandon everything he'd spent the last few weeks convincing himself of. He screws his eyes tight as a stab of pain darts through his lower back. The pain meds are wearing off and he should be in bed resting up after a long shift at Calico's. Hell, he's still wearing his flouncy pirate shirt.

The doorbell rings.

Jones's breath solidifies in his chest as he stands and makes his way to the door, half convinced it's a prank, or a trick caused by the weariness and ache in his body. His hands tremble as he turns the lock and opens the door. His heart all but leaps out of his chest.

"Hi," she says, her eyes instantly darting down to the spot above his belly where the deep V points to.

He's a mess, he knows he is. It was a long shift and he hasn't showered, he's covered in spilled beer and sweat. His beard is windblown and he's dressed like a pirate for fuck's sake.

But Liz is perfect, so perfect that he doesn't deserve to want her. Beneath the glow of the porch light, her brown hair shines, fluttering in the nighttime breeze. Her beautiful dark-brown eyes are fixed on him. It's past midnight, but the sun is shining on him.

Her eyes widen as they pass over him for the umpteenth time. "Wow."

"It's a work thing," he mutters, tugging the cotton away from his hip to emphasize he wants no part of it. "They make me wear it."

She can't tear her eyes from him, the heat of her gaze threatening to wilt him. Despite the pain he stands a little taller.

"I…" Her breath catches in her throat before she shakes her head and blinks rapidly. "Wow."

Jones chuckles, leaning against the doorframe as heat prickles on his cheeks. "I'm picking up some hints that you might like the blouse."

"Who knew?" Her eyes raise to meet his and her smile damn near melts him. "Apparently it's very much my thing."

It's been a long time since anyone made him blush like she does. "Do you want to come in?"

She closes the gap between them, raising onto her tiptoes as she presses her body against his, her eyes scanning his face with an expression he can't quite pin. Curiosity, maybe. She looks at him as though she has never seen another human being before, as though she never knew there was another creature out there who shared the same world as her. And she's desperate to understand him.

"I don't know what it is," she says, her voice thin, wavering, silk blown in a breeze. "I couldn't wait until tomorrow to see you again."

His hands skate along the curve of her hip, dipping into her waist. She glances down to where his hand rests, and her throat twitches as she pulls in a breath.

Without another word he pulls her gently inside along with him, smiling against her lips as they stumble over each other's feet. But as soon as the door closes their mood shifts; heated, hungry. He turns her, pressing her back to the wall. The pain is meaningless as his lips find hers. Her fingers curl at her sides like she isn't sure whether it's okay to touch him. A moment later he realizes they were simply coiled, ready to pounce. One hand goes to the back of his neck, tugging him slightly down toward her so she can kiss him deeper. The other explores him.

She runs her fingers through his chest hair, down into the opening of his shirt and over the swell of his stomach. He closes his eyes and soaks up the sensation of her hands on him, like a tree at the end of the dry season, clinging to the first rain. She brushes a lightning-charged fingertip to the silver bar in his nipple and a half groan, half growl emerges from him.

She kisses him and nothing else matters. Jones sinks into the softness of her lips, forgetting the hard, unforgiving world around them.

*I'm not worth her* the voice in the back of his mind taunts him, but Liz silences it, sliding her tongue between his lips and claiming his mouth as hers.

He's denied himself a lot over the years, but he can't deny himself her. Not a minute longer.

*You are. Tonight, you are.*

"Bedroom," he growls as he tangles his fingers in a fistful of her hair.

She opens her eyes, her pupils shot wide as her breath stills in her chest. "Is that an order?"

"Do you want it to be?"

Her throat leaps before she nods.

"You like to be bossed around?"

"Yes."

"Okay. First, tell me." His voice is edged, his heart pounding. He would be lying if he said that every inch of his skin wasn't covered in goosebumps, that he's momentarily forgotten his pain because he can't stop wanting her. "Tell me what you want."

Color flushes her cheeks as she stares up at him, but she meets his gaze without wavering. "I want to sleep with you."

"Again."

"Jones…"

"Say it again. I have to know you really want this."

She moistens her lips with the tip of her tongue as her fingers glide along the neckline of his shirt, sending shivers across his skin. Neither of them are breathing. "Jones, I need you. I need you to fuck me."

He likes this, making her pursue him, having her tell him to take charge. Jones is so big and strong, and he'd be damned before he ever makes her feel like she doesn't have a choice in this. "Are you sure?"

"Yes." Her voice is barely a whisper now and the hunger in her eyes is intense. "I want you. I can't think of anything else."

"Good," he says. "Bedroom. Now."

She rocks back down onto the flats of her feet, holding eye contact as she steps past him, and only breaking away to walk confidently toward his bedroom. He follows close behind, his heart beating out of his chest as he tries to remember to just keep breathing.

His legs are jelly beneath him as he watches her, the way her hips sway with each step, the perfume of her body blurring his senses. His fears, insecurities, reservations, his past, they all fade, drowned out by his lust, and for the first time in a while, excitement.

They're only about five feet from the bedroom door but he can't stand it anymore. He catches her wrist in his hand and turns her around, pushing her up against the hallway wall. A desperate whimper emerges from her lips as he pins her with his body, bracing his hands on the wall at either side of her head. From the way she reaches up, her lips colliding with his, the ferocity of her kiss, the seconds they spent apart was unbearable for her too.

Her arms wrap around him, and her hands skate along his shoulders, down over his back, lower and lower, past the point where the pain radiates, to work her way beneath the hem of his pants and squeeze his ass. His heart damn near stops at her touch, as she pulls his hips toward her, grinding her soft body against his cock. The knowledge that she wants him as bad as he wants her makes him just as breathless.

"Liz," he growls her name against the curve of her shoulder, nipping her soft skin with his teeth as she gasps in his ear.

And then, she pulls away.

Her body trembles as she edges along the wall, her arm spread out in search of the door handle.

"I can't wait anymore," she whispers as she finds it, and steps into his bedroom doorway.

She reaches out to grip his shirt, pulling him along with her. They stumble through the darkness for a moment before he finds the light switch, and all the while she kisses him, her teeth nipping his bottom lip, each fervent lick of her tongue against his both a promise and an instruction.

He guides her backward until the backs of her thighs touch the mattress, leaning into her to urge her down. God those thighs, thick thighs he'll lie between, rest them on his shoulders as he licks her pussy until she's nothing but a quivering, whimpering wreck.

A spike of agony shoots up from the base of his spine to the small of his back, and he grits his teeth as he tears his lips from hers.

"Shit," he hisses, face burning as Liz looks up at him with pity and concern.

"Pain?" she asks, as though it could be anything else.

"I'm fine."

And he is. He will be. He has to be. If he gives in to it now, he might not get another chance to be with her like this. It's already a miracle she wants him at all.

He takes a moment to compose himself, waiting until the stabbing sensation ebbs completely. Pulling in a deep breath, relief washes over him. He could drop down on his knees and thank every force in the universe for sparing him.

So he does.

# FOURTEEN

Liz can barely breathe as Jones lowers himself onto his knees. He's so tall that even kneeling his face is aligned with her breasts. His big, rough hands skate along her hips, beneath the hem of her shirt and along the soft, sensitive skin of her waist.

Lifting her shirt, she tilts her hips toward him, inviting him to kiss her stomach. His mouth is hot against her skin as she rakes her fingernails gently across his scalp and makes him shiver.

"Take all your clothes off," he tells her. He looks up at her, his pupils shot wide. "I want to see you."

Her body bristles at his command. She unbuttons her jeans and lowers the zipper, her throat tightening as he watches her peel off the tight denim, the hunger in his gaze matching her own. She wants him so desperately it's absurd to think they ever thought this was avoidable. Ever since that moment –God, was it really only four days ago—since she crashed into him at the festival, she wanted him.

When she steps out of her jeans, Jones presses forward,

kissing the pink mark on her stomach the waistband leaves behind. His thumbs skim her hips and the top of her underwear. He doesn't mention the lace, men rarely do, but his appreciation for her body beneath the pretty wrapping is more than apparent.

She unhooks her bra and lets it fall, and he draws a sharp breath. For a moment she thinks he might be in pain again, but he kisses a trail along the soft curves of her belly before dragging his tongue along the underside of her breast. A shiver of pleasure rolls through her body as he traces the dark ridges surrounding her aching nipples. His tongue is hot and soft, slick against her desperate skin.

She arches her back as he pulls one of her nipples between his lips and sucks, gentle at first, then hard, his tongue teasing, flickering.

"Jones," she whispers, her nails pressing into his shoulders as he hooks his fingers beneath the waistband of her panties and pulls them down to her ankles. Her knees buckle as he slides two fingers between her thighs.

"God," he whispers against her breast, his eyes closed as he explores her. "You're so fucking wet."

"That's what you do to me."

A half-growl, half-purr sounds at the back of his throat. His voice is deep, edged with desperate unrefined need. "Lie back."

She does as he tells her, sitting on the edge of the bed before lying down. She props herself on her elbows so she can watch, her heart fluttering as this man, this big man in his flowing poet shirt, holds her gaze, and a wicked, devilish smile plays across his lips.

Fuck.

She was in love with his smile before, but this grin tells

her he's about to wreck her, and she knows with all certainty she'll thank him for it. It's a smile which tells her she's bitten off way more than she can chew and that she made the best mistake of her life by coming here. Because there's no coming back from this. She knows right now there would be no getting over Jones even if she wanted to.

"Please," she whispers, desperate, agonized, wanting.

"Tell me what you want," he growls.

Heat fans across her cheeks and his teeth sink into his bottom lip as she fights for her breath. She knows he'll make her wait all night if she doesn't tell him. "I want you to lick me."

That grin again as a low groan sounds in his throat. "You want me to eat your pussy?"

"Yes."

Her nerves fire in ecstasy as he slides a finger between her labia, slow, firm, coating it in her wetness. His eyes never leave hers as he brings the finger to his mouth and licks it, savoring the taste of her like a goddamn gourmet.

"You taste so good," he tells her. "I could do this all night."

The anticipation boils over as she watches him and imagines his tongue on her. Her breasts ache, her breath stutters from her chest. And as he skates his rough palms along the soft insides of her thighs, she can hardly bear it. Desperate, she lifts her hips, tilting them toward him.

"You're being impatient," he scolds, his voice a low rumble.

"I need you."

"Then you'd better behave. I can tease you all night, have you begging me to let you finish."

She bites back the urge to swear at him, to beg, to give

him any reason at all to withhold her pleasure. It's a resolu-
tion she forgets the moment he dips his head and his teeth
graze the inside of her thighs.

"Fuck," she gasps, bucking her hips against him. The
tingling sensation of his teeth is exquisite agony.

"This isn't behaving," he says, before biting her again.

She cries out, her body jolting. "It tickles."

Jones chuckles cruelly and lowers his head once more.

This time she's prepared, gripping fistfuls of the bedsheets
and clenching the muscles in her belly to hold herself back.
He licks the length of her inner thigh, his tongue agonizingly
close to where she needs him. Goosebumps tingle on her skin
as he edges closer to her pussy, teasing her, delaying her grati-
fication.

But when that pleasure comes, she could swear her heart
stops. The moment his tongue slides against her clit, she can't
breathe, can't speak. The world beyond them is snapped
away, and all that matters is his mouth on her. He licks her,
slowly, groaning, savoring the taste of her, his hands spread
around the outside of her thighs, urging them together to
press tight around his head.

He swipes his nose from the entrance of her pussy to her
clit, nuzzling her, groaning softly as though it gives him just
as much pleasure as it does her before he licks her again.

Her toes curl as he kisses her pussy, worshipping her with
his tongue, agonizingly slow and gentle, enough to send
sparks shooting through her but not quite enough to get her
off. If he does it all night, she'll be a shuddering, sobbing
mess, and he knows it too. He raises his eyes to meet hers
and the corners of his lips curve into a grin so devilish she
half expects him to grow horns.

She's going to die. Liz crumples back, pressing her head

against the plush fabric of his comforter, one hand resting on her forehead, the other reaching down to caress the top of his head. But she doesn't dare push him. She keeps her hips down, closes her eyes and focuses on the pleasure, the soft tongue licking, fluttering, long, languid strokes, teasing circles.

Without warning he quickens his pace, as though the torment was too much for him. It begins with the arching of his shoulders, his hands sliding over her thighs until his arms wind around them. All at once the gentleness, the unbearable softness is gone and he becomes something altogether more primal.

He grips her thighs and drags her toward him, damn near lifting her ass completely from the bed as he licks and licks, sending bolts of ecstasy shooting through her body. Liz cries out, helpless, lost in bliss, and entirely his. He pushes against the backs of her thighs, pinning her legs up, her thighs against her stomach, exposing her to him as he devours her, moaning, licking, fucking her with his tongue.

All Liz can do is lie there and take it, her fingers grasping at the bedsheets, her muscles tensing, throbbing, tightening. She reaches down, desperate for release, her fingertips brushing the slick skin above her clit, pressing down, drawing back her hood so he can kiss her deeper, harder, faster.

She pulls in a breath and holds it in her chest as her body tenses, coils constricting, winding tighter and tighter until her pleasure detonates. She comes hard, head thrown back against the mattress, lips parted in a silent cry, her thighs trembling even as he keeps them pinned in place, his fervent licks turning to languid caresses. Pulses of ecstasy rock through her until she's spent and melting into the bedsheets.

She's only vaguely aware of the undulation of the mattress, of the softness of his cotton shirt brushing against the bare skin of her chest, of his mouth, glossy with her pleasure, kissing her lips. But when she comes back to lucidity, her heart skips in the best way. Jones is bent at the waist, resting his torso on top of hers, his weight braced on his forearms as he strokes back her hair. "Are you okay?" he asks, searching her eyes.

She can only nod as she reaches up to swipe her thumb across his lower lip. He catches her wrist in his hand and holds it there.

"Do you still want more?" he asks.

"Yes," she whispers without hesitation. Delicious ache spreads through her chest and her stomach flutters at the thought of more of him, more of this pleasure.

"So needy," he growls before licking the length of her thumb and bringing the tip of it into his mouth.

Arousal shoots through her, tugging a thread which seems to run from his lips directly down to her clit. Whatever spell he has put on her, she'll happily live her life in this haze. "Fuck me, Jones," she demands. "I need you."

"Are you telling me what to do?"

She shivers at the edge of darkness in his voice. Jones in the streets is a grumbly, grumpy bear, but here, like this, he's an altogether more dangerous beast. And the thought of him sinking his teeth into her is far too tempting. "Yes. Fuck me, Jones. Hard."

His lips curl into a snarl. "I should roll you over and spank your bossy ass."

She grins as she shifts her hips against him, wrapping her legs around his thighs. His rigid cock presses firm against her as he groans.

As much as she loves him telling her what to do, she does so enjoy watching him unravel. "Look at you," she whispers against his ear as his eyelids flutter shut. "So hard, so turned on." She grazes his neck with her teeth, nipping at the skin at the edge of his beard. "Can you still taste my pussy on your lips?"

The skin of his throat heats against her mouth as he presses his hips down onto her, grinding his cock against her belly. "Goddamn, Liz, I'm going to fuck you so hard. I'm going to have you coming all night."

His lips press to hers with a ferocity bordering on savage, all at once punishing and rewarding her for goading him. Liz's heart thunders in anticipation as he cups her breasts in his big, rough hands and grinds his hips against hers.

God, how long has it been since she felt like this with anyone or anything? The excitement, the delicious, nervous flutter, the confidence. He may be on top of her, but he looks at her like she's a goddess towering above him.

"Wait here," he tells her.

As fun as it is to get him riled, she obeys his command. If she has to wait a second longer to have him inside her, she'll surely die, and she knows only too well he'd relish her demise.

He pushes up off the bed, standing upright for just a moment before he gasps, eyes wide, fists clenched. The shift is as sudden as it is devastating.

"What is it?" Liz lifts herself up, her pulse quickening as the color drains from his face. "Jones?"

"Don't," he hisses through gritted teeth. "Just stay there. I can do this."

But he's frozen, gasping, his knuckles turning bloodless.

His breaths are shallow and growing faster by the second before he crumples, folding back down at the waist.

He's hurt.

Liz stands, her legs still a little wobbly. "What did the doctor tell you to do? Stretches, right?"

Jones grunts as he takes a step. And even though he protests and tries to turn away from her, she stays by his side and guides him gently to the bed.

"What are you doing?" he asks.

In truth, she has no idea, but she knows what she isn't going to do. No matter what, she isn't leaving him alone while he's hurt and ashamed. So, she takes his phone from the top of his chest of drawers, sits beside the great, wounded beast, and prepares for a night of snarls.

***

Hot shame scalds Jones's face as he pushes out a breath and arches his back. He's on his hands and knees on his mattress, repeating the same movements over and over at her command; back arched upward like an angry cat, then slowly bowed inward like an overworked mule. Honestly, right now he feels like both.

Liz sits beside him, naked and cross-legged, his phone resting in her hand as she scrolls through the list of stretches which the website claims can ease his discomfort. "Is it helping?"

"A little," he winces. The pain is bad but the humiliation, that's what really hurts. "You must be so disappointed—"

"Don't," she says, setting his phone aside. She reaches out a hand to caress the arc of his cheek. "Please don't."

"You can leave." He grimaces through a labored exhale.

Jones has never been a crier, but the burning sting of tears is far too intense for his liking. "I'd understand if you don't want to come back again."

"Jones…"

The sympathy in her voice crushes him. He rights himself, biting back against excruciating pain. He'd let his spine snap clean in half before he let her see how weak he truly is. "Just go."

"Jones—"

"Stop." Her hand is cool and soft against the burning skin of his neck, a balm to soothe his frayed patience with himself, but it isn't enough. He shrugs her off. "Go."

"What are you? A goddamn crosswalk?"

There's no malice in her tone, no mockery. It's just an attempt to lighten the mood between them, but he scowls all the same. "Hilarious."

She chuckles quietly. "I remember the doctor recommended alternating hot and cold compresses. Have you tried—"

"No."

She gives a little disappointed sigh. "Well, we can start now. Do you have any—"

"No." He shakes his head, unable to even look at her. "Liz, just go."

A relieved sigh escapes him when she climbs off the bed and picks up her t-shirt and underwear from the floor. It's for the best, he tells himself. Bad enough she has already seen him on all fours, dangerously close to tears, broken and weak after talking the big talk about fucking her brains out. Best that she leaves now.

But the other part of him, the part that defied everything his father did to chase it out of him, longs to beg her to stay.

He's sorry. He's being a grumpy asshole and he knows it, but he's hurt and embarrassed, and in truth, terrified that this is it.

Jones knows what he is; a brute, a hulking beast born to work hard and fuck hard, but if he can't do that…

He can't even look at her as she strides across the room, the click of his bedroom door striking him like a stake through the heart.

Knelt on the mattress, shaking hands gripping his thighs until his nail beds ache, he closes his eyes. As fuck-ups go it's a pretty damn spectacular one, but it's definitely for the best.

She had felt so right. The whole night was so perfectly, terrifyingly right.

Just for those few minutes he'd loved her with every atom in his broken being. Wholly and cruelly loved her. He'd burned for her, so hot and bright it scared him.

Because he isn't worth her.

Now that she's gone, he knows that for damned sure.

He pushed her away before the spark of his feelings caught and the flame spread to her. Pushed her away before he choked the life out of her like a weed stifling a flower. He pushed her away the only way he knew how, denying himself pleasure, denying himself her.

He fights to fill his aching, heavy chest with air and tries to silence the incessant urge to run out there and apologize. Fuck the pain, fuck his pride. He'd charge out there and fall to his knees before her, beg her to forgive him, if he wasn't so certain he isn't good enough for her.

"Fuck," he hisses beneath his breath as he rocks back and forth, testing his boundaries, seeing how much movement he can get away with before the pain becomes unbearable. It isn't much.

She'd felt so good, and for the first time in a long time, just for a second, he'd felt good too.

Good enough.

The shrill beep of his microwave draws his attention, pulling his face into a perplexed frown. A moment later the bedroom door opens, and Liz appears wielding two small bundles wrapped in his tea towels.

His confusion almost deadens the soar of elation at seeing her again. "What—?"

"Cold," she declares as she approaches, raising the bundle in her left hand. She then repeats the gesture with the other. "And hot."

She climbs back onto the bed, wearing nothing but her t-shirt and underwear. In his wallowing he hadn't even noticed she'd left her jeans on his bedroom floor. Of course, she was planning to return.

"Which first?" She asks, and from her tone he knows she isn't going to take 'neither' as an answer.

Jones sighs. "Heat, I guess."

"Okay." She settles down beside him, back in her cross-legged position. She takes his pillows and puts them in front of his thighs. "Get comfortable."

Jones rolls his eyes but does as she says, lying on his side with the pillows wedged beneath his hip. He's facing away from her, his knees slightly bent when the comforting warmth of the compress smothers his lower back. He closes his eyes and attempts to relax.

"Where did you find a heat pad?" he asks. "I didn't think I had one."

"I made it. It's just rice wrapped inside the towel and microwaved."

Jones scowls, unseen, but secretly impressed. Perhaps it's

one of those things which people who actually take care of themselves know, but to him it may as well be magic. Still, "You stole my rice."

"Oh hush," she sighs. "I'll buy you some rice if you're that sore about it."

"How did you even know where to find everything?"

"Because I snooped around your whole kitchen the morning after I stayed here looking for something to eat."

Jones chuckles quietly, wincing as the pain snarls. He breathes through the attack until it passes and he can speak again. "I've never met anyone like you." His heart thuds, filling the empty seconds as she doesn't respond. Perhaps it was the wrong thing to say. He can't see her face, can't judge her reactions. "I've never known anyone who cares as much as you do."

His breath stutters as she reaches around him and presses her palm to his forearm. Her skin is hot from holding the compress in place. A moment later her lips graze his temple. It's a soft, chaste kiss which socks him like a fist to the jaw.

And though he's comforted by her affection, panic still creeps into the back of his mind. Panic that at any moment he'll be scolded for being soft.

"I've never met anyone like you either," she says.

Her words alone dull the edge of his fears, but then she shifts on the bed and lies down behind him. She curls her body around his, the heat pack wedged between them.

"What are you doing?" he grumbles as she wriggles her arm under his so she can reach around and place her hand on the exposed skin of his chest.

"Spooning you."

His instinct is to protest, but he can't find it in himself to actually speak it. She's warm and gentle, and she strokes his chest with such comforting caresses he suspects he could close his eyes and fall asleep in seconds. Or he could, if he wasn't painfully aware of the pressure building inside his boxers. Her body, covered only by a t-shirt and underwear, pressed to his, her breath hot on the back of his neck, her hand stroking his chest. He's back to semi-hard in seconds.

"Oh. I've never been the little spoon," he says, just to fill the silence. "I'm not normally a cuddler."

"Well, that's just a waste."

"What do you mean?"

"You're very cuddly." She holds him a little tighter. "Is it okay?"

"Yeah. It's nice. I like it." His mouth is completely dry, and his breath shallow and unsteady as her fingers skate across his chest. They brush against one of his nipples, then across to the pierced one. She keeps her attention there, tracing the outline of the piercing until his nipple is hard and aching.

"Does that feel good?" she whispers against his neck.

He can only nod as the words snag in his chest. She kisses a trail, slowly from his collar to his ear, her mouth hot and wet against his tingling skin. Her fingers delve lower, over his soft, round stomach. Heat flares across his cheeks as she touches him, exploring the shape of him.

She drowns out his worry, his expectation of derision. She touches him with a tenderness he never, *never* permits himself. He can't stand a moment longer without her lips. Carefully, he takes the heat pack from between them and rolls over onto his back. With the pillow beneath his thighs, it's quite comfortable.

"I'm fine," he whispers in answer to the little crease

between her eyebrows. He takes her by the arms and guides her down to his lips.

God, the way she melts against him, the way she holds his face as she kisses him, her breasts brushing against his chest through the flimsy cotton of her shirt. She breaks away from his lips to kiss him lower, down his chest, lifting his shirt to kiss his stomach. His cock throbs with anticipation, his mind turning somersaults as she slides down the zipper on his pants.

"Oh," she gasps in surprise as she frees his cock from its confines.

Jones grins, waiting for the inevitable elaboration. "Everything okay?" Of course, he'll take the piercing out if it's a problem. He wouldn't want to make her uncomfortable. Some of his partners have hated it, others went wild.

She slides her thumb along the metal bar curving from his opening to his frenulum, sending a dart of pleasure straight to his core. "Do I need to do anything different for it to feel good for you?"

"No," he replies. The grin is torn from his face as she circles the head of his cock with her thumb, spreading his pre-cum as he sinks his teeth into his lower lip. "Fuck. There are condoms in the bottom drawer if you want—"

Gently, she runs her fingernails down over his balls. A shiver arches his back.

"Have you been tested?" she asks.

He nods. "Twice since the last time I was with anyone. I'm clean."

"Me too."

"And I've had a vasectomy," he says, swallowing hard as he waits for her reaction. "I understand if you still want to use condoms too."

But she lowers her head to take his cock into her mouth and the world shatters around him. He's quickly learning that Liz loves to turn the tables, to let him lead her down paths he thinks he's choosing, only to reveal she's been shepherding him the whole way.

She slides her tongue down the underside of his cock, and he's no longer in control of his body. His hand is on the back of her head, her hair tangled around his fingers, his toes curling as she works her way back up his shaft to suck the head of his cock, her tongue rippling against the piercing.

He props up his head on his forearm so he can watch her, those perfect, soft lips caressing his cock, her dark eyes on his. She licks and sucks his cock, caresses his balls, strokes his thighs when they tremble.

It has been a long time since anyone pleasured him like that, since he was the focus of the attention, and it doesn't take long for his balls to tighten beneath her palm.

"I'm close," he gasps, pressing his heels into the mattress.

She moans softly against his cock, and the sensation tips him over the edge. He comes hard, teeth bared, hips bucking, toes curling, consumed by the sensation of her. He's always extra sensitive after an orgasm, and as she kisses her way back up his body, he has to hold his breath to try not to squirm.

She curls up beside him, her head resting on his bicep, her arm draped over him, fiddling with the lace on the neck of his shirt. "Are you a cuddling convert now?"

He chuckles softly, still on his descent back to earth. "I'm anything you want me to be."

"I like you in the pirate shirt," she says softly.

"I noticed."

"I like you when you're taking care of animals, when you're smiling, and when you're grumpy too."

He pulls in a breath, "Can I ask something?"

"Sure."

"You know my real name, don't you?"

She nods. "Yes."

"But you haven't mentioned it."

Her brow creases. "No. Because *you* didn't mention it." Warmth radiates from the patch of his chest where her palm rests. "I know that if you wanted me to call you by that name, you would have told me to. You told me to call you Jones, and I respect your wishes."

"Well, I appreciate it." He holds her tighter, tilting her chin with the side of his knuckle so he can kiss her lips.

"You know we should do the cold compress now too, right?"

Jones sighs. "I was hoping you'd forgotten."

He grits his teeth and takes the cold, bunching his fists in the covers much to Liz's amusement. As big as he is and as strong as he makes out to be, he's never handled the cold well. The only thing which makes it tolerable is Liz's hand in his hair, her fingers stroking, offering comfort.

Every instinct in his body tells him to stop, to push her away so he doesn't dim her radiance. He can't be with her. He can't let himself fall in love with her, and he sure as hell can't let her fall for him.

"Is something wrong?" she asks.

"What if I'm hurt for the rest of my life?"

Her eyes dart across his features, full of trust and affection, neither of which he's worthy of. "What do you—?"

"Would you still want me?"

"I want you now." She raises onto her elbow, gently caressing his cheek.

It should be enough. But as they fall asleep later that night, he can't shake that doubt. Pushing her away now would be the kindest thing.

# Fifteen

Liz's stomach flutters again, as it has been doing since she left Jones's place that morning. She presses her teeth into her lower lip and tries to focus on the music instead, her fingers dancing over the keys. The Vixens play on, oblivious, their hearts filled with the song. And it does sound good. It does.

Mia and Étienne's vocals complement each other perfectly as they blast out the final notes of the song and Liz plays them out on the keys. They've played the song so many times it's effortless for her, ingrained in the memory of her hands rather than her mind. Even caged birds make pretty music.

Étienne woops when the song is over and she can't help but be happy for him. He's drunk on the newness of it all, the excitement, and God, she hopes it lasts for him. Because this, knowing deep in her heart she should be somewhere else but unable to move on, is hell.

"That was awesome," Mia laughs, fighting for her breath

as she raises a water bottle to take a sip. "Before we all go, we have some boring business stuff to deal with."

Anya gives an over-exaggerated sigh. "I bet Eddie Van Halen never had to deal with boring business stuff."

"Pretty sure he absolutely did," Nic frowns.

"It's not boring," Finn grumbles as he pulls a black ring binder out of his backpack and snaps open the fastening. The front of the file is decorated with a sticker which reads, *'Drummers pound hard'.*

Anya snorts, "Nice dude."

"Thanks… it's my business folder." The drummer clears his throat. "As discussed last weekend, since things seem to be taking off, we've had contracts written up to keep everything simple."

Liz's heart drops to her stomach. "Contracts?"

It sounds final. Permanent. Binding.

"Oh, that's right," Anya says with a grimace. "It was in the meeting you missed. The Saturday after the festival."

The meeting she missed because she was still at Jones's place. Right. Her temples burn as she takes the document from Finn. "Uh… is it okay if I take it home and, you know… read it first? Not that I don't trust you, or anything, I just want to know what I'm agreeing to. Not that I'm not going to sign it, but—"

Finn holds up his palm and chuckles. "Yeah, please take it home and read it. You can bring it into our next rehearsal on Friday. That goes for everyone. If there's anything at all you don't agree with or want to ask about you can call me or Mia and we'll be happy to talk."

"Too late," Anya says as she approaches Finn from behind and drops her contract on the top of his pile. "Signed it."

Finn rolls his eyes. "Do you even know what it says?"

The guitarist shrugs as she picks up her guitar and begins to pick out a melody. "Don't need to. I trust you, and I'm a Vixen for life. Whatever it says is fine."

"That's not—" Finn shakes his head. "Come on, Anya, it took for-fucking-ever to write. We have a lawyer and everything."

"I was being sentimental, Finn."

"Yeah, and what if I own your soul now?"

"So? You'd be getting a dried-up little husk, big deal."

Liz's eyes glaze over as the drummer and the guitarist bicker, her fingers clenched around the edge of the document in her hand. Of course, she trusts Finn and Mia. The contents of the contract aren't what worries her. The finality of it is.

"I'll read it through," she says as she stuffs it into her bag.

"Thank you," Finn sighs as Nic puts their contract on top of Anya's. "At least someone will."

She offers a consolatory smile as she heads towards the door, "See you… Friday?"

Finn sighs again, rubbing his hand over his face. "Saturday. Honestly, it's like herding kittens."

"Pretty sure you told us Friday," Étienne interjects.

Liz ducks out before it gets messy. Making her way down the factory's cool, quiet hallway, she takes a deep, calming breath and pulls out her phone. There are no texts from Jones, but then, why would there be? He isn't exactly talkative.

She swipes away the rest of the notifications, pausing when she reaches her emails.

>> *From: Monroe Massage Therapy Training*

>> *Subject: Re: Your application.*

Her heart stalls as she withdraws her thumb. The fact they've emailed twice means that the first time was probably an acceptance. "Fuck."

She can't do this here, not with the Vixens so close by. Speed-walking down the rest of the hallway, she bursts through the doorway at the top of the stairwell before she begins to rush down the stairs. Perhaps it's just a request for further information, or a feedback survey. It could be nothing.

Then again, it could be everything. Because the truth is, no matter how many times she tells herself she's grateful for the Vixens and for the comfort of living in the same town all her life, she can't help but gaze out of the window and dream. A new life, a new passion, helping people, making a difference. She's wanted it for so long.

But she promised Anya she would stay.

Her heart stills at the sight of a hulking figure walking through the front doors of the factory, pushing a hand truck with a large black amplifier mounted on the top of it.

"Jones?" As soon as the realization it's him settles, her heart restarts, beating a desperate, longing rhythm.

He's dressed in a dark grey, short-sleeved Henley, displaying the muscles in his arms. His pale blue jeans fit tight over his perfect pumpkin ass. Just the sight of him is enough to make her body ache for him. His eyes widen as they slide to where she stands on the stairs.

Smoothing down his hair, he sets the amp down. "Liz. What are you doing here?"

"Hi," she says for him as she makes her way down the last few steps. "I could ask you the same thing."

"Well, I asked first." He gives her a smile, the corners of his eyes creasing, showing her that beneath his attitude, he's genuinely happy to see her. It fades just as suddenly as it appears.

"Practice," she says, hoisting her purse up onto her shoulder. "This is where we rehearse. We just finished, actually."

"Ah. I'm sorry, I had no idea you'd be here."

"Don't be sorry." She takes a step toward him, breathing in the faint spice of his cologne. "It's a nice surprise."

He glances down at the amp as the corner of his mouth raises into a fleeting smile. "It is for me too."

She closes the gap between them and raises on her tiptoes to kiss him. At the touch of his lips, every sensation of their night together comes back, the ache, the need, the desperate longing. He leaves her breathless before he breaks the kiss and turns his head away.

Probably for the best. The other Vixens could come down any moment and she doesn't want to get caught making out with him.

"So, how come you're here?" She asks, steadying herself against the amp. "This looks vaguely familiar."

"Yeah, this is the one you helped me with after the festival." He gives the amp a hearty pat with the palm of his hand. "It was busted so the equipment firm was going to throw it out but I got it working again, so I'm donating it. I figured there would be a bunch of teenagers here starting their first bands who might get some use out of it." He shifts his weight between his feet and turns his attention toward the empty office desk at the entrance. "If there's actually anyone working here who can take it."

"Oh, yeah it's kind of a struggle to get anyone to actually stay at the desks. Everyone who works here is kind of an artsy type so they're off doing their own things." She presses the darkened screen of her phone against her palm, as if he'll somehow see the email and know. Raising onto the tips of her toes, Liz leans over the front desk and calls out, "Beth? Are you here?"

"One sec," a distant voice replies. A moment later Beth appears, more paint spatter than human. She has three paint brushes wedged in the spaces between her fingers. "Everything okay? Did someone try to take the cashbox again?"

Liz steps back and lets Jones handle the donation. And that's all she's doing as she stands behind him. Absolutely everything.

When he turns around her cheeks are flushed with heat. She clears her throat and asks, "Would you like to maybe get a coffee, or—?"

"I can't," he says gruffly. "I'm sorry."

"Oh." The cold shift in him is startling. Just last night they held each other while they slept. Perhaps it was too much too soon. "Well, if you want to do something some other time just let me know."

He nods once before his eyes flit to the clock on the wall. "It was nice seeing you. I have to go."

And that's it. He pushes open the front doors to the factory, letting in a blast of cold air and leaving nothing but silence in his wake. He doesn't even look at her.

The urge to go out after him, to ask if something is wrong almost uproots her, but she tells herself to stay. It's not as if they were dating, just two people who happen to keep bumping into each other, and who also, conveniently, are pretty good at giving each other orgasms.

It's not like she was planning on marrying him.

Beth eyes the amp with suspicion. "I have absolutely no idea if this is a good speaker or whether it's going to just explode the first time someone uses it." She smiles, relieved as Finn and Anya make their way down the stairs, still arguing over the contract.

"You didn't even see clause three-point-two, which states I get your firstborn child," Finn says.

Anya grimaces. "Good. If I ever have children, *please* take them all." The redhead raises her eyes to Liz. "Still here? We thought you ran out on us."

"Oh, yeah… I just had a couple of things to take care of," Liz smiles. "I'm leaving now."

"Well, I'll walk you to your car," Anya says, taking Liz by the elbow and herding her toward the door. "It'll get Finn off my case."

They head out of the door as Beth calls Finn over to inspect Jones's amp. Liz's heart sinks a little that his big silver truck isn't out in the parking lot, waiting for her. She shakes her head and tries to push past the disappointment.

"So, how are things going?" Anya asks, zipping up her jacket against the bitter breeze.

"With?"

"Him?" The guitarist narrows her eyes. "The roadie. I mean, I assume things are going, after the shelter. Did you see him again?"

Liz's ears heat despite the chill in the air. "Yeah, but I don't think it's anything serious."

"Well, his loss. But don't worry, we're contractually bound together now so we can grow old together. We'll be in our eighties someday still kicking about on the stage. Vixens for life."

A wave of nausea presses against the back of Liz's throat as she clutches her phone to her chest.

"We all love you, Liz," Anya says. "And you deserve nothing but the best."

Those words hurt worse than anything. "I love you too."

When Liz gets back to her car, she waits until the others drive away, pressing her phone to her ear so no one stops to check if she's okay. As the last of their vehicles drive away, she lowers the phone to her lap, and closes her eyes.

It could be a no, and then things would sort themselves out. She wouldn't have to leave the Vixens *or* reject the chance to get out of town. The status quo may be stale but it's safe. No one gets hurt.

She opens her eyes and stares down at the notification she dreads clicking.

*>> From: Monroe Massage Therapy Training*

*>> Subject: Re: Your application.*

Her stomach tightens as she presses 'read'.

*Congratulations on your successful application to Monroe Massage Therapy Training…*

The world tilts on its axis as she reads on, torn between elation and despair. Balancing on a ledge between the Vixens and her dreams.

*To accept your place on the course beginning December 1st, please log on to our website, enter your application ID number, fill in the information requested, and select a payment method. To decline…*

She reads it again and again, as if she somehow could have missed the option to defer, to take some time to mull it over. But it isn't there. It could be now or never.

Stay here forever, or get out of town for good.

———

Jones rubs his hands over his face and sighs, glancing at the clock. There are still a few minutes to go before his appointment. He could have stayed and explained why he couldn't get coffee with Liz. If he hadn't been so goddamn afraid to admit where he was going. But he couldn't even bear to look back at her.

Taking out his phone, he opens his messages, his thumb hovering an inch above the screen as he tries to figure out what to say to her.

"Mister Jones?" a woman's voice pulls his attention from the phone.

He raises his eyes, and immediately he knows this was a mistake. A young woman in a grey pencil skirt and a peacock blue sweater smiles at him, no older than her early twenties. She doesn't need to sit and listen to a miserable, broken old man bellyaching for an hour.

"I…uh," he stands, grimacing. "Sorry."

"It's alright," she smiles, opening her arm in a welcoming gesture. "This way."

Thoughts claw at the inside of his skull as he follows her down the short corridor. He doesn't need this, he's being dramatic, it's an admission of weakness, no one wants to sit and hear him complain.

The woman enters a room up ahead and he follows her in. Where he expected high ceilings and mahogany shelves lined with leather-bound books, there's just a small office, no larger than his own bedroom. There are no marble busts of Freud, no diagrams of dissected brains or specimens in jars. Just a comfortable blue armchair on one side of the room, and a large matching blue couch on the other.

"Take a seat, Mister Jones. Wherever you'd like."

He huffs the air from his nose, hesitating at the threshold of the room before he steps inside. His eyes trail across the sparse white shelves on the warm beige walls. In place of psychology books or tools for lobotomy there are a couple of cacti in terracotta pots and a weird abstract sculpture which could be a woman or a flame or birds…or just a bunch of swirly shapes.

Jones diverts his gaze in case she asks him what he sees in the sculpture and uses that to infiltrate and analyze his brain.

He sinks down into the corner of the couch, grimacing as his pain spikes. There's a plump cream cushion on the other end which would help alleviate the strain, but now he's seated, and so is the doctor. He breathes through the pain.

"Well, hello then," she smiles. "I'm Kim Shepherd. You can call me Kim, if you like."

Jones nods, pressing the heels of his hands into his knees. This was a mistake.

"What should I call you?" She asks. "I have your name down as Theodore Jones Junior."

"Just Jones. Please."

She smiles and makes a note. "Okay."

Jones's throat tightens. Was that some kind of test? Does she already know what a monumental fuck up he is? "I…" The pillow is so close. It would take so little effort to reach over, place it behind him. But then she would know he was hurt. He tightens his stomach muscles in an attempt to take some of the strain from his back. "Honestly I don't know why I'm here."

"That's okay. A lot of people feel that way once they arrive. Have you had any kind of cognitive behavioral therapy before?"

"No…"

She nods. "Again, completely okay. Before we start, I want you to know that everything you say here is completely confidential, unless I feel there is a risk to your safety or the safety of others. Why don't we start by talking about how you feel right now?"

How does he feel? Embarrassed, terrified, pathetic, in pain, ashamed. He feels like he wants to jump through the window and get the fuck out of here.

"I'm fine," he tells her.

The corners of her mouth lift into a smile. "Where do you work, Jones?"

"All over the place." He runs his thumbnail over the pale blue denim over his thigh. "I work most nights at Calico's… that's a bar. A pirate themed bar. Sometimes I'm a roadie… uh. I think the official title is road crew. I'm the senior technician or something, basically they pay me to lug heavy things."

"A roadie? So, you travel a lot?"

This is easy. Work he can talk about, work is simple. He breathes a little easier, his shoulders dropping a half inch. "I used to, when I was younger, but then my dad—" He snaps his jaw shut. He's nowhere near ready to go there. "I mainly just do local events now. I also volunteer at the animal shelter."

The therapist smiles. "That's lovely."

"It's easy," he shrugs, reaching over the couch to grab the

pillow. He sets it behind him, and the relief is immediate. "It's the highlight of my week, most weeks."

"And what about home?" She asks. "Do you live with anyone? Family? A partner?"

"No. I live alone, and other than…I'm not really sure what Liz is. We haven't known each other for very long. Just a week or so. I wouldn't say she's my partner… more… I don't know."

"A girlfriend?"

"No. At least, I don't think so."

"How do you feel when you're with her?"

"Like I'm enough." He laughs a little at the absurd sentimentality of it. "And like I'll never be good enough to deserve her."

The therapist nods and narrows her eyes. "Why do you say that?"

He's said too much. Jones turns his head and glances out of the window. It's November and the sun has already set. Raindrops speck the glass, glowing orange beneath the beams of a streetlight. "She pushes me, um… She took me to the hospital when my back pain got too bad and made sure I had medicine." He chuckles. "Did you know that if you wrap dry rice in a tea towel and microwave it for a few seconds it makes a hot compress?"

The therapist smiles. "I didn't."

"Neither did I."

"Do you know what caused the pain? Have you been given a diagnosis?"

"The doctor called it sciatica. A pinched nerve."

"How long have you experienced the pain for?"

"Two years, before she made me go," he says, reality hitting him full force. He had been in pain for two years before meeting Liz, and within a couple of days of stumbling into her, he had relief. Not permanent, but more than he'd had for a long time. "Shit. Sorry. I apologize for swearing."

The therapist smiles. "It sounds like Liz is quite a positive influence on your life?"

He nods, as much as it pains him. "She's something else." Clasping his hands together, warmth floods his cheeks. "But I know I'm not good enough for her."

"Did she tell you that?"

"No." He breathes heavily through his nose. *I want you now,* she had told him. Now. Even while he was in pain and couldn't do everything he wanted. Even when he's broken and tired. "She insists that I am."

The therapist nods. "I think one of the things we should work on together, are the sources of this negative core belief you have that you aren't worthy." She sits forward a little, her fingers spread in mid-air, as though she's holding an imaginary ball. "This feeling of not being good enough may have stemmed from one particular incident, or the culmination of many. It may take us a little while to discover the root of your belief, but we'll get there." She smiles. "I promise."

H e gets home early. Well, early for him. Roxy, clearly confused by her primate father being off schedule, waddles after him around the house, her long, pink tongue flickering in the air, convinced she's in for a treat.

"Your fruit bills are going to bankrupt me," Jones grumbles, reaching into his fridge and taking out a handful of raspberries and leading her back out to the living room. He sits on the couch, tossing the pink berries to the lizard, and thinking over what Doctor Kim had told him.

"She set me homework, Rox," he mutters. "I have to work on challenging my *automatic negative thoughts.*"

The lizard stares at him, expectantly so he tosses another raspberry. He checks the time on his phone and finds it's only eight-thirty. He took the evening off work for therapy, and though he should be all talked out, there's one person he desperately wants to speak to.

"She might not want to talk to me."

*Or she might.*

"After this afternoon, she might think I'm a total asshole."

*She already knows I'm an asshole, and by some miracle she still wants to be around me.*

He frowns. That probably isn't the right counterargument to the asshole thing, but it's enough.

Scrolling through his meager contacts list, he finds her name. Twenty seconds of courage. It's all he needs. He closes his eyes and hits the call button. She picks up after two rings.

"Hello?" she says, uncertainty wavering in her voice.

And God, it feels good to hear that voice. Jones lets out a breath and his shoulders relax. "Hi."

"You're... calling?"

"Yes, I'm calling." He smiles at her tone, the playful confusion. "I just wanted to apologize for earlier. I'm sorry I walked away from you without explaining what was happening."

"No, no, it's okay. You don't owe me anything."

"But I would like to explain, if that's okay?"

"Of course."

"I...I had an appointment. I didn't want to be late and I

was just… honestly, my head was up my ass. I guess I was nervous." He grimaces and closes his eyes. "I still am." As explanations go it barely even qualifies. He stares at the empty La-Z-Boy armchair ahead, and imagines his dad sitting there, beer in hand, cigarette smoke curling from his ashtray as he rolls his eyes. *Pathetic.*

"That's okay," Liz says. "Honestly, no offence taken."

"Still, doesn't excuse me from being a jackass."

"Well, I know better than to ask you if you're okay, but you can talk to me, any time."

He balls his fist and thumps it against his thigh. She could say yes, he forces himself to think. This could be the start of something good. "Actually, I was wondering if… Would you… ah. Liz." The silence against his ear is killing him. "Are you still there?"

"Yeah… yeah I'm here."

"Okay." He gets up from the couch, groaning as he stands, and makes his way out of the living room, away from his father's chair. She stays with him as he heads to his bedroom, as though he might be heard otherwise. When he's surrounded by his own things he can breathe again. "Liz?"

"Are you okay? Do you need me to take you to the hospital again?"

"No, God no." This is why Jones doesn't call. "Would you… like to go on a date?" The question hangs in the air, awkward and corny and just begging for rejection. "With me."

"Sure."

His heart empties. "What?"

She chuckles on the other end of the phone, and he can't help but smile. "Jones, I'd love to."

# Sixteen

She's going on a date. A date with Jones.

A giddy sort of feeling overcomes Liz, so much so she forgets, just for a few minutes the crushing words on her laptop screen resting on the bed in front of her.

*OFFER REJECTED.*

"So, where are we going?" she asks, clinging to this bright spot pushing through the oppressive dark clouds.

"Well…" his deep voice is like a balm to her heart and she can't help but smile. Clearly, he was nervous about asking her but she's so glad he did. "I could do next Monday… we could do something after I'm done at the shelter. Or I'm free next Thursday. I'm sorry. My schedule isn't exactly date-friendly."

Fuck it, may as well go all in. "How about we do both?" She bites her bottom lip. "Is that too pushy?"

"You know I need pushing," he says. "Okay. Let's do both. Monday afternoon and Thursday?"

"Perfect. Do you have somewhere in mind?"

There's a long pause. Liz stands, closes the laptop and shoves it back in its case. She should probably switch it off, but right now she can't bear to look at that screen one moment longer. It's done, she tells herself. The crisis is over with. She chose the Vixens, as she should have done. She's just one person in a group of eight. Her dreams don't overshadow theirs.

"I'll be honest," he says. "I wasn't sure you'd say yes. I didn't really get to the planning part."

Liz hides her smile behind her knuckles. "How about you plan one and I plan the other. I'll plan Monday and you plan Thursday."

"That sounds good to me. And when I decide on a place to take you, I'll let you know beforehand in case you want to let anyone know where you'll be."

His consideration warms her heart. "Thank you."

"Well," he says with a sigh. "Since it's us I'm sure we'll bump into each other at some point between now and Monday, but if not... I can't wait to see you again."

She bites down a smile. "I can't wait to see you either."

"Goodnight, Liz."

"Goodnight, Jones." She ends the call and crumples back onto the bed.

But they don't bump into each other.

The rest of the week crawls by slowly, almost painfully. The contract sits on her kitchen countertop and stays there during the Friday rehearsal and the Saturday morning meeting. Each time, the disappointment in Finn's eyes— nearly veiled by gentle teasing— damn near destroys her. But she can't sign her life away. Not yet.

It's still in her kitchen when she pulls up outside the

factory on Sunday morning, slipping her car between Anya's and Jordan's. The guitarist is still in the driver's seat, seemingly oblivious to Liz's presence.

The redhead's eyebrows knit together as she scrolls through her phone before puffing out her cheeks and swiping back her hair. Only then does she notice Liz out of the corner of her eye.

They emerge from their cars at the same time.

"What's up?" Liz asks.

"Internet weirdos," Anya sighs as they walk side-by-side across the lot. "Men thinking that challenging me to guitar duals constitutes flirting."

"Isn't it?"

"No. It's foreplay, and I'm not doing it with this particular guy. He plays in a folk metal band for crying out loud. Their songs are all about wizards and dragons."

"And our songs are about vampires and ghosts," Liz chuckles as she holds the door open for Anya. The pair of them make their way up the stairs. "So, it sounds like one specific internet weirdo is putting that look on your face."

"That's enough about me," Anya sighs, evading further questioning. "How are things with you?"

"Good, actually. Great." She smiles, an easy gesture with the burden of Monroe Massage Training lifted from her back. "I have a date tomorrow."

"Nice. With roadie boy?"

"He's thirty-eight. And yes. Two dates, actually."

Anya's smile widens. "Two?" she tuts. "You two are so in love already."

"Don't be ridiculous."

"Who the fuck organizes two dates? You do one, then the

next if it goes well, right? No one organizes two dates at once unless they're in love."

"Stop," Liz rolls her eyes, shoving the guitarist gently with her shoulder. Despite her indignation, she knows there's at least a pinch of truth to what Anya says. Maybe not love, but the beginnings of *something*. She's never wanted to plan ahead with someone before. "And I'm only organizing one of them. I'm planning the one tomorrow, and he's taking me somewhere on Thursday."

"Ugh," Anya sighs. "You're already too cute. What are you going to do with him?"

She grimaces. "I don't know. Maybe dinner somewhere… a movie maybe. I got my period a couple of days ago so probably no sex."

"You should cook something together." Anya glances at her as they climb the stairs. "Take the ingredients to his place, and prepare a meal together. It's a good way to see how the two of you work in potentially high-stress situations, and to find out how capable he is at taking care of himself. Plus… food."

Liz pauses as they reach the floor of the rehearsal room. "That's actually not a bad idea."

"I have over a decade of experience with guys who don't know how to cook for themselves and aren't aware that you're supposed to wash your ass in the shower. I'm getting good at weeding them out."

"So, does internet guy wash his ass?"

"To be determined." Anya shakes her head. "But we're not talking about him. Tell me more about your roadie."

"He just… I don't know. He ignites some primal cavewoman urge in me. I look at him and I think 'that man there knows where the juiciest mammoths are', and I know he'll wrestle one to the ground with his bare hands if I ask him to."

Anya's eyes narrow as they reach the rehearsal room door. "You're in love with him."

"I've known him less than a week."

"So? Sometimes you just know when you've met your person."

As the guitarist shoves open the heavy door and the corridor is flooded with the sonorous groan of Jordan's cello accompanying Nic's violin. The hairs on the back of Liz's neck stand on end as her stomach turns somersaults at the thought of seeing him again.

She knew right away when she bumped into him that he wasn't like anything else in her life, and try as she might, she can't seem to stop wanting him, or forgetting everything and running to him. It isn't like her.

Until she sent off the rejection to Monroe, she should have been standing with one foot out the door when it came to Jones, but she hasn't. Both feet are planted firmly inside. They have been since the night she took him to the hospital. Maybe he is her person.

"You coming?" Anya says, holding the door open.

Liz starts. "Yeah."

"Wow. Must be a very vivid daydream about your big, sexy caveman." The guitarist bites down a grin and turns her back before the comment has time to register.

Liz shakes her head in disgust as she files into the rehearsal room, greeting the band.

"Liz!" Finn calls as he polishes the chrome parts of his kit. The soundproofed room already smells of warm bodies and the chemical stench of polish. "Did you bring the contract in?"

Her heart plummets. "Oh… no, sorry. I forgot it." She was hoping he would forget, at least for a little while. Not that there's any reason for her not to sign. She's stuck with the Vixens now no matter what. "I'll bring it next time."

"Yeah, no problem, but if there's any issue with it, let me know—"

Étienne pulls his contract out of a navy-blue folder and presents it to the drummer with a flourish as Jordan chuckles from the opposite side of the room.

"Nerd," the cellist teases affectionately before stage-whispering to the whole room, "He bought a special pen just to sign it."

"Baby Beeeear," Finn croons as the new vocalist's cheeks redden. "You are an absolutely adorable button of a man; do you know that?"

Étienne cringes as he rubs the back of his neck. "I'm a button?"

Mia nods, hiding her smile behind her long, pointed, midnight blue nails. "Yeah, I'd say there are several buttonish qualities about you."

"Absolutely," Jordan grins.

Liz laughs along with the rest of the band, silently grateful to Étienne for drawing the attention away from her, and simultaneously filled with a sense of longing as he and Jordan lovingly tease each other.

She pulls her phone out of her purse and fires off a text to Jones:

*Still on for tomorrow?*

He replies before she even has time to lock the screen:

*Yes.*

A smile spreads across her lips. Grumpy Jones. Abrupt Jones. Straight-to-the-point Jones who she strongly suspects is smiling too.

When she raises her eyes, Anya is staring, a wide smile plastered across her face before she mouths the words, *"You sooo love him."*

And perhaps she could.

Perhaps she already does.

<hr>

Each week it gets harder and harder for Jones to put Teddy back in his kennel. Their walks together, while fun, are always tainted by the horrible, inevitable conclusion. Back into his cage, another week of waiting and being left behind.

The Pitbull curls up onto his bed, tucking his paws beneath him and staring up at Jones with… well, puppy dog eyes.

"I'm sorry," Jones whispers, hanging Teddy's leash on a peg by the door. "I'd take you in a heartbeat if I didn't have Roxy. But I promise one day you're going to find a home. You'll find someone who loves you like you deserve."

A desperate whine sounds at his back as he closes the gate on the pen. "I'll see you next week, okay? We'll go out somewhere nice."

Jones can't look back as he walks away. Barks and howls follow him, desperate and lonely, still clinging to the hope that somebody somewhere could want them.

He clocks out with Dana and gets into his truck, rubbing

his hands over his face and letting go of a sigh he's held in for the past ten minutes.

Perhaps it was a mistake organizing the date on a day he often goes home with an aching heart. He's definitely not in the mood to go out and be around strangers in a restaurant or wherever she's decided to take him. He takes his phone out of the glovebox of his truck and unlocks the screen. Her name pops up right away: *On my way.*

No going back now. He pulls in a breath and tries to look at the positives. It's time with Liz, and wherever she decides they're going, even if it's the last place he wants to be, she'll be there with him. Hell, that woman even made a hospital trip bearable.

He pulls out of his parking spot around the back of the shelter and heads home. There's just enough time for him to shower and put on fresh clothes before his doorbell rings.

Casting one last glance in the mirror, he tries to make peace with what stares back at him. He wore the grey shirt with the little buttons at his throat she seemed to like, and clean jeans which actually fit as opposed to his usual grease-stained, baggy cargo pants. At least his beard is somewhat tidy.

Smoothing back his hair, he steps over Roxy who has decided she's sleeping in the hallway for the afternoon, and goes to answer the door.

The frisson of nervous energy in his chest barely outweighs the feeling that this was a mistake, but as he opens the door, any doubts are erased.

"Hi," he breathes.

Her smile is like a shot of adrenaline straight to his heart. The moment it dazzles him his pulse beats harder, and his own lips couldn't stay downturned even if they were wired that way. Her silky brown hair is curled around her shoulders, her glasses fogging a little as the heat from his house meets her at the threshold.

"Come in." He steps aside to let her pass, and only then does he notice the brown paper grocery bags in her arms.

She's fully fogged up as he takes the bags from her. "Hi," she smiles. "Thank you."

Shrugging off her thick black coat, she raises onto her tiptoes and kisses him, an easy, casual gesture of affection which hits him like a kick to the chest. As she sinks back down, his gaze travels down with her, but his pulse rises. Beneath the padded coat she wears a burnt orange dress, covered in little white flowers. The dress is low-cut at the top and only comes down to her mid-thigh, light and summery despite the cold November weather.

"You look beautiful," he manages to say before clearing his throat. "You always do."

Her eyes trail the length of his body. "So do you. I approve of the Henley."

"The what?"

"Your shirt." Her smile widens before she points to the bags in his arms. "I hope it's okay, I thought we could stay in and cook together."

He could kiss her. It takes him a moment to realize that he *can* kiss her. She raises up to meet his lips, resting her hands on the center of his chest. She kisses him slowly, filling him with longing and it takes all his self-control not to let the grocery bags fall to the floor. His heart lunges as the weight shifts within the brown paper bag, and Liz's hand darts out to stop a bottle of olive oil from tumbling out.

Jones stands upright and takes the bags to the kitchen. "What are we making?"

"Pizza," she says brightly as she follows him. "I thought it would be cool to make the dough from scratch and choose what toppings we want. It's a fun and exciting way to spend forty dollars on what otherwise would have been a twenty-dollar takeout order."

"Sounds good." He sets the bags on the countertop as she reaches inside and pulls out a white plastic packet and hands it to him. "Rice?"

"I told you I'd replace it." She beams up at him, her teeth grazing her lower lip.

"You really didn't have to do that," he chuckles. "But thank you. I'll savor every grain."

"You'd better. That bad boy set me back eighty cents."

He laughs. Home isn't the same when she's there.

Ordinarily, home is quiet, painful, filled with bad memories which can be stirred by just a whisper. There are doors he never looks behind, smooth, fist-sized marks in drywall he'd learned to patch at a young age after his dad passed-out. But when Liz is there, it's warm, bright, filled with laughter. When Liz is there, he isn't afraid to smile anymore.

After wiping down the counter and washing their hands, they measure out the flour, salt, garlic powder, sugar and yeast, pouring the ingredients into his metal mixing bowl. He stirs as she pours in warm water and oil, trying not to grumble as the mixture grows heavy.

"Okay," she scrolls through a recipe on her phone before taking a handful of flour and sprinkling it on the counter. "Now it's time for…" She pauses for dramatic effect before adding in a seductive tone, *"gentle kneading."*

"Ooh." He arches an eyebrow as he takes the dough out of the bowl and drops it on the counter. This he can do. "So, pirate shirts and pizza making are your kinks?"

"They weren't, but I have the feeling you're about to make it so."

Hoping she doesn't see the heat rising in his cheeks he pushes the dough away with the heels of his hands, before gently pulling it back toward him. And he does it again, and again as the dough smooths beneath his touch. His arms ache a little, but he's used to feeling sore.

# Seventeen

Who gave him the goddamned right?

Liz's mouth dries out as his strong hands massage the dough, the cords of muscle in his forearms flexing as he works. She doesn't know whether to thank Anya or murder her for suggesting this. Maybe both.

But it's not just the muscles or his hard-worked hands gently caressing the soft dough. It's his competence and his quiet confidence as he sculpts the ingredients into something wonderful for the two of them. It's the little smudge of flour above his left eyebrow, it's the hint of chest hair visible thanks to the undone buttons of his Henley. It's Jones. Just Jones, in all his mysterious glory.

When he's done, she greases up the bowl with a little more olive oil and steps back to let him drop the ball of dough inside. "Okay," she says, keeping her gaze low, partly because of the recipe on her phone, but largely because if she keeps looking, she's going to pounce on him and dinner will probably be ruined. Wasted pizza is a tragedy she isn't willing to flirt with. "Now we just cover it with a clean towel and wait."

"For how long?" Jones asks as he pulls a towel from a drawer and places it over the top of the bowl.

She scrolls. "An hour and a half. Then we can either make one big pizza to share, or individual ones. What do you think?"

"Well, that depends. Do you like olives?" he asks.

"Love them."

"Then we're making separate pizzas." The corner of his lips raises into a crooked grin. "I can't stand them."

"More for me," Liz shrugs.

"All for you."

He wipes down the counter and washes the remnants of the dough and flour from his hands. Somehow, he manages to make that sexy too. Every movement is thorough, meticulous, his big hands sliding together through the suds. If she doesn't get those hands on her soon, she'll combust.

"What now?" he asks as he dries off his hands, though from the tone of his voice, she suspects he has an inkling.

"Well, now we have an hour and a half to kill." She casts a glance over her shoulder as she walks away toward his bedroom, acutely aware that the hem of her dress comes barely two inches below her ass. "Oh." She freezes at the end of the hallway, which is blocked by Roxy, sleeping peacefully on the carpet. "I see you had a speed bump installed."

Jones laughs. For a man who until recently never smiled, he laughs more and more. "You can just step over her. She's too lazy to react."

Carefully, she does as he says, turning back to face him as she reaches the three doors at the end of the hall. Bathroom. Off-limits. His room.

"Look, um…" There's no sexy way to put it so she shoots for blunt. "I'm on my period, so I'm not really up to anything intimate today."

Jones arches an eyebrow as he closes the space between them and kisses her in the center of her hairline. "That's fine. Do you need anything?"

"I'm good," she smiles. "But that doesn't mean I can't do things for you."

Sliding her hands over his big, broad shoulders, she lets them drop down over his chest, his stomach, down to his thick, sturdy thighs.

Jones takes her hands in his and holds them about an inch away from his body. "Look, I appreciate it, and God, I want you, but I want it to be good for both of us more." He crooks a finger beneath her chin, tilting her face up to meet his lips as he places a gentle kiss on the little beauty spot above her lip. "I'd rather wait." Another kiss, this one on the curve of her jaw.

"But I'm already two up in the orgasm department."

"Because your pleasure means more to me than mine does." He kisses her cheek. "I love making you come. I've loved it since the second day I knew you."

Heat floods her cheeks as memories of the day of the festival clamor for her attention. Jones was supposed to be an explosive exit, a final send-off fitting for a rock star. But he's so much more. Some part of her knew that from the start.

"So," he continues, his voice deep and husky. "How about instead, we just talk today, get to know more about each other."

"I'd love that," she says.

"And…" he glances away, his throat flexing as he swallows. "Could we… uh…" He chuckles quietly. "It's okay if you don't want to… but can we cuddle?"

Her heart just fucking melts. His softness is every bit as irresistible to her as his gruff, no-nonsense façade. She can't keep her eyes from him as she reaches behind her, gripping the door handle. "Yes, of course. Let's just lay on your bed and cuddle up and talk." She reaches out, brushing the smudge of flour from his brow with her thumb.

"Perfect. Thank you."

She pushes open the door, and his eyes widen. "Liz!" He barks her name like she's about to step in front of a speeding car, emptying her heart and causing her to twist around to find the source of the danger.

It's the wrong door, the off-limits door. Beyond the forbidden entranceway is a large main bedroom—or rather, it could be a bedroom, if it wasn't filled with boxes and piles of paperwork. Dim light filters in from the doorway, illuminating the big bed in the center of the room, made up with yellowing sheets. Beside it on a dusty dark wood bedside table is an old electric alarm clock flashing 00:00. The air is musty-sweet with the cloying scent of dust.

Jones exhales behind her. "I'm sorry."

"Why?"

She turns back to face him and finds a breaking man, head bowed as he stares at his feet. Slowly, quietly, she closes the door.

"I shouldn't have shouted. I didn't mean to scare you. I panicked."

"It's okay."

"It isn't."

Though she can't quite fit the pieces together yet, the picture on the puzzle is beginning to show. That room belonged to someone once, someone he hasn't been able to fully move on from. It's off limits because it's too painful for him to see.

She reaches out and takes his hand, leading him away from it and through the correct door into his bedroom. It takes a moment for him to arrange the pillows in the way which gives him the most relief while he's lying on his side, but once he's comfortable, she climbs onto the bed beside him so they're face-to-face.

"I'm sorry," he says again, his eyes drifting across her face. His lips seal tight for a moment as his throat leaps. "It was my dad's room."

Liz shuffles closer, putting an arm in the space between his neck and the mattress, while her other hand strokes his hair. "Do you want to talk about him?"

"Not really." Jones sighs. "And kind of."

"You know I'm here. Whenever you need me, whenever it feels right."

He nods, closing his eyes. "He… wasn't the best dad. Not to me, anyway. I have an older brother who idolized him… turned out just like him. A bitter, angry man who drinks too much. I haven't seen him for over twenty years."

"I'm sorry." It's all she can say.

"By all accounts my grandad was even worse." Jones shakes his head. "Can we talk about something else?"

"Of course."

He slides his arm across her waist, pulling her closer to him still. The soft, warm press of his lips against her forehead serves to quieten her concern. "What did you want to be when you were little? Did you always want to be a musician?"

She sighs deeply and lets go of the pieces she's trying hard to put together. "A massage therapist. I wanted to help people. I know music does that too and it's a powerful, wonderful thing, but… I wanted to help people in a tangible way. You know?"

"You mean this whole time I could have been getting free massages?"

"No, I'm not trained. I wouldn't want to hurt you even worse."

"Ah." Jones chuckles quietly. "But how did you join the band? A massage therapist is a far cry from a rock star."

"I never really wanted this. I know that makes me ungrateful, and there are people who work hard their entire life for even a fraction of the recognition the Vixens have, but it just… sort of happened."

Jones's eyes open, trailing across her face as though he can uncover some buried secret. "Are you happy?"

"Right now, yes. I'm here with you." She tightens her arms around him and before he can ask her more, she adds, "What about you?"

"Oh God…A vet… or a zookeeper. Anything which involved animals. But we couldn't afford the schooling." He swallows hard. "And my grades weren't good enough anyhow."

She could see it. Kind and gentle Jones surrounded by critters like some enormous, hairy fairytale princess. The image of it makes her smile. "Would you go back to school now? Maybe not a vet or a zookeeper but *something* to do with animals."

"Maybe." He stares at a spot on the wall above her head. "I need to figure out what. I'm scared, Liz. I'm scared that I'm getting older and my body isn't going to let me carry on doing the only things I know how to do. There will probably come a time when I'm too hurt to go on. I don't know what happens after that."

She holds him close as she rolls onto her back so he can rest his head on her chest. She doesn't have the answers. "We'll figure something out," she tells him.

"We?"

"Whatever happens you won't be facing it alone. I'll be by your side."

"Thank you." He breathes deeply, his big shoulders rising and falling as something works loose. "You mean a lot to me, Liz."

"So do you." She kisses the top of his head and breathes in the familiar scent of him.

They lie in silence for a long time, holding each other close, exchanging comfort just by being together. And as Liz strokes back his hair, smoothing the sporadic strands of silver threaded through the brown, she realizes Anya was right.

He's it.

He's her person.

"I think I'm in love. With Liz." Jones wipes his palms on his jeans as he glances around Doctor Kim's office. "No. I...I know I am."

The therapist smiles. Her sweater is maroon today, the exact same style as the peacock blue. "Do you think she feels the same way about you?"

It's the question he has been asking himself for a while, the one he can never seem to settle on an answer to. "She cares about me. I know that. And I know you're going to say

I should talk to her about it, but…What if knowing she feels the same is worse than not knowing?"

"Why do you think she wouldn't reciprocate?"

"Because I'm unlovable." The words fall from his lips far easier than anything else. He sighs as Kim's eyes narrow. "I don't think I've ever been loved."

She makes a note. "What was your relationship like with your parents?"

He doesn't want to answer. It'll hurt. But he saw the same question burning in Liz's eyes when she opened the door. Sooner or later, he'll have to tell her, and when he does, she might find that he's too broken for even her to hold together.

"My mother walked out when I was thirteen days old, and my father spent the rest of his life making sure I knew it was my fault he was forced to raise me." His breath stalls as he focuses on the neutral beige tone of the carpet beneath his feet. All at once he's disarmed. "I'm sorry."

"You know none of that is your fault."

A knot in his stomach tightens painfully as he shifts on the couch. Logically he knows it. If it were Imran or Liz, or anyone else who confessed the same to him he'd know it wasn't because of them. But a weight sits on his chest, a dark and agonizing tormentor reminding him in every moment of happiness that it's only temporary. Pain will come. People will leave. They always do.

Doctor Kim glances down at the pad in her lap, and he wonders if she's actually checking her watch, counting down the minutes before the session is over and she's free.

"I don't think today is a good day for me." He sighs. "Mentally."

"That's okay, progressing through trauma like this isn't a linear journey. There will be times it feels as though you're taking steps backward, but that's completely normal. Is there something else you'd prefer to talk about?"

"I don't know. Yeah."

"How's Teddy doing at the shelter?"

"He's okay." Jones sits a little straighter in his chair. "He's just done with the place. Needs to get out. Needs a home. Love. Nobody wants him. Well, I do… but I can't have him on account of Roxy."

The therapist offers him a half smile. "I'll help put out the word and see if I know anyone who can take him."

An idea clicks into place. "I could ask Liz."

"If she would take him?"

"No, no, I know she can't. Her apartment is too small. But she's in a band and there are thousands of people who follow them on social media. Maybe they could help?"

All at once he's lighter, excitement fluttering in his chest. How did it never occur to him?

<hr>

As soon as he gets out of his appointment, he pulls out his phone and calls Liz. The phone rings against his ear, the screen warm and smooth against his cheek as he makes his way over to his car.

*"Hi this is Liz's voicemail. Leave a message."*

He ends the call instantly. Talking on the phone with her is hard enough, but he'll die before he leaves a message on one of those things. Instead, he fires off a text which reads simply: *call me.*

He's already home and sitting on the couch with Roxy's head on his lap when his phone vibrates. Liz's name flashes on the screen, making his pulse beat just that little harder.

As he answers the call and puts the phone to his ear, her voice spreads over him like a soothing balm. "My, my, Mister Jones, how the tables have turned."

He smiles immediately. "Hi, Liz."

"Hi. Sorry I missed you, I was at practice."

Right. He cringes at himself for forgetting. "How did it go?"

She sighs deeply. "It… went. Finn cracked a cymbal, so we spent most of the time waiting for him to deal with that, and then Nic had to leave early because their partner had a migraine, so we had to rehearse without violins and just teeny-tiny cymbal splashes." She makes a frustrated sound at the back of her throat. "And then a fuse blew in the factory so it was practice over."

As frustrated as she clearly is, he can't help but grin as she vents. "Rough day?"

"Yeah." She laughs. "It was kind of funny watching Finn try to be delicate while he played. He kept forgetting and launching into full beast-mode and then yelling *fuck* when the crack got bigger… Anyway, how are you?"

"Better for hearing your voice."

"Me too." There's a long silence, broken only by the sound of her car's ignition roaring to life. "Sorry, it's cold. I need the heater on."

He chuckles quietly. "It's okay, I won't keep you long."

"You can keep me as long as you need," she says softly. "What's up?"

Oh, yeah… there was a reason he called. He's so wrapped up in the loveliness of just hearing her voice he almost forgot. "Uh, I was thinking about Teddy and wondering if you think it could work if your band posted about him on their social media? You know… try to see if people would be interested in taking care of him." He smooths his hand over the spikes on top of Roxy's head, preparing himself for rejection.

"Jones, I think that's a wonderful idea!" she says. "Are we still on for tomorrow?"

"Of course."

"Do you have any pictures of him?"

He closes his eyes and braces himself. "An embarrassing amount of them."

She chuckles. "You're so sweet. Okay, well at some point tomorrow, why don't you come over to my place and we can put together a post? I'll call Finn and Mia and let them know what we're doing, but yeah, that would be perfect. I have early morning practice tomorrow but I'll be done before nine, okay?"

"You're amazing," he says. "Thank you."

"No problem at all. I'm glad we might be able to help him. I'll see you tomorrow," she says.

"See you," he smiles. As the call ends, he keeps the phone to his ear, just a moment longer. And in the silence, he whispers, "I love you."

When he puts the phone down, he glances across to the empty recliner turned toward him. The most comfortable chair in the house which never gets sat in because it was and always will be his dad's chair. A constant reminder, a specter watching over his every moment, keeping him from moving on from the past. A silent, inanimate jury condemning his heart to a life alone.

Enough is enough.

Liz would probably tell him off if she found out, but he drags the recliner across the room grunting and gasping as spasms of pain shoot through his thighs. He'll probably pay for it tomorrow, but it will be gone.

Cold night air whips around him as he lugs the chair down the pathway of his front yard, knocking over empty flower pots and dislodging the stones lining the edge of the grass, until he reaches the curb. Someone can take it if they want to, or hell, he'll drive it to the dump himself if the trash truck doesn't take it. But it's gone. Out of the house. It's a step, one of many he needs to overcome, but a big one nonetheless. He turns his back on it and heads inside to take his meds.

# Eighteen

On Thursday morning Liz checks the clock for the fiftieth time since she got to rehearsal and finds, to her dismay, only two minutes have passed since the last time she looked. Releasing a sigh, she plays a couple of bars of *Bloodlust Beautiful* on the keyboard, and tries to pretend she doesn't see Anya staring at her out of the corner of her eye.

"How was the pizza?" the guitarist asks regardless, an innocent enough question which Liz knows is just a stack of inappropriate questions disguised in a trench coat.

"It was nice," Liz says, without taking her eyes from the sheet music on her keyboard's stand.

"Like… nice or *nice?*" She wiggles her eyebrows.

How can she answer that? The pizza was good, the cuddling was lovely. But the rest of it; Jones's anxiety, his vulnerability, the confession about wishing she was anywhere else but here dancing on the tip of her tongue… Those things have to stay inside.

"Uh…"

"Liz!" Finn calls from across the room. He's wearing his fan-made 'I heart Finn' shirt. "Contract?"

Fuck. "Oh… shoot, sorry I forgot it again."

The drummer sighs but offers her a weary smile. "It's okay, just as soon as you can, if that's alright?"

"Sure."

"Is there anything in there you're unsure of or…?"

"No, no it's all good. I just keep forgetting it." The lie sits heavy in the center of her chest as she forces a smile. She's unsure of *everything*.

Anya clears her throat. "She's nervous about putting her full name on there. Few people know that Liz is actually short for Lizard."

Nic snorts on the far side of the room as Liz narrows her eyes.

Finn scratches his eyebrow with his thumb, only partially obscuring the fact that he's holding in a laugh. After a long exhale he turns back to Liz. "Just whenever you can."

"Sure thing," Liz nods.

"Okay," the drummer says, clapping his hands together for emphasis. "So, you may remember from our meeting the other week, we discussed our next move and which gigs we wanted to play blah blah and so on and so forth. Well, we discussed applying to perform at Armand Corvo's industry party in the new year—"

Mia shimmies her shoulders a little, tapping the tips of her nails together as she grins in anticipation of the big news. Liz's stomach drops.

Finn laughs. "He accepted."

"Shut the fuck up," Anya gasps. "Are you serious?"

The drummer nods, beaming as Étienne sinks down to sit on the ground, resting his hands on top of his head. "Are you for real?" The vocalist blinks rapidly as Jordan comes to his side and ruffles his hair. "Armand Corvo… *The* Armand Corvo?"

Mia squeals before answering. "Yes, big scary guy, beard, lives in a huge mansion and possibly feeds on the blood of innocents."

"Oh my God," Étienne sighs. "This is huge."

"Why?" Liz asks. "What does it mean?"

Finn arches an eyebrow. "The last band who played at his event was Siren's Call…" he pauses, as if expecting her to know what he's talking about. When he gets no reaction, he continues. "They were smaller than us at the time. Now they have a record deal, music videos, they're about to go on a worldwide tour. Shit. This is everything we've ever wanted."

Icy cold descends over her as she feigns enthusiasm. The others hug each other, excitement written plainly all over their faces. But Liz can't muster it. In fact, this is the complete opposite of everything she wanted.

As practice ends, she hangs back, staying with the Vixens as long as possible in the hope that their happiness is contagious. It's certainly overwhelming.

"Siren's Call is a crappy band name," Anya mutters. "So unoriginal."

"I have literally no idea who they are," Étienne confesses as Jordan wraps her arm around his waist. He raises his arm to sip from a water bottle before adding, "I'm just happy to be here. Put me behind a microphone and I'll sing whatever you want me to."

"And you'd do it beautifully," Jordan tells him, pressing a kiss to his cheek just above his beard.

The new vocalist is practically glowing with the news. As he gushes, telling them all the rumors he's heard about the infamous reviewer, Liz can't help but wonder if he's the key. Perhaps, if she could just absorb one percent of his excitement, maybe the news about Armand Corvo would be less soul-crushing.

"Hey, Étienne, do you have a sec?"

The vocalist snaps the lid shut on his water bottle and smiles. "Sure."

She beckons him over to her side of the rehearsal room. "How are you finding it? Being here with us? You didn't really sing this sort of stuff before, right?"

"Oh," he chuckles and swipes his hand back through his dark hair. "No. I was a wedding singer, so… you know… not really metal, no. But I think I'm finding my feet. The fans don't seem to have noticed I'm an imposter."

She smiles with him. "Do you enjoy it?"

"I love it." He chuckles softly, wiping his brow on his forearm. "Honestly I've never been this happy before in my life."

"Oh—"

"I mean, obviously Jordan is a huge part of that, but this, making music with you all, even singing the same line over and over again, it's more than I ever really thought I'd get to experience. The fact that I get to do it with cool people is even better."

As envious as she is of his passion, she can't help but smile for him. "I'm glad you're with us."

"Me too." He raises his eyes to the ceiling for a moment before shaking his head. "Cool news about Armand though, huh? I keep having moments where I think 'how is this happening to me?' you know?"

"Yeah." She doesn't know.

"Like… What if this is it? What if we play for him and

he puts his all into us? What if after this we're just on tour all the time, ten albums, millions of fans. Rock 'n Roll Hall of Fame." He chuckles. "I guess we can dream, right?"

"Yeah. Guess so."

A vibration against her thigh gives her a welcome distraction as she excuses herself from Étienne's effusive gushing and pulls her phone from her pocket. The moment she reads the name Jones her heart skips a beat. Ever the wordsmith, the text is just a thereabouts description of a trail in the mountains, and the phrase *sensible footwear*.

"Oh… shit," Liz sighs as she slips the phone back into her pocket. "Hey, does anyone have any hiking boots?"

———

This was a mistake. Condemnation repeats through Jones's mind as he tromps through the damp undergrowth, leading Liz further from the trail markers. What was he thinking? It's muddy, and the cold, damp air clings to them like the moss clings to the trees. The sleeves of his old grey knit sweater are pulled up to his elbows, his work khakis put to use as walking pants. He tenses in anticipation of an announcement that she's turning around and going back home.

"It isn't far," he assures her, hoping he's remembering that correctly. It never seemed far when he was younger. Then again, he was half the size he is now and whippet quick. "The doctor said gentle exercise would help my back so I thought this would be a good idea."

She smiles, already a little winded from the effort of walking on the uneven terrain. Her cheeks are washed with color, that same pink she had back in his bedroom what feels like a century ago. Liz looks like she knows what she's doing; proper hiking boots, a waterproof jacket, black yoga pants which faithfully follow every curve of her thighs. "I don't mind. I like spending time with you."

With just a glance she turns his legs to jelly, and it takes all his composure to remember he has to concentrate. He definitely doesn't want to get them both lost in the woods. "I used to come out here when I was a kid, when I didn't want to be at home." He sniffs, turning away. She doesn't need to know about that, not yet. Today is for her. "I always thought it was the most beautiful place in the world."

*I figure it suits you*, he adds silently.

Liz glances around them, and he can see the uncertainty in her eyes as she tries to peer through the mud to find the beauty beneath. "I haven't been to the woods for so long. Not since I was a kid."

She sounds wistful, her statement laced with regret. Jones curls his fingers into his palms to fight back the urge to reach out for her hand.

"Between Vixens practice and working to pay bills, I haven't even considered coming up here."

Jones nods. "Life gets in the way sometimes. I thought about bringing Teddy up here one day when I can take him from the shelter. It would be good for him. New smells, new things to roll in."

Liz chuckles and sighs. "I hope we can find someone for him. He deserves to be happy."

"Me too."

His heart squeezes at the sensation of her hand, warm and gentle against his. She nudges his fingers down from his palm before interlacing her fingers with his. Suddenly the air isn't so cold or damp, suddenly his cheeks no longer feel the bitter chill. They're warm. His whole body is warm.

And it occurs to him, though he'll never admit it aloud, he hasn't held hands with anyone since kindergarten. His heart thunders as they reach an outcrop of jagged slate. They're on the right path. He slipped there once and cut open his calf. "Be careful here. It's slippery."

"Okay."

She takes small, uneasy steps, clinging to his hand as he searches out his old footholds, grateful today more than ever for the painkillers. Less than two weeks ago he could barely walk across a flat, gravel parking lot. Now he's helping her, making sure his biceps flex a little more than strictly necessary as he pulls her up the ridge. His late-night recliner haul hasn't hurt him half as much as he'd expected.

They're definitely not far from the hollow. The distant roar of water guides him the rest of the way, and as they weave their way over tangled tree roots and slate outcrops, nostalgia slams into him. His eyes begin to sting.

The days he would spend there, dreading the journey home, wondering if he could survive the night, if he could sneak back and take the blankets from his bed to build a shelter. But he never did. Every night he would go back home, back to a man whose wife had left him alone to raise a disappointing child.

"It's just up ahead," he tells her, pointing with his free hand to a huge stone outcrop. Back when this was his haven from the rest of the world those rocks were mountains to him, a sanctuary only he knew about. He had never even shown his school friends. He's never shown anyone.

Jones leads the way as they squeeze through a gap in the rocks, side-stepping through the low undergrowth. And when he sees it once more his tears draw dangerously close to the edge, threatening to spill.

A waterfall cascades before them, splashing against the stones and forming a small lagoon, an oasis in the midst of the late-fall decay. Runoff from the pool flows out into a zig-zagging river between the stones and flows down the rocks to a valley below. Though the few trees growing there are bare this time of year, the greenery around their roots is still lush. It's just as he remembers, and yet, smaller, the beating of the water against the rocks is less chaotic and destructive.

"Oh my God," Liz gasps as she emerges from between the rocks. Her whisky and woodsmoke eyes are wide as she takes it all in. "Jones…"

"Beautiful, isn't it?"

"Incredible." She steps down onto the rocks, letting the low water trickle over the rubber soles of her walking boots before she smiles up at him. She never once lets go of his hand. "Is this where you bring people to make out?"

He chuckles, despite his nerves. "Actually, I never brought anyone up here. You're the first."

"Really?"

He nods.

"Well, I'm honored. Thank you." She steps toward him, closing the gap between them and pressing her body against his. Even through her jacket the warmth and softness of her body calls to him. "Can we still make out?"

"Yes."

She raises up to meet his lips as he stoops to meet hers. At their first touch sparks flow through him, a warmth which radiates from her, straight to the parts of his heart he has always kept barricaded. All too late he realizes those defenses are being burned down.

She wraps her arms around him, holding him tight as she kisses him, as though there were a single force in the entire universe which could tear him from her, other than her word. Her tongue strokes against his, stoking the fire in the pit of his belly, making the animal part of him wish he hadn't brought her so far from his bed.

His heart aches for her. He loves her. As simple and as complicated and impossible as that. It silently pours from him to her, steady, infinite, and as patient as the water slowly carving through the rocks. He can't say it yet, won't say it, so he simply whispers the word which has come to mean love, "Liz."

When she breaks away, she gazes up at him, her eyes following the curve of his cheek. It takes a moment to realize why.

Turning away, he wipes the tear on the back of his hand and sniffs. "Fuck."

"Hey," she says in a soft, reassuring tone. "It's okay."

"It's ridiculous."

"I know, and I feel it too."

Her words stop his goddamned heart. Turning back to face her, his eyebrows furrow. "Feel what?"

She pulls in a long breath as if she's preparing to dive into the water tumbling behind them. "Like I can't stop smiling, like my heart is bursting out of my chest. When I'm with you, I feel like clouds are parting."

He stands open mouthed, searching for the right words to say back to her, but he can't. How can he? Jones has spent his life being the cloud, blotting out the light in everyone's lives, an unwelcome presence which makes people huddle down and pray he goes away.

"Liz… why would you say that?"

She frowns a little. "Because it's the truth."

"How?" He shakes his head. "How can someone like you stand to be around me?"

"Jones, you're a good man." She draws toward him, taking both her hands in his and meeting his gaze. "I love spending time with you. You make me smile and laugh, you're handsome and sexy. You give me butterflies. You make me excited in ways I didn't think I was capable of feeling. Ever since I met you, I've woken up each morning just so amped to be here, knowing there's a possibility I'll see you. And I know you don't see it, but I do, and I feel as though I'm only just scratching the surface of the mountain of things which make you wonderful."

He stands there, shoulders aching from the tension of bracing himself against the torrent. The compliments sit on the surface of his waterproofed soul, never fully sinking in.

*What would Doctor Kim say? Try.*

Maybe Liz is telling the truth, or at least the way she perceives it. Maybe she does look at him and see someone completely different to the man who stares back at him in the mirror.

"Is that really what you think of me?"

"Yes," she raises onto her tiptoes and kisses him again. "I do. And if you need me to keep reminding you, I will. You are kind, loving, caring, handsome, sexy, funny, and honestly, you eat my pussy like nothing I've ever known before, and I refuse to let you go."

A bark of laughter bursts from him as the world blurs behind tears. "What can I say? I'm a big boy, I like to eat."

She laughs with him before lifting his hands to her lips and kissing each of his knuckles in turn. "I need you, Jones. Ever since I first saw you, I knew."

"I need you too." He turns his hands around in hers so he can cup her face and stroke back her hair. "I started seeing a therapist. I had my second session last night."

"That's great," she says.

"It doesn't put you off?"

"No. I know you have things you need to work on, and as much as I want to get to know you better, I know if you ever want to tell me more about your life, it'll happen when you're ready."

"I…" The truth burns inside him like a ball of molten iron, pressing against his throat. "I was brought up to believe men shouldn't have to ask for help. We should be strong and get on with things."

She bridges the space between them in an instant, wrapping her arms around his body, holding him close as she nestles her head against his chest. He wraps his arms around her in turn.

"I'm proud of you," she whispers against his heart.

The seal breaks, and her words begin to sink in. "There are things I should tell you."

"Okay," she raises her head. "I'm listening."

"Okay." He prepares to plunge. "When I told you I'd never met anyone like you, I meant it. I've known a lot of people. I've…" he frowns, searching for the right word. "I've slept with a lot of people. Not all of them have been women. Does that bother you?"

"Not at all."

He breathes. "Thank you."

"I'm in a symphonic metal band whose entire aesthetic is an Anne Rice fever dream, Jones. I don't think any of us are actually straight."

"Oh." He chuckles. "Well, yeah, that makes sense."

He loves her. Loves her so damned much. And perhaps she truly does see him as the sun peering through the clouds, but if he is, that makes her the breeze, pushing away the dark so he can shine.

"It's only you now," he says.

"I know, I would never have doubted it. It's only you for me too." She gazes up at him as though he's even more spectacular than the water cascading from the rocks. And he feels like it. God, for once in his life he feels worthy of being looked at like that.

She pushes out a sigh. "My turn."

"Okay."

"Before you, I thought I'd seen everything this place had to offer, and none of it excited me. I love the Vixens and I know how lucky I am to be able to do what I do, but my heart wasn't here. I didn't think there was anything here for me, but I was wrong."

His heart swells, already certain of what she's saying. But he asks anyway. "What changed?"

"Everything," she tells him. "Everything changed when you came into my world."

Her words steal his breath, make his head spin. How can she see him that way? How can the version of him she sees be the same man he has to endure every damn day?

The answers don't come easily, and perhaps they never will. Maybe he'll have to spend his life challenging his perceptions, drowning out the cruelty infecting his mind. Maybe. But that doesn't make him unworthy.

He trails a strand of her hair between his fingers and clings to that thought.

# NINETEEN

What the fuck is happening to her?

When she's with Jones, every corny word makes sense, every declaration is nothing but truth. He's hurt, she's known that from the start. Not just his back either, but he's working on it and maybe one day he'll tell her what cut him so deeply, but in his own time. And she'll give it to him. She'll give him as much time as he needs. She'll wait as long as it takes.

Of course, he wasn't the reason she gave up her dreams—Liz Larkin might be many things but she certainly isn't the type to throw away a lifetime ambition for a guy she met less than two weeks ago—but he's the main reason the decision isn't crushing her to death.

"This place truly is beautiful," she says, "I can see why you used to come here."

"No one would ever find me. I used to sit here for hours just watching the water rush by."

He raises his head to glance around the hollow, following the twisting branches and the fissures in the rocks. And boy, is he ever handsome. It's been too long since she felt his touch on her skin.

"Do you think people have found it now?" she asks.

"No. I don't think so. There are no footprints, no trash."

"Good. Just so you know, my period ended yesterday."

Jones stares, realization dawning on his features. "Oh… You want to? Here?"

"Here. Yes."

In an instant he's on her, driving her against the stone wall with primal force. She cries out in surprise and the anticipation of pain which never comes. For all his strength he's gentle and so goddamn addictive. He kisses her like he's been told he has minutes to live, like at any moment the rocks will crumble down on top of them. And she's pinned, deliciously helpless between his big body and the unyielding stone.

Her hands twist in the thick, worn wool of his sweater, pulling him closer, as though the two of them could melt together. The press of his thigh between hers ignites the divine ache coursing through her, and she bears down, grinding herself against him as he sighs against her.

He sucks her bottom lip, grazing it with his teeth as he unzips her jacket and reaches up beneath her shirt to place his big, rough hands on her soft skin. She squirms beneath his icy touch, but the heat coursing through her soon warms them too.

"Jones if you don't fuck me, I'm going to die," she whispers against his lips. "I've never needed anything more."

But he draws back, pressing his forehead to hers, denying her his lips. "Before we go on, I need to ask something."

"What?"

"You don't have to answer now, but what are we doing? Is

this just sex? Am I a broken project for you to fix and send back out into the world when you're through? Because if I don't get this clear in my head, I know for damned sure my heart is going to break."

"No," she whispers. "I don't think you need to change and I know I'm never going to fix what's hurting you. Only you can do that. I want you because…"

"Because what?" His breath shivers between them. "Because what, Liz?"

"Because I think I love you." Icy cold descends over her. It's too soon, far too soon to admit how she feels. Tears prick her eyes as heat simmers beneath the surface of her skin. Shame topples on top of her as his gaze rakes across her features. She's raw, overwhelmed, filled with want and need. Half of her wants to shove him away from her, half of her is glad he wouldn't budge if she did.

He lowers his head. "Say that again."

Liz's chest presses against his as she inhales. "I love you."

He looks at her like he's watching the creation of the universe; awestruck, almost tearful. "Again. Please."

"I love you, Jones. You're the best person I ever met, and I need you. Not just now, always."

His throat twitches, and the muscle in his jaw dances as he nods, as though running her words through the mill of his mind.

"No one has ever said that to me." He fixes her with an intense gaze, stroking loose strands of hair back from her cheek and tucking it behind her ear. So gentle, so softly trembling.

"I've never said it to anyone."

"Liz, I love you." He gasps as if the words burn in the air between them. "I love you too.

She reaches up to put her hands on the back of his head, stroking his hair as he closes his eyes. Her every breath is flooded with the scent of him.

"Is it too soon?" she whispers. "We're only halfway through our second date."

He sighs. "Maybe. But I feel it Liz, I do. It's like…"

"You're my person. And I'm yours."

A chuckle shakes his chest. "Yeah. Yeah, that's it."

This time when he kisses her, it's slow, deep, but the fire in her veins burns just as bright. He cups her face in his big, strong hands, and she knows it's true. He loves her, he adores her. And she feels it too. When he breaks away his cheeks are flooded with color, and his pupils blown wide.

"I want you," he whispers. "I want you so bad it hurts, but I don't think I can do it here. If my back goes, up here, I don't think you're going to be able to carry me back to the car."

Of course. It's far improved from when they first met, but his back still bothers him. The last thing she wants to do is make it worse when he's made so much progress. "Should we head back to my place?"

He nods. "I'd like that."

"Okay."

Jones turns, casting a last glance around the serene beauty of his secret place, before turning back to her. His shoulders loosen as he gazes down at her. "Let's go."

They make their way out of the hollow, sidestepping through the rocks and following the path they took to get there. When they reach the slate outcrop, they move slower. Every second they delay is torture.

"Thank you for bringing me here," Liz says as she

searches for a foothold on the sheer grey rock. "I know it meant—"

Her heart plummets as the earth moves from beneath her, and she falls, landing on the edge of the sharp, slippery outcrop. She lands hard. Pain spears through her from her ass to the top of her thigh, pulling a cry from her as Jones whirls round.

"Liz! Are you okay?"

"Mm-hm," she manages through airlocked lips. Screwing her eyes shut, she grimaces as she lifts herself off the ground and tentatively presses her hand to her backside and brings it around to check for blood. Her fingers come away smudged with crimson, and there's a tear in her yoga pants.

"Liz?"

"I'm okay," she winces as she tries to take a step down from the slate. "I think mostly just bruised."

Why, *why* couldn't she be the type of woman who falls daintily and twists her delicate ankle? Pain throbs through her behind as she limps to Jones's side, offering him a reassuring smile and hoping it at least convinces him.

"Come on," she says as brightly as possible through clenched teeth. "Let's go back to my place."

The walk to the car and the drive back to her apartment are hell, and not just because of the pain. Every glance, every brush of his fingers against her thigh as he drives, stokes her anticipation and fear that she's too hurt to do what she wants to. By the time he finds a parking spot around the corner from her apartment, her vision is blurred by tears she steadfastly refuses to let fall.

"Liz," he says gently, reaching across to place his hand on hers. "Do you want to go to the hospital?"

"No, no it's not that bad."

Gently he reaches out and brushes her hair back from her face. Heat rolls over her as he picks a dark brown leaf from her hair. It's no use. She can't keep faking.

"I think I need some ice," she tells him, unbuckling her seatbelt and refusing to meet his gaze. "It hurts pretty bad."

"Alright."

<hr>

She leads him up to her apartment in mortified silence, throwing her keys into an abalone shell by the door, kicking off Anya's walking shoes, and heading straight for the kitchen which takes up the corner of her open living space. Jones hangs back, keeping her in sight but giving her room to maneuver. His hands are stuffed into the pockets of his khakis, his big shoulders hunched as he watches her take her ice pack from the freezer.

"I'm sorry," she mutters.

"You have nothing to be sorry for." At last, he steps toward her. There's a little hesitation in his eyes, uncertainty in his movement, and it takes her a moment to realize he's opening his arms to put them around her. Grumpy Jones is… *hugging her.*

As sore and humiliated as she is, she'll take it.

She nestles against him, listening to his heart beat against her cheek, drawing every moment of comfort from him she can get. The soft press of his lips to the top of her head pulls her downturned lips into a smile. "Thank you."

"I'll be back in a minute," he says, pushing her away to hold her at arm's length, and a moment later, he turns and leaves. The front door clicks shut behind him.

"Oh."

Liz frowns and walks to her living room, peering out of the window to the street below. From the sixth floor she gets a good view of the street, and of the spot where Jones parked his truck, but when he finally emerges from the front of the building, he doesn't head that way. Instead, he crosses the street, hands firmly back in his pockets as he walks away.

"Weird."

A petulant throb of pain in her buttock draws her away from the window. She takes the front door off the latch for when Jones eventually returns from his mission, and limps to her bedroom. There, in front of the full-length mirror, she slowly peels away her black yoga pants, holding her breath as she braces herself. There's a rip in the fabric, and blood beneath.

"Shit," she hisses as she peels the fabric away from her tender skin, revealing a long, bloody scratch surrounded by a fierce scarlet bruise the size of her palm. Gritting her teeth, she rolls her pants down the rest of the way. The backs of her legs are covered in mud too. Great. No wonder Jones ran away.

Fortunately, the scratch is no longer bleeding and doesn't need stitches. Silver linings. Shrugging off her jacket and the teal tank top beneath, she walks into the en suite bathroom and turns on the shower.

She loves him. She does. She smiles to herself as she waits for the water to heat up, pressing her fingers to her lips. Anya will have a field day teasing her if she admits it to the Vixens so soon.

Her front door is unlocked when he gets back from the pharmacy, and the distant whoosh of her shower explains her absence. Flicking the latch back on the lock, he removes his shoes at the door and pads across her apartment. Carefully, he sets two paper bags down on her cream-colored couch, and waits.

Her apartment is small, cozy. Her walls are mostly a pale neutral shade, somewhere between cream and… what would they call it? Mushroom? Inoffensive brownish-grey? One wall opposite her living room window is a deep, forest green. She has plants on her windowsill, small succulents. It takes him a moment to realize they're fake. Of course. A rock star doesn't have time to take care of houseplants when she's busy touring.

The realization that he'll be left behind too occurs to him, but that's fine. He knew what she was before he fell in love with her, and he'd never step in the way of her passion or ambition. Never. Hell, maybe someday they can buy real plants together, and it would be his honor to stay behind and water them while she tours the world. His heart would burst with pride.

The green wall is host to a framed photo of her band, and besides Liz, he recognizes a few of them from Ghoulfest. Their singer, Mia, was it? The one who actually got things organized after the short, dramatic guy bolted off the stage. He'd liked her. And the big drummer, he seemed okay too. The whole band is squeezed together in a tiny room, smiling and happy. They're all good looking, radiating confidence and a glamor he could never even hope to achieve. But, he supposes, that's why they stand on the front of the stage, while he works at the back.

*But you're good enough for her.*

*She loves you. She told you that you had changed her world.*

He lets himself smile. Taking in the rest of the apartment, he envies her this space, a space that's truly hers. He's lucky to have been left his family house, he knows that, but the pain soaked into those walls, the memories which haunt each corner. Often, he'd wished he could sell it and start afresh, but the chains of those specters were wound around him too. But now… now he's in love.

The hiss of her shower stops abruptly, halting his thoughts as he waits, clearing his throat so she'll know he's there.

"Jones?"

He follows the sound of her voice, muffled behind a door. "Yeah, it's me."

The handle twists, the door opens, and his heart just about explodes from his chest. Liz stands wrapped in a fluffy purple towel, her dark hair damp and dripping as it spreads like tendrils across her tanned shoulders. She doesn't have her glasses on, and the towel clings to her, following the broad curve of her hips and waist, glancing off the soft roundness of her stomach and breasts. He swallows hard to moisten his arid throat as she leans against the doorframe.

"I'm back," he says, cringing even as he speaks. Of course he's back.

"I see that."

"I got some things."

"Ooh," she smiles, though the pain is apparent in her eyes. "Things are my favorite."

His ears are burning, his cheek too as he turns back toward the couch and picks up the bags. He goes to hold them out for her to take, but she steps aside. "Come in."

Stepping into her room, he breathes in the soft scent of her; warm vanilla and honey. It's so different from his own bedroom. His is stripped bare, pared down to the basics he needs to get by, as devoid of those haunting memories as he can make it, but hers… the navy-blue walls are covered in paintings and photographs, lined with shelves stacked to bursting with books. A fish tank bubbles away in the corner, well planted and brightly lit.

"That's Jim," she says as she pulls open a drawer and takes out a hairbrush. "Jim, this is Jones."

Jones peers into the tank at the solitary blue and red betta fish flaring its gills at him. "He doesn't like me."

"He's just grumpy." She chuckles. "Apparently I'm drawn to grumpy men."

As he scowls, feigning indignation, Jones notices the ice pack sitting on a towel on the end corner of her bed. "Have you used that yet?"

"No," she sighs, combing through her hair. "I took a shower because there was a bit of blood and a lot of dirt, and I was hoping the pain would stop. I don't like the cold."

"Hypocrite," he teases. "I distinctly remember you putting ice on my back like it was no big deal."

She frowns at him playfully as she ties her hair up, her nose crinkling in protest. "Fine."

"Lie down," he tells her. "Let me take care of you this time."

Her scowl dissipates, leaving a curious smile as she climbs onto the bed in nothing but her towel. She folds her arms beneath her head and sighs.

His body aches at the sight of her, of her bare, curvy legs, and the way the towel stops not two inches from the curve of her backside. He'd be lying if he said he didn't still want her, desperately, almost painfully. But for now, he pushes aside his craving for her, and goes through the bag.

"Okay, first things first," he mutters as he sits on the bed beside her. He reaches into the bag and pulls out the first item. "Chocolate, because you're upset, and I've heard this helps."

She turns her face toward him and laughs. "You're amazing, but no chocolate in bed. I'll only get it on the sheets."

"Ah," he nods. "Fair enough." He sets it down on top of the nearest book case. "Well then, that's for later." Emptying the rest of the bags' contents onto the bed, he grimaces. Bruise cream, Band-Aids, more chocolate, pain relief, antibiotic ointment, potato chips, a bottle of red wine and a pumpkin spice flavored Chapstick. "I might have come over-prepared."

"Jones," she laughs as she raises onto her elbows. "What is all this?"

"Well, some of it's useful… hopefully. Some of it is just to help you feel better."

She reaches over and picks up the Chapstick, turning it over in her hands. Confusion tightens her forehead.

"Oh," he clears his throat. "I got that because of the pumpkins. It's kind of Halloweeny, and you're in a Halloweeny kind of band."

Burying her face in her hands, she laughs. "You are without a doubt, the sweetest man I've ever met, Jones."

"It was just by the register when I went to pay. I think I panicked."

She's still smiling as she peels off the plastic around the cap before pulling it open and sniffing the contents.

Warmth rushes to his cheeks as she slides the stick over her lips. He distracts himself by sorting the haul into two piles; stuff to fix her heart, stuff to help her heal. As he puts the food items to the side and arranges his makeshift first aid kit, he becomes aware of her watching him, studying his movements. And when he turns to her, she glances away.

How, he wonders. How is he the person she wants? She's radiant.

*And yet, here she is, and here I am.*

"Uh," he stammers a moment. "How do you want to do this? Do you want me to leave the room while you take care of it or—?"

"If you're okay with it, I am too," she says. "The bleeding has stopped."

"That's not why I'm asking. Do you mind if I lift the towel?"

He shouldn't be turned on by this. She's hurt and he's supposed to be helping, but the thought of it, knowing he's making her feel better, providing for her. He's hard before she even lifts it.

But when she does, he sucks in a breath. A large, angry bruise is already forming on the soft, dimpled skin of her ass, and the four-inch-gash, though not deep, is furious crimson.

"That bad, huh?" she asks.

"You're going to be sore tomorrow."

"I'm sore now," she mutters.

Standing from the bed, he heads to the bathroom to wash his hands.

The mirror above the sink is still fogged from the shower, which he counts as a blessing. It's easier not to tear into himself when his reflection isn't confirming all of his fears. When he returns to the bedroom, he feels every degree of warmth in her beautiful, dark eyes.

"I'm sorry," she says. "I know this isn't how you envisioned our date today. You shouldn't have to take care of me."

"Liz…" He lets go of a sigh. "I thought we would walk out to a waterfall and you would say it was pretty and we'd go home. And you're right. I didn't imagine this." He sits back down beside her gently stroking the back of her thigh. "I didn't imagine quite how hard my heart would be beating the second I saw you, or that I'd walk into your apartment and discover even more of the wonderful person you are." He leans forward, careful not to overstretch as a weak flare of tingling pain reminds him his relief is still temporary. "I didn't imagine you would say you loved me and that I would get to say it back. So, no, I didn't imagine it like this, and other than you being hurt, I wouldn't change a thing about it."

One corner of her mouth quirks into a half-smile. "Thank you. And I do love you."

"And I love you. So let me be your ass doctor."

"Jones!" She shrieks as she swats his thigh, laughing along with him as he takes the antibiotic ointment and screws off the cap.

If he took all thirty-eight years of his life before he met her and added together the time he'd spent smiling, it would come nowhere close to how often he smiles when he's with her. And as he applies the ointment to her cut with a square of gauze, he wouldn't want to be anywhere else.

"You're so gentle," she smiles when he's done. "I love it."

She has this unique ability to wind him, to pull the air from his lungs and turn everything upside down. In the past, people have wanted him for his strength, his size, his you-come-when-I-say-you-can-come attitude. No one has wanted him like she does. No one has ever wanted gentle Jones.

He takes the bruise ointment and squeezes some onto his fingertips, rubbing it between them with both hands to warm it for her. Carefully, so as not to get it in her scratch, he spreads it over the site of the bruise as she sighs.

"I'm such a klutz," she murmurs.

"Between us we have almost a whole working body. I think we're doing okay."

"Is your back sore?"

He bites back the urge to dismiss her concern. "Not right now," he says, truthfully. "A twinge here and there, but it's much better lately. Thank you. For everything you've done."

"I like taking care of people," she sighs. "And I like being taken care of."

Taking the ice pack, he wraps it in the towel and places it on her bruise as she grumbles in protest. "It's for your own good," he tells her as he takes a pillow from her bed and places it beneath his hip. He lies on his side, facing her with his head resting on the heel of his hand and his elbow braced against the mattress. There's a little discomfort but only slight.

"How does it feel?" he asks.

"Still sore." She lifts her head and chest, shuffling on her elbows to be closer to him. "Not so sore that I don't still want you."

Electricity tingles along his spine as she kisses him, soft and oh-so sweet, and his. No matter how often he tells himself or challenges those negative thoughts like Doctor Kim told him, he'll never get used to knowing she loves him back.

"I don't want to hurt you," he says, ache billowing between his thighs as her breath flutters against his throat.

"You won't. You can sit back against the headboard and let me ride you."

"Oh—" His breath snags in his chest at the thought of it. Reaching out to place his hand on the back of her neck, he lets his fingers trail down her back, to where the towel presses against her skin. She shivers at his touch, leaning closer to him to kiss him, her lips demanding his.

She shuffles closer still, until their bodies touch, hands grasping, breaths catching, kiss deepening. He belongs to her, heart and soul. She wriggles out of the towel and tosses it to the ground, letting the ice pack fall with it. And God, he's missed her. Every inch, every crease and dimple and line are exactly how he remembered.

She climbs onto her hands and knees, her breasts brushing against his chest as she kisses him, hands reaching beneath his sweater to gently caress his stomach. It's so good to have her hands on him, but not enough. Never enough. He stands from the bed, pulling off his sweater, then his pants, socks and boxers. The seconds he spends away from her as he takes off his clothes are torture, but hunger burns in her eyes as they trail across him, feasting on the sight of his body.

She strokes her hand between her thighs as she watches him, teasing herself, torturing him. "Tell me what to do," she says.

"I want to taste you," he growls as he lowers himself onto his knees at the foot of the bed.

Her breath quickens. "I can't lie on my back."

"Then get on your hands and knees, ass in the air."

She does as he tells her, backing up to the edge of the bed. She's on her knees with her chest against the mattress, spread in front of him, already wet and flushed by desire.

This time he doesn't tease her. The moment she's in reach he hooks his hands around her thighs, holding her in place as he presses his face to her pussy and licks. God, how he's missed the taste of her, the copper and salty sweetness of her. She cries out against the crook of her elbow as he presses his tongue into her, pumping it in and out before licking down to her swollen clit.

He could spend hours like this, making her whimper and moan, making her twitch and pulse and grind against his mouth. Hell, he'll spend every day of his life like this if she'll let him. He reaches around her thighs to stroke her clit from above as he licks from below, coaxing a broken cry from her as her toes curl against his chest. More, more, more. He can't get enough of her, pressing his whole face against her, licking, sucking, strumming his fingers until she shatters against him, gasping his name against the bedsheets, her pussy throbbing beneath his lips.

"Oh, God, Jones," she breathes.

He kisses his way up her thighs, along her back, his hard cock pressing against her. His back feels good, he could take her from behind so his piercing would hit her G-spot, but not today. This time he wants her face-to-face.

"Are you ready for more?" he asks.

She nods, her cheeks and chest scarlet as she raises back onto her hands and turns to face him. Her hair is disheveled, strands sticking to her face as she kisses his chest, licking the silver bar in his nipple.

His heart thunders as she curls her hand around his rigid cock, and whispers, "I need this. I need you."

He can barely breathe. "Do you want me to take the piercing out for our first time?"

"No," she says after a moment's thought. "I want to

know what it feels like."

"Okay. But if it hurts you tell me."

She nods. "Ditto. You've had a vasectomy, right?"

"Yes."

"Okay. Good." She strokes her hand along the underside of his shaft, her fingertips teasing his balls. "I'm ready."

It pains him to leave her side, but he does, stacking the pillows against the headboard to make it as comfortable as he can. He won't let his pride ruin this for them.

"Come here," he tells her as he sits, settling back against the pillows. His cock stands firm, curving toward his soft belly as he runs his thumb over the metal bar.

She pulls back her hair, so it hangs back behind her shoulders and edges toward him on her hands and knees, kissing her way up his body. Deliberately ignoring his aching cock as it brushes between her breasts.

"I love your body," she tells him, kissing his stomach with light, ticklish flutters. "I can't get enough of you."

He lifts his head, lost in the sensation of her lips on him, reminding himself to keep breathing as she licks his pierced nipple once more. And then her lips are on his throat, her thighs astride his hips, her chest to his, and the ache coursing through him is more than he can stand.

"Are you ready?" she whispers.

He is. God, he is. He was ready for this the moment he saw her. And it doesn't matter that he can't fuck her hard. She's here with him, desperate for him, her face flushed from the desire to have him, her lips a darker shade of pink from his kisses. She wants him right now, the way he is now, not ten years ago, not 'fixed'. She wants him.

"Yes," he sighs against the warm skin of her neck. "I'm all for you. I'm yours."

# Twenty

Jones is a big man. Big body, big heart. But as Liz straddles his hips, grazing her fingernails over the cropped sides of his hair, he trembles beneath her.

Her breath leaves her in shuddering gasps, never quite reaching the bottom of her lungs. Rough, strong fingers skate along the lengths of her thighs, along her hips, her sides. He cups her breasts, kissing beneath them as his thumbs stroke her nipples.

"I need you," he whispers.

She can't stand it any longer. Slowly, she sinks down onto him, her spine tingling as the head of his cock pushes through her entrance, then down, down. He fills her, the firm press of the piercing barely noticeable. The sensation of him far outweighs it. He groans against her breasts, shoulders tensing and color rising in his cheeks as she takes all of him, inch by inch. Frissons of pleasure travel through her body as she grinds her hips against him.

His eyes open, drinking in the sight of her as he leans back against the pillows, fingers gripping her hips, a silent plea for her to keep riding him, as though she could ever stop. They're helpless, besotted, drunk on love and pleasure and each other. With every thrust she breathes him in, her hands on his chest, his lips on his, their bodies bound together in bliss.

He slides his hand down between them, determined to draw more ecstasy from her, rubbing his calloused fingers against her clit as she thrusts onto him, savoring every second of his pleasure, chasing the peak of hers.

Her second orgasm isn't as explosive as the first, but it freezes her in place, bowing her back as he strokes her. He gasps as her pussy pulses around his cock, and a moment later he's moaning, tilting his head back against the pillows as he comes undone.

She collapses against him, still joined, her head resting beneath his chin as he gently strokes her back.

They lie there, broken and spent as their breathing settles, holding each other.

Jones laughs quietly. "I've never cuddled after sex before."

"A fucking travesty." She traces her fingertip around the brown, pebbled skin surrounding his pierced nipple. "But I'm honored to be your first."

She smiles as he kisses the top of her head, wrapping his arms around her to hold her tight.

"You know, you still need to keep that ice pack on," he teases.

Liz frowns and sighs in protest, but he's right. The pain in her butt cheek is thrumming in time with her heartbeat. "Fine." She lifts herself off him and climbs down from the bed. "I need the bathroom first. Do you want to get the laptop started so we can post about Teddy?"

Jones strokes a hand down his chest as he nods. "Sounds good. Thank you."

"The laptop is right there," she says, pointing to the space between her bedside table and the bed. "I'll be back in a second."

---

He's happy. Truly, completely happy.

Jones swallows hard, trying to push down the knot forming in his throat as he reaches for the laptop. The day has been a lot. A lot of emotion, a release of the feelings which have been building up inside him.

A thought bounces relentlessly through his mind, a simple truth, evidenced by the person he trusts with his life. He's not unlovable. He never has been.

Pulling the bedsheets over his body, he sets the laptop on his thighs. He presses the power button on the device and is met with silence. The battery is completely dead but he finds the charging cable coiled at the side of her bed.

She keeps her cables neat, he learns. The roadie in him likes that. One more thing to love about her.

He plugs it into the outlet beside her bed and waits a moment before pressing the power button again. This time he's met with the low whir of the fan and processors, bright light shining beneath the keys of the keyboard. And then the screen lights up, opening the last thing she was doing before she closed the laptop.

It's a webpage for a massage training college two states away. His heart drops at the sight of it. Was she planning to leave?

She'd said she never wanted to be a rock star, that she had

always dreamed of being a massage therapist, but even worse than the thought of her leaving to go to school are the words printed across the screen:

*OFFER REJECTED.*

She applied, but turned it down.

Jones sets the laptop on the bed and stands, palm pressed to his forehead as he tries to make sense of it. She was leaving. She was following her dream. She had been accepted onto the course she'd always dreamed of. But she stayed.

She told him back in the hollow that she wanted out of town, to pursue a life she had always dreamed of. But he came into her life and changed it. That's what she said.

*He* held her back.

*He* broke her dream.

Panic tears through him, emptying his lungs, draining the blood from his face. Cold seeps beneath his skin, replacing the warmth he'd basked in just minutes ago. The urge to run, to get away from the horrible truth pulls at him, just as it always has. Run, hide, wait out the terror.

The bathroom door clicks open, and his heart jolts back to life, galloping in his chest as Liz's deep brown eyes stare up at him.

"Jones?" The concern in her voice kills him. "What's wrong?"

He looks ridiculous, he knows he does. Naked and wide-eyed, his face drained of color, his hands clasped on the top of his head.

When he doesn't answer she glances down at the computer on top of the bed sheets. "Oh."

"You were going to go to college."

She sits on the edge of the bed and pulls the laptop toward her. "You weren't supposed to see that."

"Liz…" His chest aches. "I'm so sorry."

"Why?"

Doctor Kim was right. He's a burden, dead weight in the lives of everyone he cares for. "I held you back."

She frowns. "What?"

"You rejected your place because of me."

"No!" She gives a huff of breathy laughter. "No, no, Jones. It wasn't you." She stands and puts her arms around his shoulders. "Love, please don't think that. I rejected my place because I felt guilty leaving the Vixens. Anya made me promise I'd stay."

He closes his eyes and forces himself to breathe slowly, to tear down the black shroud suffocating him, convincing him he's everything terrible in the world.

"Jones," Liz says quietly, pressing her palm to his cheek. "I stayed for the Vixens, but you are the reason that decision isn't destroying me."

He opens his eyes and looks into hers, warmth returning to his skin once more. His hands loosen on his head, and he lets one drift down to her cheek, grazing his rough fingers against her smooth skin. "I'm sorry."

"It's okay," she says as she leans into his touch. "You've never held me back."

She takes his hands in hers and leads him back to the bed, curling beside him and holding his head to her chest. Her heart beats steady against his ear as she strokes his hair, sending shivers of comfort and pleasure through him.

"I love you," he whispers. Panic shoots through him a moment before dissipating. It's okay for him to say that to her now, as often as he feels it. No one will call him soft, that part of his life is over, it has been for a while. It'll just take a while for the reality of the present to set in.

"I love you too," she replies. Her chest rises as she pulls in a deep breath. "I don't know what to do, Jones."

"I find talking it through helps."

Another breath. "I love the Vixens. We've played together for nearly a decade but…"

"But you want to go to school. You want to be a massage therapist."

She trails her hands over his shoulder. "I don't want to be a Vixen anymore. I don't want to tour the world or have ten albums or play at Armand Corvo's party. I don't want fans screaming at me or trying to discover more about who I am. I want… God, I just want a normal life. And it seems so silly to want that when I have so much."

"It isn't." He raises his head to meet her eyes, his heart squeezing at the sight of tear tracks shining on her cheeks. "Liz… Have you told your band this is how you feel?"

"No. Because I know it would devastate them to know I want to leave. As far as they're concerned this is forever. This is our life." She laughs a little. "More like a life sentence."

"I think it would hurt them worse to know what you're giving up to make them happy."

Her lips press together as she stares back at him and she draws a shallow breath. "I'm afraid to go out on my own."

"You won't have to," he tells her. "You don't have to face any of it alone. That's what you said to me, isn't it? You told me I'm not alone because we'll figure it out together."

She nods.

"Well, that goes both ways. I love you, and that means I want to see you succeed, I want you to be happy, and God,

Liz, I'd do anything to make that happen. You mean the world to me."

Wiping her tears on the heel of her hand she sits a little straighter as Jones shuffles up the bed so they're face-to-face.

"What do you think I should do?" she asks.

"What do you *want* to do?"

A muscle in her jaw clenches as her gaze falls to the computer. Weighted silence settles around them, broken only by the gentle whoosh of her sigh. "I don't know."

"That's okay. It's a big decision." He presses his lips together and moistens them with the tip of his tongue. It's wild to even consider it, but maybe if she went, he could go with her. Sell the house, figure out what he wants to do with his life. The two of them together, figuring out their futures. "*If* you do go to college—"

"Would you come with me?"

A breathless laugh escapes him. "Are you serious?"

"I know... I know it's so soon but... would you come with me? Maybe not to Monroe because it's far away but you could bring Roxy and I'll bring Jim and... no... I know it's ridiculous—"

"Yes." He takes her hand in his, smoothing his thumb over the peaks of her knuckles. "Wherever you go, if you want me, I'll go too. I'll find a school nearby and figure out what comes next for me and we'll face whatever comes next together."

"Really?" Her voice quavers as she turns to him. "You'd do that?"

"You're my person, Liz." He smiles, ignoring the tears stinging his eyes as he pulls her into his arms. "And I'm yours."

He holds her for as long as she needs him to, breathing in

the honey vanilla warmth of her hair. Doubts stir in his mind like dry, decaying leaves buffeted by a breeze. He's too old to learn something new. He'll embarrass himself. Liz won't want him forever. All of them are untrue and unnecessary. He rakes them away and weighs them down with what he does know. Liz is in his arms, she loves him, she thinks he's good enough. Deep down, he knows it's true.

"Thank you," she whispers against his shoulder. Lifting her head, she gazes into his eyes. He could spend a lifetime finding new shades of brown and gold in her eyes, and his heart squeezes at the realization that he can. "We should make that post for Teddy and find him a home."

"Yeah."

They get up and sit together, scrolling through Jones's phone to find the best pictures of the dog, the ones which really show just how gentle and wonderful he is, despite everything he's endured. He sends them to her laptop as she types out their desperate plea.

"I think it's perfect," Liz smiles as they create the post. "Someone is bound to want him."

"I hope so," Jones sighs, swiping away a tear on the back of his arm. The dam is cracking, and he can't hold back much longer. "My dad's name was Ted too. That's why I don't go by it. I'd change it completely, but… sometimes I wonder if my mom might someday search for me. Better to keep it."

The sensation of Liz's hand curling around his is a comfort, a much needed one. He tells her the parts of his life he's only recently dared to speak aloud, and every word is like choking on marbles lodged in his throat.

She leans her head on his shoulder and brings his hand to her lips, sitting silently beside him as the pages of his life lay open. She doesn't try to tear them out or diminish the heartache, doesn't try to fix things for him or tell him what he already knows. She listens, and holds him.

And as the notifications start pouring in, as people start to talk about Teddy and wish they could love him, Jones cries freely, for the first time in over thirty years. Because he and Liz and Teddy will all be where they're meant to be. At last.

# Twenty-One

The engine of Jones's truck rumbles as warm air blasts from the dashboard. Through the partially-fogged windshield a giant inflatable turkey bobs its head at them from the roof of the tiny shelter office.

Jones blows into his hands, his blue eyes bright in the morning light as he impatiently scans the parking lot.

"I'm so excited for them," Liz sighs, glancing in the side mirror to see if Finn's van is pulling up yet. The clock on the radio shows they're almost three minutes late, and she just knows Jones is inwardly tallying every minute as a misdemeanor.

"I'm nervous," Jones grumbles, picking up an insulated coffee cup from the dashboard and taking a tentative sip through the hole in the lid. "What if they don't get on?"

"Then I guess we try again. It's not like they're complete strangers and we can never contact them again."

"Well, I've never met them."

"He's Finn's cousin."

"Yeah, and I barely even know Finn. For all I know they could be a family of dog murderers."

Liz presses her lips together to suppress a laugh as she reaches for his free hand. "It'll be fine. The pair of them volunteer as firewatch people in the summer, so Teddy will have miles of forest to walk through, all kinds of nasty crap to roll in, and a mom and dad who love him."

"They'd better." His big shoulders drop as he releases a breath and glances in the rearview mirror. "Crap. They're here."

"Okay," she says as she reaches for the truck's door handle. "Just try to keep an open mind."

"No, I'm going into this assuming they're planning to eat him. They have to prove otherwise."

"Jones!" Her eyes widen as the driver's side door closes, and the soft crunch of Jones's steps fades. Shit. Over the past few weeks, he has personally vetted every single applicant who enquired about Teddy, conducting interrogations via video-chat if they couldn't make it to the shelter in person. But Finn's cousin Simon, and his girlfriend Vanessa did *something* to make the cut. Until now, it seems.

Opening the truck door, she steps out into the cold air and heads over to the group. Jones stands with his back to her, his legs parted to shoulder-width and arms folded over his broad chest. Finn waves from behind the steering wheel of his van as his cousin climbs down from the passenger seat.

"Morning," the man says, a brief smile crossing his lips before it disappears. Like Finn, Simon's a big guy, tall and handsome in an ursine kind of way. And oh-so broody. He wears a grey knitted hat and a red, sherpa lined flannel jacket, comfortable blue jeans, brown work boots, and a perpetual heavy brow.

Vanessa climbs down from the middle seat and stands beside Simon. She's short, curvy and ginger, and she's practically beaming from ear to ear. "Good morning!" she says enthusiastically, glancing between the two big, grumpy beardies before her eyes settle on Liz. "We're here to meet Teddy."

Liz chuckles. "This way." She gestures toward the office and waits for the woman to fall into step beside her. "I'm so glad you reached out to us. We've been looking for weeks to find someone suitable for Teddy."

"I can't wait to meet him," Vanessa says, the excitement in her voice palpable. "We've been talking about rescuing a dog and when we saw his picture on the forum, we knew we had to apply." She chuckles. "And it's great to see you again too. I think the last time I saw you in person we did the Macarena in the parking lot after Finn and Beth's wedding."

"Oh," Liz cringes as the memory floods back. "Yeah, that's right."

"The other woman…Anya? I think she was super drunk. She was the Macarena drill sergeant making sure we did all the moves properly."

"Yeah, no she wasn't even drinking. That's just how Anya is."

She glances over her shoulder to Jones as he walks behind her, hands thrust into his pockets as he watches his feet. It's hard for him, she knows. In an ideal world he'd be taking Teddy himself. Vanessa and Simon are right for this, that much is clear, but that doesn't mean it doesn't still hurt. When they reach the door to the office, she opens it to let the other woman step inside. "Can you just give us a second?" she asks.

"Sure."

She offers them a reassuring smile as she lets the door close and turns to face Jones. "Are you okay?"

A long sigh emerges from between his lips as a cloud of fog in the cold air. "Yeah, I'm alright. Just… I don't know. I want him to like them, and I want them to like him." He lowers his head. "And I'm nervous for you too."

"Oh." Her chest tightens a little at the thought of what she has to do tonight, but she has put it off for far too long. Tonight, after they're done at the shelter she's heading to rehearsal with Finn, and then, she'll tell the Vixens she's leaving. Her stomach slithers for a moment, but her determination overwhelms the sensation. "I'll be fine."

He arches an eyebrow. She needs to remember that in Jones-world 'fine' means 'death is imminent but I don't want to be a bother'. "You're sure you don't want me to stay out in the factory parking lot?"

"No. Just… pick me up when we're done and be there for me then."

He closes the gap between them, pulling her into his arms as he breathes in deeply. "I'm proud of you. And I'm so glad Monroe let you back in."

"Me too," she gazes up at him. "As of January fourth, I am officially a student. That's so weird to say."

The corners of his lips pull up into a smile for a moment before his eyes flicker to the office. "Come on, let's get this over with. Quick and painless."

They step into the office and find it silent and empty. Dana's computer monitor is turned off, and a sign on the counter reads 'back in five!!".

"Shit," Jones hisses as he thunders across the tiny office. "She's taken them out there to meet him without me. What if he panics, or he isn't on his best behavior? What if—"

"Jones?" Liz calls as she glances out of the window, the one where weeks ago she had first seen his smile. The warmth of his hand on the small of her back lets her know he's there to see what she sees.

Teddy sits attentive and proud, the nub of his tail wagging so hard it's little more than a blur as Vanessa crouches and offers out a hand. The Pitbull hesitates just a fraction of a second before raising his paw to plop it in hers to shake. Simon crouches by her side, offering out his hand as the dog stands and walks toward them, pressing the top of his head to the man's palm and giving him a friendly lick.

"Aw," Jones breathes softly at her back. "Look at him."

"He's doing great," Liz replies. "I think he's ready to go home."

She leans back against him, resting the back of her head on his chest as they simply stand back and watch.

"He's going to be okay, isn't he?" Jones asks.

"Are you kidding? He's going to be the most spoiled old puppy dog in the world." She turns around to face him, smoothing her hands over his shoulders. "And you are going to be an amazing veterinary assistant, and help so many other animals."

"Maybe. I have to pass the admissions exam before I even start to get excited about that."

"You will pass," she tells him. "You've been studying so hard."

Raising onto her tiptoes she kisses him, sinking into the warmth of his lips as his arms wind around her. Over the past couple of weeks, they've kissed *a lot* and every time it knocks the air from her lungs. Grumpy Jones. Sweet Jones. Her Jones.

The tinkle of a chime above the office's back door breaks

them apart. Dana beams as she pokes her head through the door. "I think they're going to take him."

"That's great," Jones says, smoothing down his beard. "Do they seem nice?"

"They're lovely. They're just taking him for a walk around the field right now and then they'll be back to fill in the paperwork and we can finally bid farewell to Teddy."

His throat twitches as he stares back out of the window. "Good. That's good."

It's about half an hour later when the door opens again, and the sound of clomping shoes and the *huff-huff-huff* of excited dog breath fill the tiny office. As soon as he sees Jones, Teddy pulls toward him, nub wagging as he greets his friend.

Liz remains by his side as Jones lowers himself onto his knees and lets the Pitbull slobber on him.

"I'm going to miss you," Jones mutters as he pets the dog between the ears. "You be good for them, okay?"

It takes all Liz's composure not to cry, but somehow she manages it, focusing instead on making sure Vanessa and Simon have everything in order and holding tight to Jones's hand when he waves them off in the parking lot.

Finn sticks his head out of his van's window and calls out to her as they load Teddy into the back. "See you at rehearsal in about an hour, yeah?"

"Yeah," Liz nods, heart hammering as she forces a smile.

"Don't forget…"

"Contract. Yep."

It hurts to lie to him, but she needs to tell the Vixens all at once. Just get it over with, tear off the Band-Aid.

She snakes her arm around Jones's back and leans against him. "You okay?"

"Not really," Jones shakes his head. "But I will be."

His eyes are glassy as he presses a kiss to her forehead, and together they head back to his truck.

---

It takes a lot to rattle Liz. Ever since they first met, he's known she was the strongest person he's ever met, caring to a fault, ready to stand at his side whenever he has needed to lean on her. It's just one of the things he loves about her.

But sitting in his truck outside the factory, it's the first time he's seen her truly afraid.

"What if they hate me?" she asks. Her breath stutters as she stares ahead, as though she can see anything through the fogged window.

"They're not going to hate you," he assures her, placing his hand on hers and lacing their fingers together. She's wearing the same skirt she wore at Ghoulfest, the long, flowing, black one. "They'll probably be sad, but if they're your friends they'll understand. You have to do what's best for you."

She huffs air out of her nose as a muscle in her cheek leaps. "Okay. I can do this."

"I'll be back in a little bit to pick you up, okay? If you need me sooner, call me."

"Will you answer?"

He shrugs playfully. "Since it's you. Maybe."

That gets at least a hint of a smile out of her, and as she leans over to kiss him goodbye, he wishes more than anything he could go with her, hold her hand through this and shelter her from the outcome. But he can't. And besides, she doesn't need him to.

She walks away from the truck without turning back, her steps steady and resolute. If he didn't know better, he'd think she was brimming with confidence about this. Strong, kind, wonderful Liz.

When she enters the factory's doors, he pulls out of the parking lot and heads back to his house, sighing as he turns off the ignition. Imran's car and trailer are already parked outside, and the mustachioed man stands at his front door, shaking his head in mock-disapproval as Jones climbs out of the truck.

"Where the hell have you been?"

"Shut up," Jones replies as he lumbers up the path, scowling even as he throws his arm around the smaller man.

A muffled grunt sounds against Jones's shoulder as Imran laughs. "Jonesey, are you… hugging me?"

"What did I just say?"

Imran sighs, resignation leeching the tension from his body. "Okay, okay."

Jones smiles as Imran gently pats the top of his back. "Thank you."

"For?"

"Helping."

"Oh." Imran pauses before adding. "You said you'd pay me in beer… This better not be instead—"

"I got your beer. It's in the fridge. Shut up." A moment later Jones breaks the embrace and unlocks the front door.

They step inside, greeted by the sight of Roxy sprawled across the couch. The iguana doesn't give half a fuck that half the furniture in the house has already been removed and donated or sold.

Imran chuckles, straightening his moustache after being crushed against Jones's shoulder. "Have I mentioned how

# TWENTY-TWO

Painful crescents glare from the center of Liz's palm; marks left by her nails after clenching her fist so hard. The rehearsal room door muffles the sound of the band's warmups, but if she closes her eyes and concentrates, she can picture them so clearly. Faces eager, excited, actually happy to be there, desperate to take the band further and find the recognition they deserve.

That isn't her. It hasn't been for a long time.

She pulls out her phone and opens her email app, tapping on the confirmation from Monroe. Elation rises in her chest at the sight of the school's logo. It's the right choice. It has always been the right choice, and now it's one she doesn't have to face alone.

She draws a few steadying breaths and opens the door.

"Liz!" Finn calls out over the racket as he stands behind his drumkit. "Do you have it?"

"No. I'm sorry."

The drummer tilts his head as he folds his arms over his chest. "Liz…"

Pressing her back to the door, her heart thrums as Anya turns to face her, then Nic, Tamika, and within seconds the whole band is looking at her. Cold fear washes over her face, and every muscle in her body tenses in anticipation of what's to come.

"What's wrong?" Anya asks, her usual smile slipping from her lips as she takes a step toward Liz.

"I…" She gulps down a shallow breath, fighting back the urge to run. She has to do this. She has to face it. "I'm leaving."

Anya's eyes narrow as an incredulous laugh bursts from her. "Leaving rehearsal?"

"No… the band."

The words hang in the air, heavy in the resounding silence as seven faces stare back at her. Brows etch with confusion, then mouths open in realization. The borders of her vision darken as she waits for their anger.

"Liz…" Anya whispers. "Please don't do this to me."

"I'm not. I'm not doing this to you, I'm doing it for me."

"Alright," Finn says, glancing to Mia as though she holds the script he's supposed to read from. Color rises in his cheeks as he covers the top of his head with his hand and glances up at the ceiling. "Shit. Okay. Uh… was it something in the contract? Something you're unhappy with?"

"No." Liz pushes off from the door and takes a step toward them, putting herself in the circle opposite the drummer. "This is something I've wanted for a long time. I'm going to college." She chuckles as a miniscule tingle of excitement breaks through the cold fog of fear. "Playing with you all has been amazing, and getting to work with some of my best friends should be a dream come true. But I need this. I need to follow my heart and be what I always dreamed of."

Mia nods, folding her arms over her chest. "You've got to do what makes you happy, and if this is it then we can't stand in your way."

"Thank you."

The singer dips her head. "Can you still play at Armand's party? It's New Year's Eve."

"No… No, I'm sorry. But I'll call him and explain why. My course starts January fourth and we have to move two states over."

"We?" Anya asks, her eyebrow raised in suspicion. "Does that mean the roadie boy talked you into this?"

"No. I applied way before I even met him. I've applied for this so many times, different schools, different courses, and every time I've rejected my place because of tours or festivals or recordings."

"But he's going with you?" Anya scowls as she lifts her guitar strap over her head and sets the instrument on a stand at her side.

"He's going to college too, yes. We're doing it together."

"You're just leaving town with a guy you met less than a month ago?"

Liz nods. "I know it sounds reckless, but I have to do this. I have to do something for myself."

Every breath is like drawing in smoke as she stands waiting for more questions, more judgement. The phone in her hand is a lifeline he clings to, an escape if she needs it, a way to get out of explaining further. She'd known Anya would be the hardest to convince, fearless, no-bullshit Anya.

The guitarist rakes her hands through her tousled red hair and glances toward Finn. "Look," she sighs. "I've known you were in love with him for weeks and I've seen the way he looks at you. I think you two are probably the real thing."

A sigh of relief bursts from Liz's lips. "Thank you."

"But if he hurts you, undermines you, breaks your heart, or even momentarily inconveniences you, Finn and I will be barging down your front door in less than half an hour ready to kick his ass, right Finn?"

Finn's eyes widen. "I mean, yeah. I guess. He's a pretty big guy…"

"I'll help," Nic adds.

"Same," Tamika sighs.

"I'll swoop in from behind and take out his knees," Mia promises.

Jordan nods. "I'll be there too. I have, like, three antique swords we can take."

"You can use me as bait or something," Étienne shrugs. "Or I'll just wait outside and keep the car running, but you know… I'll be there in spirit."

Liz chuckles, tears pooling in her eyes as Anya crashes into her, wrapping her arms around her waist. "I'm going to miss you all so much."

"You better fucking come back and visit," the guitarist sniffs. "And you have to come to every gig we play down there, okay? We'll get you backstage passes so you can hang out."

"Obviously," Liz laughs as the rest of the band pile around her. "This isn't goodbye forever, it's just… I'm no longer a Vixen."

"You're always a Vixen," Anya mutters. "We're like a cold sore, you can't ever truly get rid of us."

When the majority of the group peel away and go back to preparing for rehearsal, Liz, Mia and Finn head out into the corridor to discuss the finer details of what her leaving means.

"I'll have an agreement written up we can all sign, saying you'll get your fair share of any royalties for songs you've recorded," Finn tells her. He stands with his back to the wall, his big shoulders slouched under the weight of what's happening. "Our lawyer is going to fucking kill me. When I told him we'd been playing together for ten years without a contract I thought he was going to cry."

"I'm sorry," Liz says, pushing her hands into her pockets.

"No," Mia says gently. "You have to do what's best for you and live the life you want. We don't want to keep you here with us if your heart isn't in it. We'll be sad to see you go, but it would be far worse making you stay and seeing how unhappy you are."

"Thank you," Liz smiles. For the first time she can remember her breaths come easily. "Can I get a number to contact Armand? I do want to call him and explain why you're down a keyboardist."

"You don't have to," Finn tells her as he shakes his head. "He's pretty terrifying and kind of a massive dick."

"I want to."

Honestly, she doesn't, but if there's a chance it can assuage at least a little of her guilt then she'll risk it.

Standing alone in the hallway after Finn and Mia return to practice, she hesitates just a moment before hitting the call button. Each muffled trill against her ear makes her heart skitter as she waits.

"Yes?"

The man's voice is deep and smooth, his tone sharp and to the point. "Mister Corvo?"

"Speaking. Who is this?"

She swallows hard. "My name is Liz Larkin, I'm the keyboardist with Vixen's Wail."

There's a slight hesitation before he says, "Ah."

"I'm… um… sorry. I'm calling because I wanted to thank you for your invitation to perform at the New Year's party, but unfortunately, I won't be attending."

"Is that so?"

"I'm leaving the band."

In the silence she's acutely aware of the beating of her heart, the blood rushing through her veins. The last words she spoke echo through her mind, each repetition just as painfully real as the last.

"And will the rest of the band be in attendance on New Year's?"

"Yes, they're very keen—"

"Good," he says sharply. "Well, I'm sure your absence will barely be noted among my guests."

She frowns. "Oh." Asshole.

"Tell me, Liz Larkin, are Vixen's Wail looking to replace you?"

"I… think so? I imagine so, yes."

He chuckles, and the sound of it is like a gate to the underworld opening beneath her feet. "Have Mia call me," he says. "I have someone in mind who could comfortably fill the position."

"Okay…I—"

"Might I ask why you're leaving?"

She fills her lungs, pushing away the darkness descending over her. "I'm going to college."

"Ah. For?"

"I'm training to be a massage therapist."

"Hm," he chuckles. "Well, I hope for the sake of your future clients you're a better masseuse than you were a keyboardist. Have Mia call me. *Not* the drummer."

The call disconnects.

"Wow," Liz breathes, shoving her phone in the pocket of her skirt.

If that's the kind of guy the Vixens are trying to win favor with, she's more certain than ever that her decision to leave is the best one. She takes a step toward the rehearsal room door, stopping as her palm presses against the wood. If she closes her eyes, she can hear them, playing *Bloodlust Beautiful* without her. And they sound good, even without the keyboard. They sound really good.

Every one of them has their whole heart dedicated to the song, to the music, to the band. But not Liz. Her heart belongs elsewhere.

She takes her phone back out of her pocket and fires off a text to Jones. A text which simply reads:

*I'm ready to go.*

---

She's quiet on the ride home. He doesn't push her, doesn't try to fill the silence with chatter and questions about how it went. If she wanted to talk about it, she would, but the gentle smile on her lips tells him all he needs to know. It's done. It went as well as it could. She's free.

When they pull up outside her apartment, she turns to him and says, "You coming in?"

"Do you want me to?"

She nods. They're barely even through her door before she's on him, her lips demanding his, her hands beneath his shirt, so damned hungry for him, so perfect. She makes him lightheaded, makes him burn.

Her bedroom might as well be a thousand miles away, so instead he guides her to the kitchen, hooking his hands beneath her thighs to help her hop up onto the countertop.

"Goddamn Liz, I love you," he says as she pulls him by the belt toward her, wrapping her thighs around him.

She kisses him hard, her tongue stroking his as he reaches beneath her skirt, fingers skating through her slick warmth until her back bows.

There's still a voice at the back of his mind telling him this can't be forever, sooner or later she'll realize he's not the type of person to waste her love on. But she quietens it with her eager lips, with the want in those beautiful brown eyes, with the way her body reacts to his touch, the goosebumps pebbling her skin as he worships every inch of her.

"I love you so much," she whispers against his ear as she unbuckles his belt. She slides down his jeans until they stop at the top of his thighs, her hands skating round his hips to grasp his ass.

He can barely breathe as she pulls him into her, his chest shuddering at the sensation of her, hot and wet and wanting him. Him. Jones, the man who once thought himself so broken that even if he managed to piece himself together, the result would be unrecognizable.

But he isn't.

Jones is still Jones, and she wants him just as he is. That she's with him, standing on the precipice of the rest of their life together brings tears to his eyes.

She whimpers as he strokes her clit and fucks her, not as hard as he once promised, and perhaps he'll never get back to that, but it's enough. He's enough.

In that moment nothing matters beyond them, beyond the sensation of their bodies united in bliss, in the sensation of each other. His thighs smack repeatedly against the cabinets. She reaches out to steady herself and knocks a coffee mug from a hook on the wall, sending it shattering on the floor as she comes, moaning his name. It's beautiful and messy, all-consuming and as simple and necessary as breath. He holds her to him as he comes, teeth bared and eyes squeezed tight as one thought pulses in his mind; *Hers. I'm hers.*

The sensation of her hands softly stroking his shoulder blades as he leans against her pulls his lips into a smile.

"I can't stay long," he says, his voice made faint by his breathlessness. "I'm sorry. Imran's still at the house and we have a lot of stuff to go through."

"That's okay," she says, stroking back the strands of hair falling onto his forehead. She presses her lips together for a moment, her eyes darting back and forth over his face. "If you give me some time to clean up, I can come too, if you like?"

"Are you sure? It's dusty work, and not much fun."

Her smile widens. "You'll let me help you?"

She'll see things, artifacts of his life before he's kept locked away for so long. Evidence of a life he's strived to forget.

"Sure," he says, pressing his lips to her forehead. "I'll let you help me."

# EPILOGUE

Her phone is vibrating in her pocket before her last client of the day is even out the door. She smiles as the device buzzes against her thigh.

"I'll see you next week Susan, take it easy," she says, waving the lady out the door and only pulling her cell out once she's completely alone. Monroe Wellness Spa has a hard and fast "no phones" policy, but within a week she'd worked out which managers were cool with her just keeping it silent in her pocket and which were sticklers for the rules.

She gives a resigned sigh as a name flashes across her screen. Of course, it's Anya. Anya's the only one who ever calls during work hours.

She smiles as she accepts the call and presses the phone to her ear. "What's up?"

"I just miss you. How was your day?"

Liz's smile widens to a grin at the sound of her voice. It's been almost a full year since she and Jones left for Monroe, and they're well overdue a visit. Since finishing their courses, they both got swept away into jobs they couldn't refuse. "It's good. Just finishing actually."

A shrill squeal pierces her ear. "Okay, okay when you get a second Google the following words... Vixen's Wail European Tour."

"Get the fuck out!" Liz gasps. "That's so cool."

"Isn't it? We're hitting Oslo, Helsinki, Budapest... uhm..."

"London," a faint male voice chimes in.

Liz narrows her eyes. "Who was that?"

"No one. Nothing. What do you mean?"

"You have a boy..." Liz grins as she wipes down her table and turns off the speaker playing soothing, ambient sounds. "That's gross."

"I'll call you back," Anya snaps, and the call ends.

Chuckling, Liz puts her phone back in her pocket and switches off the light. Her back aches, her eyes are tired, but she's happier than she has ever been.

She plays the Vixen's new album in her car on the way home, silently judging their new keyboardist. That ass, Armand Corvo was right. Liz's absence is barely notable in their music, and that makes her happy. They're thriving, and so is she.

* * *

"There you go," Jones whispers as he gently places Candy, Miss Lambert's semi-conscious fox terrier in a cage and strokes a hand between her pointed ears. "You'll be feeling better in no time, I promise."

The dog sighs as she snuggles against the soft, padded bed, completely unaware of the plastic cone around her head, or the stitches in her leg. Brave little soul. Jones glances at the clock. Just five minutes left of his shift before he gets to go home. Working as a veterinary assistant is far more enjoyable than lugging amps backstage, and far, far better suited to him than bar work. But still, he can't wait to be home.

Those five minutes feel like years as he triple-checks that all the animals who are in overnight have everything they need to be comfortable, and indulges Bobby, the Davidson's African Grey parrot in what must be their hundredth rendition of *If You're Happy and You Know It Flap and Screech* since his shift began. The bird is still whistling the tune as Jones leaves the building.

Despite living in Monroe for almost a year now, he'll still never get used to the traffic on the evening commute, or the sight of the vast gray ocean greeting him as he heads home. All his life he's been watched by mountains. Now the world lies before him, inviting him to explore.

Maybe one day they'll venture further, he and Liz, but for now, this works. Their house is pretty hard to miss this time of year, what with the veritable army of skeletons posed outside, illuminated by ghostly blue light and carved jack-o-lanterns. It makes him smile every time he pulls onto their street. Liz may have left Vixen's Wail, but Vixen's Wail never left her heart.

And, it seems, neither did her taste for theatrics inside the house. Faux candle light flickers on the walls as he opens the front door, illuminating a path from the foyer through the entire house toward the back door. Excitement bristles through his body as he follows the path, the scent of burning charcoal making his stomach preemptively grumble.

"Are we grilling tonight?" he asks as he steps out the back door and into the dusky evening.

Liz sits on the swing seat on the back porch beneath a thick yellow wool blanket. She tears her eyes from the stars to look across at him, her lips curving into a smile, making his heart skip a beat. No matter how many times he comes home to her, or how many mornings he wakes up beside her, he'll be forever amazed by her.

"I got it started," she sighs. "The steaks are marinating in the kitchen. But I couldn't finish them."

"Why?"

She flashes a wry smile before lowering the blanket covering her, just enough to reveal Roxy snuggled against her chest, sleeping soundly. "Lizard mom duties."

His heart soars as he crosses the deck and bends down to kiss her. The pain in his lower back and thighs is more noticeable after a long shift at work, but nowhere near as bad as a year ago. Still, her lips are more than worth the mild discomfort, and as he strokes back the strands of her hair, pressing his palm to the warm curve of her cheek, he can't help but smile.

He heads back to the kitchen to grab the steaks and the ears of corn wrapped in aluminum foil, setting the vegetables on the grill before taking a seat beside her.

"How was work?" he asks.

She sighs, content. "Good. Tiring but…worthwhile."

"Same for me," he says. "The best kind of tiring."

"Second best." She grins, reaching out to take his hand, and pressed her lips to his knuckles.

He loves when she flirts with him, just as much as he loves taking care of her and being taken care of. A cool breeze flutters against them, carrying the sound of the ocean crashing against the rocks. In a couple of weeks, it'll be too cold to sit out at night and watch the stars together, but for now, they make the most of it.

The seat groans beneath him as he sits beside her, listening to the pop and hiss of the grill, the roar of the ocean, and Liz's contented sigh as she rests her head on his shoulder, smoothing her hand over his belly. These days, Jones never stops smiling. The here and now with her, the paths branching before them make the past nothing more than a fading shadow far, far behind.

Nothing can take this from him.

# Sneak Preview

Keep reading for an exclusive preview of *Feedback*, the next installment in the Vixens Rock series…

# FEEDBACK

"Elise?"

She almost drops her phone. That voice. That fancy movie-villain voice. She has spent years trying to forget it and even longer dreaming of it. "Armand?"

"Do you still play?"

Her throat is tight, every breath hard-won. "Yes."

"Good. Very good."

His approval rolls through her, kneading every part of her body and turning her to putty. Even after all those years she responds as if she's still his pupil, clinging to whatever praise she can get from him. She swallows hard and closes her eyes, trying not to imagine how he looks now. He was handsome ten years ago, a big, broad man, well-groomed, dark hair and beard. He always smelled so good.

"I have a proposition for you."

"Oh?"

Her heartbeat fills the empty seconds as she waits. She checks the phone to make sure he hasn't been disconnected.

He hasn't. God, she can almost smell the cool spice of expensive cologne.

"Have you heard of Vixen's Wail?"

"Uh…" Elise frowns. She's seen their posters around town. They headlined the Halloween festival. "The metal band?"

"Symphonic metal, yes. They're looking for a keyboardist and I thought of you."

An uncharacteristic swell of excitement balloons in her chest. "Of me?"

"Yes. They're making quite a name for themselves so I thought it would be a good opportunity for you. Not awfully sophisticated so they should suit your abilities quite well."

There it is, the reason she quit his piano lessons and decided to teach herself. "I'll think about it."

"Please do. I remember our conversation about how much you longed to play on the stage." His voice is almost a purr. She loses the battle with her imagination and pictures him sitting in a black leather wing-backed chair, his exquisitely tailored suits devoutly hugging every curve of his body as he gazes down at her. And she would be on her knees between his thighs, showing him just how much she missed him, earning that praise she so desperately craves.

Ten years. A decade of realizing all too late that she had almost, *almost* forgotten him. But never quite.

He speaks again. "Vixen's Wail are playing at my party on New Year's Eve."

The heat flooding her cheeks courses lower. That means they'll be at his house. In his own very-Armand way, he's inviting her to play for him, to spend the evening in his world. And in his very-Armand way, he's setting an obstacle course for her to scramble over to get to him.

She shouldn't. She mustn't.

She is.

"Send me the contact details," she says, scolding herself even as she speaks. "I have a lot going on at the moment but I'll see what I can do."

"Very well. It would be good to see you again," he says. "I'm curious to know how you play these days."

The world drops out from beneath her as she squeezes her eyes tighter and leans forward, balancing her forehead on her hand as she braces her elbow on the desk. His voice has aged, deepened, roughened, like her need for him. But so has she.

"I play perfectly well, Armand. All my teachers have been very happy with me."

"Teachers?" he says, drawing out the S. "Were you happy with them?"

"Happier than I was with you."

It's a cheap blow, one she very much needs, but he chuckles nonetheless.

"I hope I'll see you soon, Elise."

# Acknowledgments

Whew boy, this book kicked my ass in every conceivable way. Telling Jones and Liz's story was far more difficult than anything I've written before, and there were times I didn't know if I could give them the HEA they deserved.

Thank you to Sabrina for your help and insight into CBT. The things you taught me about Jones and his way of thinking have helped me immensely in my own life and I'm so grateful that you took the time to talk to me.

Thank you so much to Jake for taking me away from my laptop from time to time and for listening to me talk nonsense about imaginary people. I love you.

A massive thank you to real life Liz for your generosity and wonderfulness and to the organizers and participants of Romancing the Runoff.

Thank you to Jack Habron for his beautiful formatting.

Thank you to all my wonderful patrons over on Patreon, including the Vixens For Life, Emily H, Katie B, Melanie, Linda W, Janel A, Deanna S, and D Mayo-Wells. You are amazing!

And thank you to you, if you are reading this. Your support means the world to me and I'm so grateful to have you along for this journey.

# ABOUT MARIE LIPSCOMB

Marie specializes in writing romances with plus sized heroines and plus sized heroes. She is the author of the *Hearts of Blackmere* and *Vixens Rock* series as Marie Lipscomb, and also writes short, bonkers, high-heat romances including *No Getting Ogre You* and *Santa Claus is Going to Town On Me* under the pen name M.L. Eliza.

Originally from Bolton, UK, Marie now lives in North Carolina, USA. When she's not writing, she can usually be found playing the same three video games on a loop (*cough* Dragon Age)

# ALSO BY MARIE LIPSCOMB

The *Hearts of Blackmere* Series

*The Lady's Champion*

*The Champion's Desire*

*Forever His Champion*

*The Harpy and The Dragon*

The *Vixens Rock* Series

*Strings*

*Rhythm*

**Writing as M.L. Eliza**

*No Getting Ogre You*

*Santa Claus is Going to Town On Me*

www.ingramcontent.com/pod-product-compliance
Lightning Source LLC
Chambersburg PA
CBHW071240190726
48292CB00007B/2370